LEVITATE

one touch changes everything.

kaylee ryan

Cover Design: Sommer Stein Perfect Pear Creative Covers
Cover Photography: Perrywinkle Photography
Editing: Hot Tree Editing
Formatting: Angela McLaurin, Fictional Formats

LEVITATE

1

Kensington

MY EYES ARE fixed on the red digits that light up my room from the bedside table. I watch as the numbers slowly climb and grow closer to the midnight hour. Tomorrow is a day I wish I could sleep through. I wish I could erase it from my mind. No, actually that's not true. I wish she were still here. I wish I didn't have to live through this day without her. In just twelve short minutes, it will officially be my mother's birthday and she's not here to celebrate it.

I fight off the memories of why that is. The pain slices through me. Hot tears race down my cheeks and I make absolutely no effort to wipe them away. There is no use. The next twenty-four hours is going to be a struggle. This will be the fourth birthday Dad and I have celebrated her life without her. They say it gets easier and the pain eases. They, whoever they are, are full of shit. The pain is there, front and center in my chest. I can feel it pound like thunder. This is the same pain I felt that night, the night we lost her. It does, however, get easier to hide. I have become a pro at hiding how her death and that night still affect me.

I hear my roommate and best friend, Nicole, pacing outside my bedroom door. She knows tomorrow is my mother's birthday. Freshman year, I was a total basket case. I wasn't ready to talk about that night, but I had to give her something. I told her about my mother dying, but I didn't want to talk about the details. Nic is amazing and has never pushed me for specifics. She always just lets me know she's there for me. There is no way I could have survived college without her. I know it bothers her that I haven't opened up and given her the details. Honestly, it's not that I don't want her to know, but that I don't want to think about it or talk about it more than I have to. I don't want to explain the terror of that night, the terror that still haunts me. We've been inseparable for the past four years and I haven't told her what happened. My chest aches with guilt that I'm keeping it from her. I just don't talk about it to anyone, ever. Dad and I don't even discuss it. We talk about her and how much we miss her, how much she would have enjoyed this or that. Never do we talk about that night. Neither one of us want to bring the pain that close to the surface. I know this day, her birthday, affects him just as much as it does me, but we still don't discuss it.

Nic has an idea in her head; she knows that whatever happened to cause my mother's death haunts me. I'm a twenty-two-year-old college senior and I don't date. It's hard for me to trust men and I can't seem to find myself caring enough to put forth the effort. Tragedy does that to you. Makes you change the course of your life, your actions, and responses to normal every day activities.

Deep down, I realize my fear of dating and trust issues are irrational at best. I understand not all relationships turn out the way mine did. I also know that to me, it's just not worth the risk. I get that my ex, Justin, is not to blame for what happened, but he was supposed to be there. I can't help but think that if he would have been there, like he was supposed to, if I hadn't been alone… I roll over onto my side and watch as the red numbers turn again.

Two more minutes.

I try to blink back the tears hot behind my eyes. As the second round falls, there's a light knock on my door. She doesn't wait for an invitation as she quietly pushes open the door. A gentle glow of light flows into the room. I bury my head in my body pillow, trying to burrow deeper. The bed dips behind me as Nicole climbs in and hugs me tightly.

"I'm here, Kens. You are not alone. I'm here." Her soft voice filters through the room. Her words break me open even further and the warm flow of tears turns into a waterfall of emotion I usually keep locked away. This has been the norm for us. She is always there offering support. I often tell her she is getting the short end of the stick with this friendship. She just laughs and says friendships are not about quantity but quality. She assures me I give as much as I take. Although it may be true, I still feel bad for the drama I bring.

We lay there with nothing but the sound of my sobs for company. She never eases her hold, and I thank God every day that she was assigned as my roommate. Nicole Martin has brought me back from the dark side more times than I can count. She is my family. I will forever be by her side for anything she needs. Maybe that's why when she asks, "Do you want to talk about it?" just as she does every time, I find myself wanting to finally tell her everything about my past.

"It's okay, Kens. I don't expect it, but I'm here for you," she whispers into the night. "It might help to talk about it."

I can't talk about the details. I won't. I do feel like I need to tell her something; she deserves that. It's been four years of her picking me up and dealing with my emotional mood swings. I take a deep breath and spit out the words that I have avoided saying since the day we met. How I have lasted this long, I'm really not sure.

"My…" My voice cracks, so I stop to regroup. Nic doesn't say anything; she just lies next to me patiently waiting for what I'm about to say. "My mom was murdered. She was protecting me and he killed her." I barely get it out before I'm bursting into sobs for the third time tonight. This is going to be the norm for me over the next twenty-four hours. After that, I will wear my perfectly practiced mask into place and take each day at a time.

I hear her deep intake of breath. "Life sucks ass," she says. I can hear the emotion in her voice. My best friend is always surprising me. I expected her to go with the norm. "I'm sorry for your loss. I can't imagine what you are going through." I cannot tell you how many times my dad and I heard that after… that night. I get that people don't know what to say in these situations, but my bestie summed it up. Life sucks ass. Neither one of us says anything else. She gets me and I love her for it.

I have no idea how much time passes before I hear her breathing even out. I'm envious of the slumber she has slipped into. I know I will do nothing but toss and turn, so I slip from the bed, trying like hell not to wake her. Grabbing my Kindle off the bedside table, I quietly slip from the room. The apartment is eerily silent and I need noise. The silence makes it possible for the memories to flood my mind, to consume me. Grabbing the remote from the coffee table, I burrow into the couch, pulling the chenille throw over me. There is nothing good to watch at this hour, but I don't care. I just need the background noise, something to fill the quiet void. Skimming through my Kindle, I find my next book boyfriend. I decide on *That Girl* by HJ Bellus. Nic read it last week and insists I will fall in love with Lincoln. I have no doubt that she's right. We have the same taste in books.

Settling in, I try to focus on the words, but no matter how hard I try, I just can't stop my mind from racing, can't stop the memories from that night. It's not just the memories of what happened, it's the worry that I carry with me every single day. I worry I will forget what her voice sounded like, the smell of her sweet perfume, and the way it felt to have her wrap her arms around me and tell me she loved me. I was always close with my mom. The day after prom my junior year, I admitted I had had sex for the first time. I was so afraid she was going to be disappointed in me. I should have known better. She asked me if I was safe and if it was consensual. Looking back now, I can see how she might think it might not have been. I was a sobbing mess when I told her. The fear of seeing the disappointment on her face had me an emotional mess. The guy, my first, his name was Greg and we were not even really dating. He asked me to prom; I accepted. He was one of the nicest guys you will ever meet and it was his first time as well. Neither one of us felt pressured; it was just something we wanted to do. Sort of a rip the Band-Aid off and get it over with kind of moment. One thing led to another, and well… you know. I don't know why I even told her. Most teenagers go out of their way to hide that kind of information. She and I were sitting on the couch watching a movie and I just blurted it out. The following day, she called and made me a doctor's appointment so I could start birth control. She talked to me about safe sex and how you should share the act with someone you love. That giving your body to another person was a gift, just like giving them your heart.

The memories and the worry take over again as more tears start to fall. My Kindle long since abandoned. The low filtering of light coming from the morning sun alerts me that it's time to get my ass in gear. I always meet Dad for breakfast, even though neither one of us have much of an appetite, but that is how we always start this day together. After that night, neither one of us wanted to stay in that house in the same town. Dad rented us an apartment and put the house on the market. He started applying for jobs, and that's what brought us to our new life. I enrolled in college close to home. I couldn't muster the courage to go far away. Too much had changed too fast. I needed to know he was close if I needed him. Neither one of us looked back. We left the past and the haunting memories behind us and did the best we could to start a new life. Just the two of us.

I am an only child; my parents struggled with conceiving for several years and two miscarriages before I came along. My mom always used to tell me that she was blessed with a healthy baby girl and that was enough for her. I know she would have loved to have more children, but it just wasn't in the cards for them. It's a shame really; a girl couldn't ask for better parents.

Tears once again begin welling up. I climb off the couch and head for the shower. My only hope is to occupy my mind with mundane tasks to get through the day.

2

Maxton

THE ANNOYING BEEP of my alarm blares from the nightstand. I didn't get in until after three this morning and I have to be back in for a delivery by ten. Dad did this for years, ran the bar on only a few hours of sleep at a time. It pisses me off that I never noticed. I never realized what he did to keep the family business alive. The woman I refuse to refer to as my mother, never had to work a day in her life. He busted his ass to provide for us, to make sure we never went without. It's been two years, and every time I think about her and what she did, I see red. Looking back, she was always self-absorbed and seemed to be constantly nagging. I, however, was a teenager and she pretty much left me alone. Dad seemed to always be the one she felt needed improvement. It had been that way my entire life, so I never thought much of it. It wasn't until I learned all of her secrets, until she killed the soul of my father, that I realized she was the devil incarnate.

Kids aren't supposed to hate their parents. I can tell you that I do. The woman is heartless. Always looking out for number one, manipulating to get what she wants, how she wants it. My dad gave her the world. Would have tried to give her the moon, if she had asked. I'm fucking surprised she didn't.

When Dad died, Mom was already moved on to her newest conquest. She came home for the funeral and to say she was livid when she found out that everything was willed to me is an understatement. The house, the bar, everything. He left her nothing. I was expecting nothing, not because he didn't love me, he did. He was the best dad a guy could ask for. No, I didn't expect it, because he was never able to tell her no. Even though they had been divorced for almost three years, I just assumed it would all go to her.

She whined and tried to make me feel guilty that she had nothing to remember him by. I made sure I reminded her that she had his heart, always did. Her new flavor didn't like that comment too well. Truth hurts, and it got them both out of my hair. It's been two years, and I have not seen her since. She calls on occasion and I avoid her calls. Like I said, not a normal relationship, but she is not a mother. Egg donor, that's how I should refer to her.

I took over the house that I grew up in. I was working construction at the time and quit to run the bar. Cooper's is now a third generation establishment. My grandfather opened it back in the day and Dad took over when he was about my age. I never really gave much thought to taking over the family business. College wasn't my scene, so after graduation, I went straight into construction. I enjoyed the work and liked being able to see the end product. When Dad's attorney told me that he left everything to me, I knew I had to keep the Cooper name alive. I called and gave my boss notice and started on the unknown adventure of bar ownership.

My best friend, Brighton, worked at the same construction company. When I told him my plans to run Cooper's and asked him to hop on the crazy train, he didn't hesitate. We've had each other's backs since kindergarten. That's what family is all about. Too bad the egg donor didn't get the memo.

Not only did Brighton jump in and help me run the day-to-day operations, he became my new roommate. The house is way too big for just me, and we easily split the expenses. Brighton and I are just two bachelors living the dream.

I force my tired ass out of bed and into the shower; the warm spray helps wash away the grogginess. I throw on a pair of worn jeans and a black fitted t-shirt and call it good. I find Brighton in the kitchen, head over a huge bowl of cereal, serving spoon in one hand and his phone in the other.

He stops chewing long enough for a simple "Morning," and resumes the consumption of what looks like an entire box of Fruity Pebbles. Bastard, those are my favorite.

I settle for Pop-Tarts. "I have a delivery at ten. What are you getting into today?"

"You off tonight?" His mouth is still full and the visual is almost enough to make me lose my appetite, almost.

I hope so. "Yeah, as long as everyone shows up for their shift. I'm ready for a night off."

Brighton picks up his bowl, or should I say trough, and slurps the remaining milk. "It feels like we have been going non-stop for the past couple of months. The renovations are complete, and the staff is hired and trained. Now it's time to kick back and supervise."

"I'm in. What were you thinking?" I ask, because I know he has something brewing in that brain of his. Brighton always has a plan.

He wipes his chin with the back of his hand and grins. "I was actually thinking of calling Nicole and seeing if she wanted to meet up somewhere. Maybe Studio 57."

"Nicole? Is she the one you met at Jacob's bonfire?" I watch as his grin grows wider and he nods. "You've been talking to her?" I question because he has not mentioned anything. We've been busy as hell since that night with the renovations to the bar and hiring new staff. How in the hell did he find the time?

"Not really, just a phone call or text here or there. We've met at the coffee shop a couple of times. She's been busy with school; this is her last year. We both said we would like to hang out; it's just been hard to find the time. Since we're free tonight, I figured I would call her. I know her roommate is also unattached." He raises his eyebrows and winks.

A night out sounds awesome, and Studio 57 is always a good time. "You needing a wingman, Bright?" I decide to fuck with him. He seems really into this girl.

This causes him to throw his head back and laugh. "No. Nicole and I have talked enough the past three months, I feel like I know her. However, I'm sure she will want to bring her roommate along. She's mentioned before that the girl doesn't get out enough. I want to be able to whisk her off to the dance floor without her feeling guilty. It would help if I also had a friend there to help her not feel left out."

"I'm in. As long as I'm not the one who has to issue last call, kick out the drunks, clean up, and cash out." Before I even finish, he has his phone to his ear. I assume calling Nicole to set things up for tonight. It's been way too long since I've been out, and just as long since I have had the sweet release that only a beautiful woman can provide. Studio 57 is just what I need.

I wave as I grab my keys and wallet off the counter. The delivery isn't going to sign itself in.

3

Kensington

BREAKFAST IS DELICIOUS. Neither one of us eat much, but what we do eat, we both comment on how good it is. I was dreading this because of the day, but I have to admit I miss spending time with my dad. He's the foreman for a road construction crew. His shift is never the same, changing due to the traffic patterns of whatever area they are working in. His job also causes him to travel long distances. More often than not, he will stay out of town until the job is complete. Lucky for him, the company covers all costs. In other words, my dad is one of the guys behind the orange barrels on the highway. After we finish eating, Dad insists on taking me to the mall. I tell him it's not necessary. I know he lives on one income and I have my part-time job as a tutor to cover what my scholarship doesn't. Thankfully, it's enough to allow me and Nicole to share an apartment off campus. Dorm life is not where it's at. Of course, he blows off my concern and says it's his God-given right to spoil his little girl.

I learned a while ago that when shopping with my father, you can't show interest in anything. If he thinks you want it, he buys it. He was the same way with my mother. They both worked hard every day for what they had. Growing up, I knew we were not rich, but we never wanted for anything. I can remember one year I wanted a pair of boots that were expensive. I didn't ask for them because spending that much on boots is ridiculous. Several of my friends had them, but I just didn't have it in my heart to ask my parents to spend that kind of money. That year at Christmas, much to my surprise, my boots were under the tree. I was stunned and insisted they were too expensive. Of course, when they said it was nonsense, I tackle-hugged both of them. I can remember Dad plopping down on the couch and pulling Mom into his arms. He dropped a kiss on the top of her head and they shared a smile. Mom then said, "Kensi, life is short. You have to live each day to the fullest. You can't take money with you when you're gone. You work hard for what you have and enjoy every second of it." The memory has emotion clogging my throat. I swallow it down. Dad and I are having such a great day; I don't want to ruin it with tears. Those will come later.

After dragging me in and out of every store, asking if anything catches my eye, I ended up with a new pair of jeans, a sweater, and a scarf. It's early October and the weather is starting to get cold. We stop on the food court on our way out and grab a slice of pizza. We were in the mall for over five hours. I know what you're thinking—a man in the mall for five hours? Yes, my father is relentless when he wants to be. He hates to shop, but he loves me and loves to spoil me. My mom used to say that was one of the things she loved about him best. She used to say that behind all the brawn is a heart of gold; he loves with everything in him. She always told me that if I ever found a man like that, I needed to hold on tight with both hands and never let him go.

I see that in my dad. My issue is letting myself get close to anyone else to find out what his heart is made of.

After inhaling our food court pizza, we head to our final destination of the day. My mom loved horses. As soon as we moved here, Dad and I found a riding stable that let you rent a horse for the day. It was something we thought we could do and it would seem like she was with us. We were both reaching for anything that would make us feel closer to her. We stumbled upon a beautiful lake along the trails. The view is serene and I immediately knew Mom would have loved it. Dad agreed and we come back as often as we can. It's odd to think that coming to a place she has never been makes us feel closer to her, but for me at that time in our lives it worked. I still feel close to her when we are here. I like to think she is watching over us, and she really is.

"I called ahead and reserved Savannah and Charlotte for us today," my dad says as we pull into the long lane that will lead us to the stables.

I'm excited to see the two horses that we have grown attached to. I'm ready to feel like she's with us. "Awesome. I can't wait to see them." And feel close to her. I don't say that aloud though. Today has gone really well. Both of us have held in the emotions, grounding each other from the pain. My dad is really the only one who has ever been able to do that.

The owner, Ray, as he insists we call him, greets Dad with a man hug and me with a kiss on the cheek. "I got the girls all saddled up and ready for you."

"Great, thanks," I say over my shoulder. I'm headed toward the barn. I love horses, love being outdoors really.

A few minutes later, Dad joins me and places the lilies in the saddlebag on his horse. He will be riding Savannah. She is huge; Ray referred to her as being sixteen hands or something of that nature. That's horse speak for tall. Dad is over six foot, so they work well together. Savannah is a beautiful horse; she is white with red spots. I believe Ray said she is a paint... again more horse speak that I don't understand but can repeat and sound as though I do. It does kind of look like she has blotches of red paint all over, so I can see the logic in the name.

My horse is Charlotte. Ray says she and Savannah are sisters. Where Savannah is red, Charlotte is black. Charlotte is also smaller, coming in at fourteen hands. She's sweet and gentle and I love her. Dad and I fell in love with both of them on day one, and he has called to make sure they are reserved any time we visit.

The trails are beautiful and peaceful. The stables are not very busy today, because it's October and starting to get colder. There are over five hundred acres of trails that we can ride. I think over the years, Dad and I have traveled them all at least once. We always travel to our lake and toss some lilies in for Mom. Her name was Lillian and lilies were her favorite flower. Dad always called her Lilly, and when I was born, he decided he was going to call me Kensi even though everyone else shortened my name to Kens. Mom was the only other person who called me Kensi. A few have tried, but I am always quick to shut them down; that was something the three of us shared. Dad doesn't call me that as much as he used to.

"How's school, baby girl?" His question brings me back to the present.

"Good. Classes are good this semester. My advisor informed me that I need to be looking for a local business that I can volunteer with next semester. Apparently, the professor for my advanced business practices class requires all students to volunteer at a local business to get some hands on workforce experience. She likes to keep it local as a way to give back to the community. There are a lot of small businesses around and the extra free help is a perk for them."

"I think that's a great idea. Do you have any ideas yet?" he asks.

"No, not yet. I still have a lot of time. I'm sure I'll figure something out. I think Nicole is just going to work at her sister's salon."

"How is Nicole?"

That's Dad. He's always taking interest in my life, even my friends. He knows how much Nic has helped me over the last four years. He was worried when he moved me into the dorms. We were both going to be on our own. It was scary for both of us.

"She's good, keeps me on my toes." I don't say anything else. I know he can read through the lines. We let the silence fall between us, and before I know it, we are stopped in front of the lake. We tie the horses off to the hitching post and Dad pulls the lilies out of his saddlebag. He hands me half of the bouquet, keeping the remainder for himself.

I follow him to the edge of the bank and we both take a seat. I toss one of my lilies into the water and watch as it slowly drifts away.

"Kensi..." His voice is gruff. "I'm worried about you."

I turn to face him and I can see the lines of worry across his forehead. "I'm good, Dad. Promise," I try to reassure him. I've actually done really well today and I'm mentally giving myself a high five for keeping it together.

"I'm worried that what happened is keeping you from living life. I know you don't really date and I understand your hesitance to let someone in. I want to see you fall in love. I want to walk you down the aisle and someday hold my grandbabies in my arms. That is what we both wanted for you; I still do," he says this as he throws his first lily into the lake. It's almost as if he's speaking for her.

These are the same kinds of conversations Mom and I used to have all the time. She was always the one to touch on these types of subjects with me. Dad let us do our thing... this is a first for us. It's not as awkward as I always imagined it would be.

I lean my head against his shoulder and let his words sink in. "I used to want that. I just don't think it's in the cards for me. Maybe one day. I'm not opposed to it completely, but it's going to take someone who is willing to put in the time and effort to prove he's worth it. For now, I'm good with one man in my life. Besides, if and when that happens, he will have some pretty big shoes to fill." I feel his shoulders lift with the chuckle that escapes his lips.

Dad wraps his arms around me and holds me tight. "I love you, baby girl. I just want to see you live a full, happy life. It's up to you what will make that happen, just know that sometimes the risks are worth the reward."

We continue to sit by the lake and slowly toss our lilies into the water. Dad tells me the story of how he and mom met, and then tosses in a lily. I tell him how I miss the talks she and I used to have and toss in a lily. Within a few hours, we have managed to talk about her, about the good times and some of the bad. The pain is there, but there is just something about this place that helps ease the sting.

I hear the low grumble of his belly and a giggle escapes my lips. "Oh, you think that's funny, do you?" he says as he climbs to his feet. The next thing I know, he's lifting me off the ground and throwing me over his shoulder. We reach the horses and he gently sets me on my feet. "It's not nice to laugh at a man when he's hungry." He winks at me.

Back at the stables I smile and shake my head today turned out better than I had expected. We unsaddle the horses and brush them down. This is not something that is required, but I love it. Ray says he doesn't mind having someone spoil the "crew" as he calls them. We finish up, and with one final hug, Dad and I climb into our vehicles and go our separate ways. Somehow, throughout the day, the pain in my chest shifted. It's still there, but the dread I was feeling is gone. Maybe I was wrong, maybe talking about her, about what happened, is therapeutic. Maybe it does get easier after all.

Walking into the apartment, I find Nicole stretched out on the couch. Her eyes take me in. I know she's prepared to see me in full breakdown mode, but I'm not, much to her surprise and mine.

"Hey, how was your day?" I can hear the hesitation in her voice. I chew on my bottom lip to keep from laughing at her. She's wigged out because I'm not a blubbering mess. It feels good and it's taking all the effort I can muster not to bust out laughing at the situation.

"It was good, actually. We went to breakfast then the mall." I hold up my bags to show her my new purchases. "Then we went to the stables and road down to the lake." She knows about the stables and the lake. I've told her how I feel closer to my mother there. I don't keep everything from her, just that night. Everything else, I'm an open book.

"You seem... I don't know, lighter somehow," she comments as she continues to watch me.

"Yeah, I'm not sure what happened really. Dad and I talked a lot. We talked about Mom, the good times and the... bad. He even broached the 'I want to see you married with kids' subject. He worries, but I assured him he has nothing to worry about."

"I worry too, you know?"

"I know you do. I'll tell you what I told him. I'm not opposed to dating. I just need to know that the guy is into me for the right reasons. I need to see that he is willing to put forth the effort to really be with me. I know that makes me sound like a spoiled brat, but… my past… he needs to be able to take me as I am." I smile thinking about my conversation with Dad. It eased the pain. "I told Dad that any male in my future has big shoes to fill."

Nicole throws her head back and laughs as well. "No shit. He spoils you rotten. What's in the bag?"

"I tried to argue my way out of it, but you know how he is. He was having no part of it." I toss the bags to her. Just as she reaches for them, the alert from her cell phone announces a new message. She reaches for her phone instead.

I watch as she reads it and a smile crosses her face. Interesting.

"All right, you're holding out on me. Who is that?" I ask.

"It's Brighton. He's the one I met a few months ago at the bonfire. You remember the one you were supposed to go to, but decided last minute that you weren't feeling it." She scowls at me.

"I didn't say I wasn't feeling it. I wasn't feeling well. If you remember correctly I had a stomach thing for over a week." I remind her of my illness. "Brighton is the one who has met you for coffee a few times on campus?"

"Yes. He's been texting me all day asking if we want to meet up at Studio 57 tonight. I told him we couldn't make it. He's been trying to get me to change my mind all day."

I can see she really wants to go. I think about the day with my dad and what he said. I do tend to shy away and keep others at arm's length. I know he's right that Mom would want me to live life to the fullest. "So tell him you changed your mind."

"Kens, we always spend tonight together," she says softly. She's afraid that mentioning it will set me off. I'm just as shocked as she is that it doesn't.

"Who says we aren't? I have this new outfit that needs to be broke in. Put the guy out of his misery and tell him we will meet him there." With that, I head to my room to shower and get ready. I pass a picture of me and my parents sitting on my dresser. I miss her so much. I miss our family. Today was the first day since we lost her that I felt like Dad and I are back to being us. It's nice. I kiss the frame and place it back on my dresser. Time to strap on a smile and be the wing woman my bestie needs. I think I need this night as much as she does.

4

Maxton

THE DELIVERY TRUCK was late. By the time the truck arrived and I had everything signed in, the staff were starting to arrive to prep for the night. I was bombarded with questions, so I'm just now getting home at a little after six. I walk into the house and I can immediately see that Brighton is not in the best of moods.

"Hey, man, we still on for tonight?" I ask. I would love to grab a quick nap.

I wouldn't really classify what comes out of his mouth as a reply. It's more of a grumble with a little bit of a growl thrown in. I toss my keys, wallet, and phone on the table and head to the kitchen to grab a sandwich. I should have eaten at the bar, but I was in a hurry to get out of there. My staff is perfectly capable of handling things; however, they rely on me when I'm there. Me taking the night off is exactly what they need to learn how to step up and make decisions on their own. As long as they don't burn the place down, everything else can be fixed.

I'm mid-bite of my turkey and Swiss when I hear Bright yell, "Hell yeah!" from the living room. I make my way to him to see what the fuss is about. I find him sitting in the same place grinning from ear to ear, staring at his phone. "What's up, man?" From the sound of his yell, you would think he just hit the fucking lottery.

"She's in. Apparently, her roommate changed plans so we could all meet up tonight." He hops off the couch and passes me to head to his room. He slaps a hand on my shoulder wearing a smirk. "I'm hopping in the shower." With that, he is gone and with a little more of a pep in his step. I do believe this Nicole has really gotten under his skin. This is going to be an interesting night.

I inhale my sandwich and grab a quick shower. The nap that I have been dreaming about all day will just have to wait. I throw on a pair of jeans and a white t-shirt. It fits tight against my arms; the ladies seem to love it, so I don't bother putting forth any more effort. I run some gel through my hair, throw on my boots, and call it good. Bright is walking out of his room at the same time as I do mine. His grin is still firmly in place.

He's completely distracted by his phone, so I head toward my truck. No way do I want to ride with his ass while he's distracted by technology or maybe it's not technology that he is so enthralled with. It might be female and have a completely different appeal.

We arrive at Studio 57 and the crowd is impressive as always. As we walk through the crowd to find a table, I observe the ladies who take in our appearance. Bright and I are not hard to miss. We are both well over six-feet tall and can't help but stand out in a crowd.

While I appreciate the level of ladies who are undressing us with their eyes, Bright is busy scanning the crowd. He doesn't seem to notice the come-hither eyes and fuck-me heels that are chomping at the bit to have a piece of him. No, he has singular taste tonight. That taste being a girl named Nicole. I've never met her, well, not sober anyway. Apparently, he introduced us at the bonfire; however, I was three sheets to the wind. I knew the next few months were going to be filled with twelve and fourteen hour days, seven days a week. I woke up in the bed of a red head that morning with no recollection of how I got there. I couldn't even remember her name. I try not to make that a habit. I hook up, but I like to remember it. Hooking up with random girls while drunk is a risk I don't like to take. You never know what they will try and to trick you into. You can't trust women. My mother is a prime example. After, what she did to my dad, no how no way. I enjoy them, but I have no need for anything more than a roll in the sheets.

My buddy, on the other hand, I'm not so sure about. If you asked me before today, I would have told you we were the two amigos. Never going to settle down, never willing to fall into the trap of what a permanent woman in your life has to offer. However, watching him now as his frowned face surveys the crowd, I feel another of the mighty just might have fallen. My thoughts are justified as I study him and watch as his face lights up. I follow his gaze and see a blonde pixie coming our way. Her smile mirrors his and she only has eyes for Bright. I watch as she reaches us. She stands on her tiptoes as he leans down and places a kiss on the corner of her mouth. What the fuck? These two seem way too comfortable for just a few text messages and a coffee. I make a mental note to question him when we get home tonight.

I watch as she reaches back and places her arm around the girl who is standing behind her. She's a fucking knock out. Brown hair that skims her shoulders and those eyes… blue—a sparkling blue unlike any I've ever seen before. I'm staring at her, because again she's stunning. I feel a hand clamp down on my shoulder and I realize Bright is talking to me or maybe about me; hell, I have no idea. My brain just short circuited.

I pull my gaze from the friend to face Bright. He chuckles.

"As I was saying, Nicole, this is Maxton. Max, this is Nicole and her roommate, Kensington," he introduces us, still smiling.

Kensington, fuck, even her name is hot. I extend my hand first toward Nicole; she accepts my handshake. This is not normally how I would say hello. Usually, I would just acknowledge them with a nod of my head, maybe hold my drink up in greeting. However, I know if I offer my hand to Nicole first and she accepts, then the lovely Miss Kensington will feel she needs to do so as well. This means I get to touch her. I need to establish that connection for what I have planned. I offer her my hand

and she takes it politely in hers. When she goes to pull away, I tug her hand to my lips and place a soft kiss on her knuckles. I pull back just as fast, and act as if nothing happened. I watch as she fidgets from one foot to the next. Not the reaction I was hoping for, but we've got all night. I need to give Bright tomorrow night off. He just gave me an in with a beautiful woman who has my neglected dick standing at attention.

"Ladies, it's nice to meet you," I finally say.

They both smile in acknowledgement at my greeting.

"I called and reserved us a table," Bright says as he places his hand on the small of Nicole's back and leads our little party of four to the back of the club. I follow his lead and do the same with Kensington; however, my attempt is not as well received as Bright's. I feel her entire body become rigid at my touch. This is not what I'm used to. I've never had a woman act this way toward me before. It doesn't sit well with me.

We reach the table and Bright pulls a chair out; he motions in offering to Nicole. I follow his lead and do the same. I'm a little out of my element here. This girl has only been in my presence for ten minutes tops and has me off my game. I need to regroup. I've never really had to work for it. I'm sure once she warms up to me, it will be game on.

We all settle in and I offer to grab us some drinks. Bright asks for a beer, and I look toward Nicole. I can feel Kensington watching me, which is why I'm making her wait until the end. "Nicole?" I say her name in question. She just shrugs and says to bring her a beer as well. I then turn my gaze on Kensington. I take in her blue eyes and high cheek bones. This chick really is a stunner. I lean in close and whisper in her ear, "What about you, what do you want?" My voice is gruff as I place a gentle kiss just below her ear. I feel her stiffen. What the fuck? It's been a while since I've been out. Have I lost my touch?

"I'm actually the DD, so just a bottle of water please," she replies, not making eye contact. She's looking at Nicole. I watch as Nicole mouths the words "Are you okay?" Kensington nods once. If I was not so enthralled with this chick, I would have missed it.

Without another word, I stand and make my way to the bar. I order three beers and a bottle of water. Two lovely ladies dressed in clothing that leaves nothing to the imagination saunter up on either side of me. I offer the blonde a wink and she moves in closer. She runs her nails up and down my forearm. "Hey handsome," she coos. I want to roll my eyes at her antics. Instead, I wink at her and watch as her eyes light up. It's easy to see that if I wanted her, I could have her. I glance over my shoulder at the table and see Bright and the girls deep in conversation. I'm not sure what this girl's issue is, but it bugs the hell out of me. I wrack my brain trying to think of if I've met her before. Did I sleep with her and not remember? It wouldn't be the first time. No matter how much I like to avoid that situation, it, indeed, has happened a time or two. Her eyes pop in my head and I know if that were the case, I would remember. You don't forget eyes like that.

The bartender passes me our drinks. I give him some cash with a hefty tip and turn to leave. Blondie stops me with her hand on my arm. "Got one of those for me?" she asks. Surely her voice isn't naturally that low. She's trying way too hard and my already surly mood from Kensington's brush off isn't earning her any extra points.

"No can do, these are already spoken for." I hate being a dick, but sometimes it's just the way things need to be.

I make it back to the table and pass out the drinks. Both girls are laughing at something Brighton has said and that irks me even more. I take my seat next to Kensington and she acts as if I'm not even there. The DJ says he's going to slow things down, which prompts Bright to hold out his hand to Nicole. She doesn't hesitate. She places her hand in his and allows him to pull her to her feet. She glances over her shoulder at us and Kensington offers her a small wave.

I stand up and offer my hand as well. Seems it's working for Bright. My usual game doesn't seem to affect this chick. She stares at my waiting hand, but makes no move to accept. "Dance with me?" I ask.

She studies me for what seems like hours then says, "No, thank you. I've had a long day. I think I'll just sit this one out."

I give her a nod that I understand and turn and walk away. I don't need this shit. I don't know what crawled up this girl's ass, but I'm so fucking over it. I have not had a night out in months and I'll be damned if I'm going to let this girl ruin it.

I find myself back at the bar ordering me another beer. I killed mine on the way here. The blonde and her friend are still there, still on the prowl. At this point, I don't care. She's offering what I need.

Release.

Maybe that's why I'm letting this Kensington chick mess with my head. It's been way too long since I've been buried deep. I catch the bartender's attention and motion to the girls. He nods in understanding. They both move in close and thank me. "Trust me, ladies, the pleasure is all mine." I can tell they know the score. I only need one of them. I'm not greedy. The blonde doesn't seem to be holding a grudge from my brush off earlier. After the bartender serves their drinks, she picks it up and downs it. I follow suit and slam back the beer I just ordered. She grabs my arm and pulls to me to the dance floor.

I don't think about how rude it was of me to leave her sitting there by herself. I don't think about how pissed Bright is going to be that I left her there. All I think about is the warm willing female grinding against me, giving me a preview of what's to come. The release I have been yearning for is right in front of me and that's all I want.

5

Kensington

MY EYES FOLLOW him as he walks away from the table. He is definitely not someone who will take me as I am. I can't believe he's pissed off that I didn't want to dance. Sure I wasn't exactly Miss Hospitality, but his cocksure attitude rubbed me the wrong way. I could tell from the moment he saw me what was running through his mind. I don't have the time or the energy to be another notch on his bedpost. Maybe it's just that I'm not in the best of moods today, but he's arrogant! The blonde at the bar slides up next to him, pressing against his arm. Maxton says something to her; she smiles and licks her lips. He stands and I can't pull my eyes away as he leads her out to the dance floor. She grinds up against him as his hands roam her body. I watch in fascination as they move to the beat. Strangers… touching, grinding, and groping as if they have been intimate for years.

I watch as his big hands glide across her back. Yes, I noticed the size of his hands. How could I not? He's a big guy. Well over six feet tall, broad strong shoulders and chocolate brown eyes. Just because I think he's an arrogant ass munch doesn't mean I can't enjoy the view.

I want to look away, I do, but my eyes are glued to them. Their bodies move in sync, like they've moved together a thousand times before. My eyes follow the muscles in his arms as her pulls her tight against his chest. The way his jeans hang, just right on his hips as they grind and roll into hers. For an instant, I envy her. I'm jealous that his hard muscular body is not grinding up on me. When Maxton turns and catches me staring, he smirks, leans down, and kisses her neck. GAH! Cocky bastard.

My envy turns to pity. I feel bad for her that she has so little self-worth that she feels like she has to offer herself on a silver platter to guys like him. Then again, who am I to judge? To each their own.

Still, the way he smirked at me, like he could read my mind, pisses me off. I hate guys who think they're God's gift to women. What happened to romance, to conversation, getting to know someone? Old fashioned? Maybe. However, with my past, I need that. I'm not looking for love, but I'm not opposed to it either. I just need to be able to fully trust, and that's hard for me.

Suddenly, I feel warm breath on my ear. "Dance with me," a deep voice rumbles. I turn my head to catch a glimpse, and the guys... not bad. He's about six foot, dirty blond hair, and by the way his shirt is pulled tight against his arms, I can tell he's built, although a little too preppy for my taste. I start to say no, and then I remember the look on Maxton's face when he caught me watching. No way am I going to let him think I'm pining away for his affections. This is what I came for. To break out of the sorrow that this day holds. To continue living one day at a time. Besides, I love dancing.

"Lead the way," I reply with a wink.

Mr. Preppy grabs my hand and leads me out to the dance floor. I get a whiff of his cologne as he pulls me against his chest. He smells good. Leaning down, he whispers in my ear. "By the way, I'm Lance," he says in his deep voice.

Not giving him the chance to stand to his full height, I turn my head and reply, "Kensington. Nice to meet you, Lance."

A broad smile crosses his face just as the first beats of Ginuwine's

"Pony" begins to play. His hands are on my hips as we begin to move. It only takes a few beats for us to find our rhythm. Finding the give and take of our hips. He thrusts forward; I thrust back. Lance has got some moves and I'm enjoying them. I turn, placing my back to his front, as he snakes his arms around my waist. I raise my arms in the air and wave my hands from side to side. Lance thrusts forward. Taking the hint, I grind back against him as we fall right back into rhythm in this new position.

Lost in the moment, Lance places his head in the crook of my neck. I can feel his hot breath against my already heated skin. I lean my head back against his chest, allowing him better access. I don't know why I do it, but I open my eyes. Standing in front of me is Maxton and the girl from the bar. Her back is facing me, which means I have a direct line of site to Maxton. Our eyes lock, neither one of us willing to look away. The image of his smirk comes to my mind and I want him to know he doesn't affect me. I want him to know what his cocky ass is missing out on. I bring my arms down behind my head and wrap them around Lance's neck. I exaggerate the sway of my hips as I rock against him. My eyes never leave Maxton. His jaw clenches and it takes everything I have to not let the smile break across my face. Take that!

Childish behavior, yes I know. I also know that guys like him deserve a taste of their own medicine. The beat changes as My Darkest Days' "Porn Star Dancing" blares from the speakers. Lance places his hands on my hips and spins me to face him. He pulls my body tight against his and we again find our rhythm. I don't know if Maxton is still behind me; I don't know if he's watching. I do know I want to continue to give him a show. I twist my hips and bend my knees as I lower myself to the floor. My hands are resting on Lance's hips. I hope it looks like I'm using him as my stripper pole. As I work myself back up, Lance moves in as close as he can and we sway our hips to the beat. I straddle one of his legs and just let go. I clear my head of worry and sadness. I just feel the beat of the music and enjoy holding onto the muscular arms of my dance partner.

The song ends and a slow one begins. I gently pull away from Lance and look toward the bar. I've managed to work up a sweat. "Let me buy you a drink," he says over the music.

It's so loud I nod my agreement. Lance places his hand on the small of my back and leads me to the bar. I perch myself on a stool while Lance stands behind me. He's close; I can feel the heat radiating from him. "What can I get you?" he asks.

"Just water. Thanks."

Holding up two fingers, he says, "Waters," once he has the bartender's attention.

After guzzling half of my bottle of water, I survey the crowd. I've lost track of Nicole and Brighton. I finally spot them heading back to our table. "Hey, I need to go check in with my friend; would you like to join me?" I ask Lance. I'm having a good time with him. He's gorgeous and has killer moves. From what I can tell, he's a nice guy. He has yet to make a rude comment or hit on me. He's exactly what I needed tonight.

"Lead the way, Kens," he says, already adopting my nickname. He's so laid back it's refreshing.

After making our way through the crowd, I take my seat. Lance takes one of the two empties beside me. Brighton looks up and a bright smile crosses his face. "Lance, how the hell are ya?" He holds his fist out across the table. Lance meets him in the middle and they "bump."

"Good, man. Just working, same old same old. I haven't seen you out much lately," he tells Brighton.

Brighton looks at Nicole and winks, almost as if Lance is confirming what he's been telling her for months. That he's been busy. "Yeah, Max has been renovating the bar, hiring new staff, things like that. We've been knee-deep in it for the past few months. Everything is finally back up and running, so I convinced him to take a night off from it all."

"Max is here? I haven't seen him," Lance comments just as Max plops down in the vacant seat between Lance and Brighton.

"Hey, man, I was just asking about you. It's been a while," Lance addresses Maxton. He offers up his fist, Max half-heartedly returns the gesture.

I avoid making eye contact with either of them. Instead, I turn to

Nicole. She immediately starts talking about me and Lance on the dance floor.

"You two were hot!" she says. Her shoulder bumps against mine as she winks.

Before I can even answer, Maxton raises his voice. "I need another beer." Loudly, he scoots his chair back from the table.

Good riddance, asshole!

6

Maxton

FUCKING LANCE. SERIOUSLY? She turned me down cold but was grinding all up on him. It's bad enough I had to watch her sexy curves move against him. Had to watch him slide his hands against her flat stomach, bury his face in her neck. Watching the show has me frustrated, not even the warm willing blonde could get me to tear my eyes away from them. I can't believe she brought him back to our table. She did it to rub it in my face, I'm sure. To make matters worse, her friend, Bright's girl, just had to give us a play by play of how hot their little show was.

I'm standing at the bar waiting for my beer when Bright walks up. "What's up?" He sounds more annoyed than concerned.

"Needed a drink, man." My answer is clipped. I'm not in the mood to shoot the shit.

"If you say so," he quips.

I don't say anything else and neither does he as we wait for the bartender to deliver our drinks. I continue to pretend that Bright doesn't know me better than I know myself.

Bright takes his drinks back to the table. I decide to take up residence at the bar. I'm pissed off that I'm letting this chick and her decision affect my night. So what if she turned me down; there are plenty others willing and able. I tell myself it's because I haven't been out in so long and her rejection hit my ego. Hell, I've never been turned down before. The feeling of rejection is not one I am accustomed to.

I feel a warm hand on the back of my neck. I can smell her, the blonde. She's back and ready for whatever I'll give her. I need the release; it's been months. I pull a twenty out of my wallet and throw it on the bar. Standing from my stool, I snake may arm around her waist and bring my lips to her ear. "Ready to get out of here?" I breathe against her ear.

Her answering purr is all I need. I drag her out to my truck, sending Bright a message that I will be back to get him in an hour. I've had a few beers in quick succession, so driving for a while is not an option. Instead, I have blondie pull the truck around to the back of the building. It's dark and secluded. Perfect for what we are about to do.

As soon as she parks the truck, she's crawling across the seat and is straddling my lap. She leans down to kiss me and I turn my head. If you kiss them, they think it means more than what it actually is. It's just a release. We're just two consenting adults enjoying each other for a small amount of time. Women do whatever they can to get their claws in you and then you're sunk. Hell, just look at my dad. My mother destroyed him. No way will that ever happen to me. I always have the upper hand. Speaking of that, I need to make sure she understands exactly what this is.

"Hey," I say, grabbling ahold of her shoulders and pulling her body away from mine. I need her to look me in the eye. I need to be certain she knows the score. "This is just for tonight. I don't want you to get any romantic ideas about us; this is just sex," I say bluntly. If she changes her mind, I'm good with that.

She runs her hands up my abs and licks her lips before she says, "Just sex, got it. Now can we get to the sex part?"

I study her to make sure she really understands and her heated gaze pretty much tells me that sex is all she's thinking about right now. Good enough. I caress her thighs as my hands find their way up her skirt. Before I can go any further, she leans forward and slides out of her panties.

Instead of sitting back down, she turns so her body is facing out the window of the truck. She sits on my lap and grinds her hips back and forth. "Are you ready to come out and play?" she asks, her voice filled with want.

I lift her hips and pull myself out of my jeans. I grab a condom from my wallet and suit up. Taking ahold of her hips, I guide her back down and that's all it takes. She's riding me without a care in the world. This is actually perfect. I don't have to avoid eye contact or kissing her. The intimacy is not a factor with this girl; she takes what she wants with no apologies. I relax against the seat and enjoy the ride. It doesn't take long before I can feel my release. I slide my hand around her waist to help get her to where I am. It's been way too long and I'm not going to last.

With a few more quick thrusts, we fall over the edge together. Blondie slides off me and back into the driver's seat. She slides her panties into her purse. Flipping down the visor, she checks her make-up. Finally, she looks at me. "Thanks, that was great," she says. The next thing I know, she has the door open and she's sauntering back into the bar.

That is most definitely a first for me, and after the huge hit to my ego earlier, well, let's just say the satisfaction the release gave me is now gone. I'm wound tight.

I quickly dispose of the condom in a napkin and tuck myself back in. I pull the truck back around to the front of the bar and park. I want to go back in. I need another drink, but I've had about all I can handle for one night. I decide to send Bright a text letting him know I'll be in the truck when he's ready to go. It's already half past midnight and last call is in thirty minutes. I'll just catch a quick nap until then. I'm over this night!

7

Kensington

AFTER MAXTON LEFT with the blonde, the atmosphere at our table picked up. I enjoyed talking to both Lance and Brighton. I even let them both take me for another spin around the dance floor. Lance and I move well together, and Brighton... well, let me just say that I can see why Nicole is so smitten. They are both really nice, down-to-earth guys. I wonder how they became friends with Maxton.

The bartender announces last call. That's when Nicole speaks up. "Do you have a ride home?" she asks Brighton.

He nods, taking a sip of his beer. "Yeah, Max is out in the parking lot in his truck. He said he was going to take a quick nap while he waited on me."

"Really? That seems like an odd thing for him to do," Nicole comments.

Brighton shrugs. "Not really. Max and I have been working our asses off the last several months on the remodel. It took a lot of convincing to get him to come out tonight. It's been longer for him than it has for me. He's running on fumes," he explains.

I try to place that guy in my head. The one who puts his heart and soul into rebuilding his family's legacy. I don't see Maxton when I picture that person. It's hard for me to reconcile the man I met tonight with the one Brighton is describing to us now.

The guys walk us to the car. Lance thanks me for a fun night. We really hit it off. We have a lot in common. He has a degree in business with a minor in finance as well. We exchanged numbers earlier. He said if I ever need any help with school to call him. He leans down and gives me a warm hug. There is nothing romantic about it. He's a great guy, but I have no interest in taking things further. He's fun to hang out with. I hop in the car while I wait for Nicole and Brighton to say goodbye. I figure this will give them a little privacy. Ten minutes later, she is finally strapped in her seat, and we are headed back to our apartment.

"You and Brighton seem to be hitting it off," I say to Nicole. The smile has not left her face all night.

"Yeah. He's nice. We've gotten to know each other slowly. I kept waiting for him to call and want to hook up, you know, but tonight he didn't even try anything," she replies, almost disappointed.

"Do you call that lip-lock nothing?" I'm sure if it wasn't dark in the car, her face would be flushed.

"No, that's not what I meant. I mean, look at him, look at all of them. At first glance, they don't appear to be a group of guys who want more than a quick tangle in the sheets."

"Pft. From what I can tell, both Brighton and Lance are great guys. Maxton on the other hand..." I trail of remembering how cocky he was. Like he just knew I would be falling at his feet. As if!

"Maxton is so damn hot. Did you see his arms? All that dark hair and the scruff on his face. Not just anyone can pull that look off. Maxton, well, he makes a day's worth of stubble sexy as hell."

"Oh, he's sexy all right. That man is definite eye candy, until he opens his mouth. He's cocky as hell and he was actually pissed off that I wouldn't dance with him," I scoff.

"What? Why in the hell would you turn him down? We are talking about the same guy, right? Brighton's super-hot best friend, Mr. Tall,

Dark, and Sexy. Not to mention, the badass vibes he throws off. I can't believe you turned him down," she scolds me.

"He's cocky and so sure of himself. He just assumed I would fall to his charms and worship him. That's not me. Then he seemed pissed off that I was dancing with Lance."

"Is that why he stormed away from the table? Sounds to me like he was jealous."

"Men like Maxton don't get jealous. He was mad that he got turned down, nothing more, nothing less."

Nicole doesn't comment, and the remainder of the drive home is quiet. Once we pull into our complex, she grabs my arm before I can get out of the car. "I'm proud of you, Kens. You faced this day and kicked its ass. You're living life just like she would want you to," she says softly. Her eyes find mine. "I know if she was here, she would tell you how proud of you she is. Proud of the person you are."

Taking in a shuddering breath, I try to stop the tears from flowing. "I hope you're right." I force the words, fighting against the tears. "Dad said the same thing today; he said she would want me to live each day to the fullest. He's worried about me never letting myself fall in love. He and I don't talk about those kinds of things; it was always Mom's territory."

"Smart man, your dad," she says.

"He is, and today was a good day for us. I don't know why he started opening up, or why I did, but I think it was good for us," I tell her.

"For what it's worth, I agree with your dad. She would want you to let yourself fall in love, have the forever kind of love that she had with your dad."

"I want that, I do. It's just not going to be an overnight thing for me."

"As long as you are open to the idea, you never know what can happen."

I am open to the idea. I'm scared as hell to trust someone that much, but I think if I had time, I could. Only time will tell.

8

Maxton

I TRY TO take a nap, lay my head back against the seat and just chill. Even though that's what I want to do, it doesn't happen. Instead, I think about the last several months. Dad would be proud to see the renovation of Cooper's—our legacy. I've put everything I am into making Cooper's a success. When I took over, I knew absolutely nothing about running a business. Sure, I'd worked there for Dad when he needed help, but manning the bar is nothing compared to having it all on your shoulders. I refuse to fail. Refuse to let the blood, sweat, and tears of my grandfather and my father fade away into nothing.

Staring into the darkness, I see that people are starting to clear out of the bar. I watch the door for Brighton. I sent him a text, but he didn't reply. I'm sure he's pissed that I walked away from his date and her friend like that. All I know is that I couldn't listen to Nicole replay Kensington and Lance out on the dance floor.

I finally spot Bright and the girls… and Lance. They are walking toward a silver Honda. I don't want to watch what happens. I am so off-kilter tonight, that I don't know how I will react if I see him touching her again. This is not me. I'm not that guy, but tonight with her, I am. I

35

squeeze my eyes shut and try to wrap my brain around why her turning me down, and not him, affects me so much. It has to be because this is my first night out in months.

I hear the truck door open and Bright climbs in. "You good, man?" he questions.

I know what he's asking. He wants to make sure I'm okay to drive. I've sobered up and I'm golden. A night full of rejection will do that to you. Well, technically, the blonde didn't reject me, but she did walk away as soon as I pulled out. Becoming a dedicated business owner has softened me up. I've lost my appeal to women. Shit! Now I'm gonna have to work for it.

"Yeah, I'm good." I start the truck and head toward our house.

As soon as we make it home, I head straight to my room, strip down, and take a steaming hot shower. Something about being with the blonde… damn, I should have gotten her name. I just want to wash the night away, forget the entire night ever happened.

Twenty minutes later, I'm on the back deck, beer in hand, just watching the night sky. The weather will turn cold before long and sitting out here will not be as pleasant. I hear the patio door slide open.

Bright walks out, hands me another beer, and takes the lounge next to me. His phone beeps and he fumbles to check it. I watch in fascination as his face lights up once he reads the message.

"That her?" My voice is loud against the calm of the night.

Smiling like a fool, he answers, "Yeah. They're home." I nod my head, tip my beer back, and take a long drink. "I'm glad we were able to hang out tonight. Not sure what happened, but I wish you could have spent more time with her. I like her."

Bright and I don't really talk hearts and flowers. It's not our thing. We've been best friends our entire lives and we just know the other well enough it's not needed. For him to volunteer that he's into this girl is a huge deal. I feel like an ass that I didn't take the opportunity to get to know her better. I need to make it up to him.

"Tonight… was… odd for me. I guess I still have a ton on my mind with the new renovation and the next step for Cooper's." I don't want to tell him that multiple rejections will do that to a guy. I don't want to hear him tell me how big of an ass I was. We both know it to be true, so talking about it seems pointless. Besides, I can't handle that after the night I've had.

Brighton doesn't respond; he just smiles as his fingers fly over the screen of his phone. I watch my best friend in fascination. I never thought I would see the day. He's let this one get under his skin. His phone beeps and his face lights up.

"Invite her over tomorrow night; we can throw some steaks on the grill. I have a feeling I'm going to be seeing her around a lot."

"I hope so," he says.

"Let me know. I have to be at the bar in the morning, but I can stop by the store on my way home. That's the least I can do for how I acted tonight. I was just… off my game."

"All right, man, I'll check with Nicole," he says, his fingers again flying across the screen. "See ya in the morning." He climbs from his chair, holding his fist out. I push mine against his, and then it's just me and the stillness of the night. I chug back the rest of my beer and decide to head off to bed. Putting this day behind me cannot happen soon enough.

The next morning, just as I'm walking out the door, Bright yells for me.

"Max!" he says as he comes rushing into the kitchen, phone in his hand. "I just talked to Nicole; she'll be here at seven. She's bringing Kensington as well. Please be nice," he pleads.

I nod. "I'll stop by and pick up what we need on the way home." With that, I walk out the door wondering how my second interaction with the sexy Kensington is going to go. I tell myself that I'm just going to ignore her and her rejection. Bright is counting on me to not fuck this up for him.

9

Kensington

AS WE WALK up the front steps of their house, I wonder how I got myself into this. I glance over and see the smile that has been permanently etched on my best friends face for the last twenty-four hours and I admit defeat. Nicole has been there for me more than I can count. When she asked me late last night, as I was drifting off to sleep, if I would come to Brighton's with her tonight for an impromptu barbecue, I said yes at the sound of the joy in her voice. I also said yes, because I just wanted to go to sleep. Ready to put the day behind me. In the light of day, as I watch Nicole knock on the front door, I question my sanity.

Before she even finishes knocking on the door, it flies open, revealing the glimmering eyes of Brighton. His face is lit up just like my best friend's. I can't help but feel lighter about the night, just seeing how they both feel the same way about each other. I want her to be happy. She deserves nothing but that, true happiness. "Hey ladies," Brighton says as he leans in and kisses Nic on the corner of her mouth.

"Thanks for having us," I say, because Nicole seems too busy cheesing from ear to ear to speak at the moment.

"I'm glad you could make it. Come on in. Max is on the back deck starting the grill. I hope you brought your suits for a swim later," he says. I follow behind and watch in fascination as he reaches for Nic's hand and laces their fingers together. Good man.

Max turns to face us when he hears the patio door open. I turn my head and take in my surroundings. This place is really beautiful. It's not at all what I expected of two bachelors. The back of the house is like a private oasis. A huge multi-tiered deck leads down to a concreted area and the in-ground pool. One of the sections of the deck also holds a hot tub. I walk to the edge of the deck, we are on the upper most level, and peer out below. There are lots of trees surrounding the property and a decent size pond with a gazebo toward the back of the property. I hate to admit it, but I'm impressed.

"Kens!" I hear Nicole yell my name. I whip my head around to see all three of them watching me. "I've been saying your name over and over," she tells me. I see the concern in her eyes.

Taking a deep breath, I push off the railing and head back over to be sociable. "Sorry, I was just enjoying the view."

"I'll give you all a tour later. He's done a great job with it," Brighton tells me.

Even though I try to fight it, my eyes find Maxton. He's staring right at me. "It's beautiful." I decide to keep the compliments to a minimum. This is yet another side that I never would have guessed would be a part of the great Maxton Cooper. I guess it's possible he was just not having a good night.

He studies me. "I have all sorts of… special skills." He smirks at me.

Gah! And I was actually trying to give him the benefit of the doubt. Maybe there is a twin around here, the nice twin. I have to be missing something with this guy.

Brighton hands Nicole and I both a bottle of water. "Can we do anything to help?" Nicole asks.

"Yes, we are at your disposal," I tell Brighton.

"Nope, we've got it all taken care of. You ladies just have a seat and relax. It should be ready in about fifteen minutes." He winks at Nic before heading into the house.

"Come check out this view." I grab her arm and lead her to where I was just standing minutes ago.

Nicole gushes and Maxton yells, "Thank you," over his shoulder.

I fight the urge to roll my eyes. Sexy, infuriating man. It's a shame really, such a waste of good eye candy. He's great until he opens his mouth.

"What?" Nicole asks, shocked.

Shit! I must have said that aloud. Great. Shrugging, I answer, "I just call it how I see it." The corner of her mouth lifts in a smile and I know what's coming next. Me and my damn big mouth!

"I think he's hot as hell," she says, bumping her shoulder into mine.

"I'll give you that; he's fucking beautiful to look at. It's when he opens his mouth that he loses appeal." Just as the words leave my mouth, Nicole's eyes go wide and I know I'm busted.

I feel his hands on my hips and his breath on my ear. "I'd like to show you what I can do when I open my mouth, sweetheart." He places a kiss on my neck just below my ear and then he's gone. I instantly miss the heat of his body and it pisses me off. Guys like him are all the same. I know this. My body is betraying me because he looks so damn edible.

The sound of Nicole's low chuckle breaks me out of my trance. "See what I mean?" I ask, exasperated.

This causes her to throw her head back and laugh. "Oh, I see all right. That man has you twisted," she says through her laughter.

"Really? He's an asshole."

"Time to eat, ladies," Max yells out.

Nicole slips her arm through mine and leans in close. "I just call it how I see it," she throws my words back at me.

This time I let my eyes roll back in my head, letting her know what she's insinuating is ridiculous. We reach the table and Bright pulls out a chair for Nicole. I make my way around the table to take a seat, and Max is suddenly there, pulling out my chair with the ever present smirk on his face. My manners rule in this situation as I whisper, "Thanks."

Max leans down, his lips once again against my ear. "You smell fucking edible," he whispers.

I shudder at his words. Before I can regain my composure and reply, he's already seated in the chair next to me as the bowl of salad is being passed around.

What the hell was I thinking coming here?

10

Maxton

I SHOULD HAVE never got close enough to smell her, to taste her. I couldn't resist taunting her when I walked up on her saying she thought I was sexy. My cock was instantly hard, begging to take her. The gentle kiss of her neck just about had me blowing a load in my pants. I need to fuck this girl out of my system. I'll need to be careful so I don't piss off Bright's girl. I don't want to mess things up for him. He's really into her and was even talking about making things more permanent. Why he would want that, I will never know. He saw what happened to my dad, but he's still falling for the feminine charms. At least he can't say I didn't warn him. I did, just this morning. He took it well as he laughed at my warning. He then proceeded to tell me how one day I would fall to those charms and he was going to sit back and enjoy the show when it finally happened.

I need to come up with a plan to get her under me, or on top of me, I'm not picky. I just need to work her out of my system. I watch her face as Bright pulls Nicole's chair out for her. I could swear I see longing on her face, but it's gone before I can really study her. My feet are moving on their own accord and I find myself beside her, pulling out an empty seat for her. The wind picks up and I get a scent of her, her sweet flowery scent with a hint of coconut.

I quickly take the seat next to her so I don't embarrass myself with my rock-hard dick standing at attention. Fuck! I reach for the bowl of salad that Bright is offering and quickly place some on my plate. I sit the bowl in front of her and reach in to grab a steak and baked potato. I busy myself adding butter and sour cream, dousing my steak in A1. I shift in my chair to try and get more comfortable. Nothing is working. Shit, my mind races for a distraction, and that's when my dad runs through my mind. He loved my mother with everything in him and she killed him. He used to tell me I would find the one and just know. That nothing would be able to keep me from her. I used to believe him. I used to believe in that fairy tale he talked about. That all ended the day he ended his life, because of her. The anger I feel toward my mother does the job. My dick is effectively deflated.

Both of the girls thank us for dinner and say how great the steak is. I can grill a mean steak, if I do say so myself. They insist on helping us clean up since we took care of dinner. Bright and I both protest, but they want no part of it. Cleanup is fast with the four of us working together. I take every chance I can get to rub against or touch Kensington during the process. I need to work on wearing her down.

Bright asks the girls if they want a tour of the property. I watch as he grabs a sweatshirt off the back of the chair and I know what he's doing. He's taking every opportunity to get his girl close. He's being a gentleman. I decide this is my best bet. Kensington seems to like Bright as does Nicole. Maybe I need to change up the game to get this girl in my bed. I run down the hall to the laundry room and grab a hoodie from the dryer. I meet back up with them as I slip it over my head. The girls don't seem to notice that he and I are both prepared for the night air, but didn't offer them the same. They are too busy admiring the landscaping. Once we reach the pond, Bright takes them across the bridge to the gazebo. He leads Nicole to the other side and I watch as she shivers and he wraps her up in his arms. I'm thrown off by this behavior. He and I have always been the same. Take us like we are, you don't like it, move on. There are plenty out there that do. This is not what he's doing with Nicole.

Kensington remains on the same side as me. I watch her as she leans against the railing and looks out over the water. She rubs her bare arms and I watch as she shivers. I move next to her. Gripping her hips, I turn her to face me. I expect her smart mouth to unleash on me, but she doesn't. Her eyes follow my movements as I lift my sweatshirt over my head. I turn it around and pull it over her head. She immediately places her arms in the sleeves. My eyes never leave her and she leans down and inhales deeply. She's sniffing my fucking shirt! She's smelling me, and from the look on her face, she likes it. My cock is again standing at attention for this girl.

I step closer to her. She peers up at me and smiles. "You smell fucking edible," she says and I cannot contain the smile that crosses my face. She fucking gives it right back to me and that only makes me want her sassy smart mouth even more. Makes me want to bury myself deep inside of her. Makes me want to worship every inch of her until I've got her out of my system.

She looks away, a slight blush against her cheeks. I bend my knees so I'm more her height. Placing my index finger under her chin, I lift her face so she's looking at me. My left hand moves to her hip. I stand to my full height and tug her close to me. My right hand slides behind her neck. I caress her cheek with my thumb as her eyes find mine. I'm just about ready to make my move. I lean in, closing the distance, when I hear footsteps against the creaky boards. I've been meaning to get out here and fix that, but with the remodel, I just haven't had the time. I'm thankful and pissed all at the same time. I'm glad I stopped before our best friends were witness to what I would have done, witness to how bad I want her. I'm pissed off because my fucking mouth is watering at the thought of tasting her.

11

Kensington

HOLY SHIT! WHAT am I doing? He was going to kiss me and I was going to let him. My heart is racing as Nicole bounds up to me, wearing Brighton's sweatshirt. She smiles at me and tugs on the sleeve of Maxton's. I thought for sure, me throwing his words back at him would set off his cocky attitude. Instead, it had the opposite effect. I could see the heat in his eyes. He wanted to devour me and I wanted to let him.

I link arms with Nic and we walk back across the bridge. "That man looks like he's going to eat you alive. What the hell did I miss?" she whisper-shouts.

"I lost my head for a minute, that's all. He was… close and smells… amazing and it threw me off. Just a minor lapse in judgment that will not happen again," I tell her.

"Uh huh. Anyway, Brighton is… I can't even describe it. I really like him," she says.

She doesn't need to tell me this. First of all, she has said this before, and second, any fool could see that the two of them are smitten. "He seems like a great guy. I'm happy for you."

The guys catch up to us, but stay behind. "Now, let's give you a tour of the house," Brighton says. You can tell he's not ready for the night to end. Nicole didn't think this through. If I had not ridden over here with her, she could be curled up in his bed. We all know it's going to happen.

Nicole stops and turns to face them. "Sounds good," she tells him. He steps forward and reaches for her hand; he gently pulls her toward the house. This leaves me trailing behind with Maxton, yet again.

We try our best to ignore each other, at least I try my best. I follow along and ooh and ahh at the right places. It's not a hardship. This house is amazing. I'm again reminded of my initial thought when we arrived earlier. This does not feel like the house of two confirmed bachelors; this feels like a home. Something I miss more than I realized.

We stop at a door. It's at the end of the hall. I realize Nicole and Brighton are in the room directly across. I feel him come in close behind me. "This is mine," he says as he slaps me on the ass with one hand and reaches over my shoulder with the other to push the door open.

Once we are in the room, he walks around me and sits on the edge of the bed.

"You couldn't handle me," I mumble under my breath as I walk further into the room. Taking it all in. It appears that Maxton has supersonic hearing. He stands and stalks toward me. Two steps and he's right in front of me, once again invading my personal space. My body reacts to him as my nipples harden and I press my legs together. Suddenly, his "this is mine" statement means something completely different.

He bends down and his shoulder hits my belly as he picks me up. I protest by beating my fists on his back. It's a short ride with his long legs and I find myself sitting on the bed, Maxton between my legs leaning over me. I lean my head back to look at him and he takes advantage of my exposed neck. He runs his tongue from my collarbone to my ear. "I can handle you, sweetheart. The question is… can you handle me?" I can feel my legs quivering; apparently, so can he. He places his big hands on my thighs and runs them up and down. "You're quaking for my touch."

I realize I'm sitting on his bed, two seconds away from letting him seduce me. I'm about to become another one of many, something I said I would never be. What is it about him that reduces my brain to mush?

Placing my hands against his chest, I push with all of my strength and he doesn't move. He's a big guy, but I'm not afraid of him. "Maxton, please," I say. I thought maybe, if I was nice, he would relent and let me up.

Instead, his eyes flame with lust as he moves in closer. I can now feel his erection against my center and I want to moan at the simple contact. Jesus! What is he doing to me? "Are you begging for me, pretty girl?" His voice is deep and laced with the same desire I see in his eyes.

"No! Please, let me up. This is not happening," I tell him, pushing again on his chest. This time he steps away from me. He runs his fingers through his hair, and for a split second, I think he might be just as affected. I know he wants me. I could feel the evidence, see it in his eyes. But for that one split second, I thought I could see that it might be more than that. However, the look on his face is gone just as quick as it arrived.

It's just my mind playing tricks on me. I want him; he's sexy as hell— tall, muscles in spades, strong jaw line, all that thick dark hair, the scruff on his face, and let's not forget about those eyes! He has my hormones working overtime, and I need to keep my head clear. I know he sees me as a challenge. He just needs to realize I'm one challenge he is not going to win.

Taking a deep breath, I rise from the bed and walk out of his bedroom. I hear Brighton and Nicole across the hall. I just keep walking until I'm back in the kitchen. I sit myself down on a stool at the island and wait. I pull my phone out of my back pocket and tap on the Facebook app. I leisurely scroll through my newsfeed. I'm not really paying much attention, just trying to look busy.

I hear footsteps as Maxton joins me. He reaches into the fridge and pulls out two bottles of water. He sets one in front of me as he downs the other.

"Thank you."

He nods before taking the stool next to me. He too pulls out his phone. I assume he's doing the same thing as me. Trying to look busy.

Trying to avoid the elephant in the room. Trying to avoid the chemistry that sparks between us. I will admit to that, but I want more. I know from my body's reaction to him that even one time with Maxton and I would be destroyed when he walks away.

12
Maxton

I DOWNED THE entire bottle of water, trying to cool my shit down. I had to stay back in my room for a few minutes to talk my dick down. Fuck, the sight of her leaning back on her elbows, her legs around my hips. I want nothing more than to sink inside her and stay there... for days.

I noticed when I came in that she was on Facebook. I take the stool beside her and pull out my phone. I tap on the search button and search for her name. Immediately, I see her picture pop up.

Kensington James.

I click the button to send her a friend request. Out of the corner of my eye, I see her phone vibrate on the counter with a notification, I assume. I watch as she picks it up and slides her finger across the screen. A small smile plays on her lips. My phone dings with a notification. Looking down, I see "Kensington James has accepted your friend request."

I lean over and bump my shoulder against hers. No words are said as we sit and play with our phones. The silence is comfortable. I scroll through her friends list and see Nicole. I send her a request as well. Brighton is head over heels for her, and maybe if I get to know her better,

I can find out what it's going to take to crack my new friend Kensington.

After I've exhausted my daily dose of Facebook, I close out the app and slide my phone back in my pocket. "Why don't we go start a fire? It's hard to tell what they're doing in there," I suggest.

"Sounds good. I love bonfires," she says, standing. Her eyes glance back at the hallway. "She really likes him," she states as she turns to head outside. I grab a blanket from the back of the couch, as well as my sweatshirt, which she folded and placed on the table by the patio door.

Once we are outside, I make my way down to the patio and throw a few logs on the fire before lighting a match. The blaze starts a slow burn. I take the lounger next to Kensington and hand her the sweatshirt. She happily slides back into it and burrows her arms in front of her. Once she seems to be settled, I stand and shake out the blanket. I drape it over her legs and tuck it around her. I don't want her getting cold.

Once I have her covered and wrapped in a cocoon, I sit back on the lounger and watch as the flame starts to grow. "He really likes her too, just so you know. I don't think I've ever seen him the way he is with her."

"How long have you guys been friends?"

"Since kindergarten. We met on the first day and we've been inseparable ever since. How about you and Nicole?"

Her face lights up at the mention of her best friend. "Our freshman year at college. I was in a rough place and Nicole… she saved me."

I wait for her to elaborate, but she doesn't. I want to know more about her. What had her in a bad place and what did she mean by Nicole saved her? I have a million questions running through my mind.

"Bright and I have been through some shit together, that's for sure," I offer that little tidbit, hoping she'll elaborate. She doesn't. "So Bright said you are both seniors this year?" I inquire. I want to keep her talking.

"Yeah. I'm kind of sad about it, if you want to know the truth. I don't know where life is going to take us. I hate the thought of losing touch with her."

"Sounds to me like the two of you are tight. It's hard to break that bond," I tell her.

"So you own Cooper's? I've been there a few times, but I've never seen you."

"Yeah." I hesitate to tell her more. I decide to go with it and skip over the details. "My dad passed away a few years ago. He and my mom were divorced and he left the business and this place to me." I point toward the house.

"This place is amazing. Honestly, when I first walked in, I was shocked. It's not what I expected for two bachelors," she says sheepishly.

I throw my head back and laugh at her assessment. "You're right." I shrug. "I just… I grew up here and construction was my thing, what I was doing before I inherited the bar. I just wanted a nice place to come home to. Dad and I always worked on projects together. In a way, it felt like each time I fixed up something else that he was here with me. Sounds crazy, huh?" I'm an idiot. I want this girl in my bed and she's fighting it. Then I go and tell her the crazy shit bouncing around in my brain. She's really going to run from me now.

I sit up on my lounger and study her. Her head is tilted back and her eyes appear to be closed. She's so fucking beautiful bathed in the moonlight. A gust of wind blows and a shiver runs through me. I look at Kensington all cozied up in my sweatshirt and blanket. She's on the double lounger, so there's room for me. Decision made, I stand up and walk to the other side. Her eyes pop open when she feels my weight beside her.

"What are you doing?" she asks. Her voice is soft as she watches my every move.

"It was starting to get cold, so I thought we could share." I point toward the blanket. I hold my hands up in front of her. "No funny business, I promise."

She chews on her bottom lip, debating. "I promise," I repeat. She gives me a slight nod of her head and reaches for the cover and lifts it. I scoot in beside her and she drops it on my lap.

We sit there in silence, both watching the night sky. After several minutes, she takes a deep breath and starts to talk. "It doesn't sound crazy. My mom, she umm… she passed away a few years ago, and I like to think that she's here with me, you know?"

She's still looking at the sky and I'm looking at her. I watch as a lone tear slips over her cheek. I reach over and gently wipe it away with my thumb. "We have something in common," I whisper. It's then that her sad eyes meet mine. The devastation I see guts me. Leaning over, I place a tender kiss against her temple.

Leaning back against the lounger, I return my gaze to the night sky. I feel Kensington tilt her head against my shoulder. "Yesterday was her birthday. It's a hard day for me. I'm sorry if I came across as a bitch. I just… I'm a mess."

I reach over and link my pinky with hers. "I've never seen a mess more beautiful," I tell her. I have no idea where the words come from, but I believe them with all that I am. I've never been that guy, the one who passes out compliments or sits with a girl and watches the stars. Tonight, I am. The game is changing and I'm in uncharted waters.

13

Kensington

I FEEL HIS pinky link with mine and my heart melts. Maxton Cooper has just shocked the hell out of me. I was sure he wanted to sit with me to make his move, but he didn't. Instead, he offered me comfort. Something that no one other than my father and Nicole have ever offered. I've never given anyone else the opportunity. I don't know if it's the dark of night, sitting with him under the moonlight. Maybe it was his confession about feeling like his father is here. I can't pinpoint exactly, but I allowed him to learn more about me tonight than anyone else.

I hear the patio door open. Finally! I love my best friend, but shit is getting too... just too much for me right now. I feel a tug on my hand as Maxton pulls it to his lips and places a soft kiss against my palm, then releases me. He folds his hands behind his head as I sit there with my mouth hanging open.

What the hell was that?

"Hey, you two." Nicole's chipper voice rings throughout the night. Brighton sits down on the lounger that Maxton was using before he invaded mine. He pulls Nicole onto his lap. "You two look cozy," she says to me.

"We've been out here for over an hour. It got cold, so we shared the blanket," Maxton explains, pointing to the blanket.

The wind picks up as soon as the words are out of his mouth and Nicole sinks back against Brighton. "Brrr. It's freezing. I guess we should go." She's talking to me, but looking over her shoulder at Brighton.

"I'll walk you out," he says, allowing her to pull him up from the lounger. I stand and fold the blanket, then hand it to Maxton. "Thank you." I lift my arms to take off his sweatshirt, but his hand on my arm stops me.

"Keep it. I'm sure I'll be seeing you again with the way those two are acting. I'll get it another time," he tells me.

I turn and follow Brighton and Nicole out to the car. As I reach the passenger door, I feel his hand on the small of my back. Maxton reaches around me and opens the door. I didn't even know he was behind me. "See you soon," he says.

"Thanks again for the sweatshirt," I tell him before climbing into the passenger seat. Maxton leans in the door and fastens my seat belt. He looks over to Nicole who is already sitting in the driver's seat.

"Drive safe," he says. Then he's gone. He pulls his big frame out of the car and gently shuts my door. He taps twice on the roof and walks back toward the house. My eyes follow him all the way. I hear Brighton tell Nicole to text him when we get home, another quick kiss and her door is shut, too. The blast of the heater immediately warms the inside of the car. Nicole reaches over and turns it down.

"Sorry I left you for so long. Brighton... his kisses."

"It's fine. Maxton built a fire and we just sat and talked."

"You too looked pretty close when we walked up."

"Not really. He had only been beside me maybe ten minutes. He was on the other lounger the rest of the night. At first, I thought he was trying to make his move, but he didn't. He just sat beside me and we kept talking," I tell her.

"What did you all talk about?" she questions.

I debate on telling her. Nicole will read more into this than what it really is. I can't, however, lie to her, even by omission, more than I already have. Someday soon, I need to sit her down and tell her everything with my mom. Someday. "He just talked about how he lost his dad a few years ago and he left him the house and the bar. I told him that I lost my mom a few years ago as well." I keep my answer simple. It doesn't feel right telling her Maxton's thoughts about his dad being near. She already knows I feel that way about Mom, especially when I go to the stables.

"Wow," she whispers. "I can't believe you told him. Kens, that's a huge step for you. Do you like him?"

"Yeah, I guess. First impression, he's a player with a cocksure attitude. Today he was… not. At least, not like he was at the bar last night. He seems like an all right guy." An all right guy who has my hormones in overdrive and makes my heart race, but it's whatever. I know he's still that first impression guy. At least, that's what I keep telling myself. "I just… I don't know… something about how he was telling me about his dad. The words just came out before I could really think about them." That is the honest truth. I was thinking it over, contemplating if I should say anything when the words just spilled out. Telling him was not as bad as what I had imagined. Only one lone tear escaped, but Maxton took care of that.

"They both seem like great guys. He has to be for you to open up like that." She doesn't say anything more. I know she wants to. She wants to talk about how great we would be together, but she knows better. She knows that if and when that happens, it will take time.

"Classes start Tuesday," she says, changing the subject. This girl knows me so well.

"Senior year, here we come! What's on the agenda for tomorrow?" I ask her. I'm sure she and Brighton have something planned.

"Nothing right now. You?" she asks.

"I got nothing," I tell her. "I figured you and Brighton would take full advantage of an extended weekend."

We pass under the street light close to our apartment and I can see her happiness has faded a little. "He didn't mention it. I didn't either. I didn't want to sound needy or clingy."

I laugh aloud at her comment. "First of all, I've never known you to be either. Second of all, the guy is freaking crazy about you. Maxton even said that he's never seen Brighton act this way about a girl. He's into you, just as much as you are him. Trust me," I tell her.

She pulls the car into our complex and shuts it off. Turning her head to face me, she demands, "You have to tell me everything."

I chuckle at her excitement. "I already told you. Maxton just said that Brighton really likes you and that it's the first time he's seen him like a girl this much. That's it, I promise," I tell her.

"I know it's too soon to like him this much. I'm not in love with him or anything, but he's just… gah! His kisses…" She touches her lips as if she can still remember the feel.

I run my fingers over my palm as I remember the tender touch of his lips there. That wasn't the only time his lips touched my skin tonight. It also wasn't the only time I wanted them to. I wanted him to kiss me in the gazebo. Hell, I wanted him to kiss me in his bedroom. I'm glad he didn't. I'm not sure I would have found the will power to resist his hard body. I need to be very careful around one Maxton Cooper.

Nicole and I end up sitting in her car, just listening to the radio and talking. We eventually decide that ice cream sounds good, so we drive to McDonalds and get a McFlurry. When we get back to the apartment, we grab our treats and head inside. Just as we are getting out of the car, a big black truck roars into the parking lot. We both freeze as we watch Maxton climb out of the driver's side and Brighton the passenger.

"Where in the hell have you been?" they say in unison.

Brighton is beside Nicole within a few strides of his long legs. Maxton is on his heels, rounding the car and pulling me into his chest. I feel him release a shuddering breath and kiss the top of my head. I step away from him and look over the car to see Brighton with his hands on both sides of Nicole's face.

"You were supposed to call. You said you would call when you got home and you didn't. I tried calling your cell, but there was no answer. I didn't have Kensington's number." He pulls her into his chest and wraps his arms around her. I can tell by the look on his face that he was worried sick about her.

Maxton tucks a loose hair behind my ear. He doesn't say anything. He doesn't need to. The embrace when he got here tells me he was worried as well.

"Sorry, we sat in the car talking, and then decided to go for ice cream," I say, holding up my McFlurry.

Maxton grabs my spoon and takes a big bite, returning the spoon as if nothing happened. I ignore the move and walk around the car to join Nicole and Brighton, Maxton right behind me.

"You want to come in?" Nicole asks Brighton.

"No, babe." He runs his fingers through his hair. "I was just worried. I wanted to make sure you were okay." He leans in and kisses the top of her head, then turns to me. "Can I please have your cell number, so the next time my girl forgets to call me and her cell dies, I can at least try you before I freak the fuck out?" he says.

I smile at Nicole as I recite my number to him. Maxton places his hands on my shoulder as he tells Brighton to text him my number. I roll my eyes at his request, but I don't argue.

I hear Maxton's phone beep behind me and he gives my shoulders a gentle squeeze. "All right, let us walk you to the door and then we'll go," Brighton says.

"Bright, we can—" he places his finger up to her lips to shush her.

"I need to know you're safe and sound. I'm already here; there is no reason for me not to make sure of that," he says, pulling her toward the entrance of our apartment.

Maxton turns me by my shoulders and I lead him to the door. I take my time, letting Bright and Nic have a minute. They are pulling out of a lip-lock when we reach them. Maxton leans in; his lips are next to my ear and his hot breath sends shivers throughout my body. "Goodnight, Kensi," he says. His hands leave my shoulders, and just like that, he's gone.

14

Maxton

AT FIRST, WHEN Bright started pacing the floor checking his phone every ten seconds, I chalked it up to him being smitten with Nicole. After twenty more minutes of pacing, I started to get concerned as well. Two beautiful girls alone at night, my mind started racing with what could have happened to them. I'm not used to worrying about anyone other than Brighton. This is yet another first for me. The look of relief that crossed Bright's face when I grabbed my keys and told him to get in the truck had my adrenaline pumping. He was genuinely worried. Apparently, over the last three months, any time Nicole said she would call or text, she did. Brighton insisted that this was not normal for her and he was worried about his girl. He said that. "Max, I'm worried about my girl."

Oh, how the mighty have fallen. I didn't say anything else and neither did he. He just continued to call her cell every twenty seconds until we reached their apartment.

We pulled in just as they were climbing out of the car. Bright was out of the truck and had Nicole in his arms before the truck stopped. I was right behind him. I had worked up a million different scenarios as to what could have happened and I was relieved to find them both okay. I stalked

58

around to the passenger side and pulled Kensington against me. I wasn't thinking about getting her into bed, or how good her tight little body felt against mine. The only thing I felt was relief that we found them safe.

Emotions that I'm not used to are stirring and I don't understand the sudden change. I've worked my ass off the last few months. Every spare minute was devoted to the bar and the remodel. I finally see light at the end of the tunnel and try to get back into a normal routine and my world tips on its axis. It's all too much to handle. I say a quick goodbye to Kensington and walk away. This entire weekend has been weird as fuck. I needed to walk away.

I climb into the truck and wait for Bright to say goodbye. I pull out my phone and program Kensington's number into my contacts. I can see she went inside already.

Me: Glad you're okay.

Kensington: Maxton?

Me: Who else would it be?

Kensington: Thanks!

She ignored my question. I want to ask her who else would be texting her from a strange number, but I don't. First of all, I don't have the right, and second, that's not me. I don't care what else she has going on.

Brighton climbs into the truck and leans his head back against the seat. "Fuck!" he roars. I sit there behind the wheel, just waiting to see what his next move will be. "What are we waiting for?" he asks me.

I raise my eyebrows at him, but don't comment. Instead, I start the truck and pull out of the complex.

"I can't even... Shit! I just... fuck, that girl she's got me," he says.

I know what he's trying to say. This is new for him; this is not what happens to us. Not what we ever said we wanted. I keep my mouth shut and just drive.

When we pull into the drive, I see Bright place his phone up to his ear. "Hey, babe, we just got home." He listens to what she's saying and the corner of his mouth lifts at whatever it is. "Okay, I'll call you tomorrow." He ends the call and climbs out of the truck.

Once in the house, he walks straight to the fridge and pulls out two beers. He slides one across the counter to me, then screws off the top of his and tips it back. He doesn't stop until the bottle is empty.

"She wanted to make sure we were home. She wanted to say thank you for being worried and coming to check on them." He laughs. "Fuck, man, I was about to lose my fucking mind worrying about her. I don't even want to think about what could have happened to them." He reaches in the fridge and grabs another beer. He doesn't kill this one all at once. Setting his bottle down, he braces his hands on the counter and hangs his head. I stand and wait. If he wants to talk, he will. If he wants to scream and yell, well, he'll do that too. I let him work it out on his own. I wouldn't know what to say even if I wanted to. My mind is fucked up with my reaction to Kensington. This entire weekend is fucked... for both of us.

Bright raises his head and looks at me. "Did I see you hugging Kens?" he asks.

What the hell? This is not what I expected to come out of his mouth. "Uh, yeah. I just thought it was the right thing to do. You know, since you were making sure Nicole was okay. That's what chicks want, right? To feel important?" I try to blow it off. I can tell by the look on his face that he's not buying it. Damn it. He wasn't supposed to be paying attention, not when he had his girl in his arms.

"Listen, man, Kensington is beautiful, I get that. From what Nicole has told me, she's been through a lot. I don't want to cock block you, but as your friend and as the guy who I'm pretty fucking sure is falling in love with her best friend, can you please not fuck with her? Don't break her heart. It would make things really awkward." His voice is pleading.

I shouldn't be surprised by his words, but I am. "You love her?" I ask him.

"I'm falling hard, man. I've gotten to know her the past three months, actually talking and getting to know her, and the past two days of being with her... I think about her all the time. Fuck, look at tonight. How many times have I worried about if a date made it home? None, never, zero, zilch!"

"She's home safe," I tell him. I can see he's getting worked up again.

He peers across the counter at me. "They both are. Something is different with you when you're with her. Tread lightly, brother." He picks up his beer and empties the bottle. Throwing both empties in the trash, he mumbles a goodnight and heads off to bed.

15

Kensington

ROLLING OVER, I look at my alarm clock, ten o'clock. I'm usually up and moving by now, but it took me forever to fall asleep last night. My cell beeps from its place on my nightstand. I unplug the charger and adjust my eyes to look at the screen.

Facebook notification: Brighton Jones has sent you a friend request.

I slide my finger across the screen and wait for the app to load before clicking confirm. Nicole comes into my room and bounces on the bed, phone in hand. "So, Bright invited us to the movies today. It's supposed to rain."

"Why don't the two of you go?" I know she's just being nice by including me, but honestly, I'm good with staying in. This weekend has been filled with enough social interactions for me. "I have laundry to catch up on and we need to go to the grocery," I tell her.

She sticks her lip out as if she's pouting. "Come on, Kens, he was going to ask Maxton to go as well."

Hell no! I need a break from sexy Maxton and his multiple personalities. One minute he's being cocky Max, trying to get me into bed, and then he's sweet and comforting Max, and let's not forget flirty, friendly, fun Max. "Really, I have a ton of laundry to do and I just want to chill."

"Fine! I get it. I got you out two nights in a row. I guess I shouldn't push my luck." She stands to leave. "You know, Maxton is probably going to be sad that you decided to stay home." She turns and quickly walks away.

I chuck a pillow at the door and hear her laugh all the way down the hall. I'm sure Maxton couldn't care less if I went or not.

An hour later, I'm showered and dressed for the day. I have on yoga pants and a racer back tank top. As I finish blow drying my hair and pulling it into a ponytail, my stomach growls.

I'm in the kitchen toasting a bagel when Nicole walks in. "Brighton just called; he should be here any minute," she says as she transfers her debit card, Chap Stick, and cell phone into her small wristlet.

"Have a good time. Tell Brighton I said hello."

There's a knock on the door. Nicole skips over stops, takes a deep breath, and then opens it. "Hey, babe," he says as he grabs her by the waist, pulls her close, and kisses her cheek.

I can see her blush from here. Standing to his full height, he looks over her shoulder. "Hey, Kens, you sure you don't want to join us?" he asks.

I briefly think about spending the day with the two of them and Maxton. I definitely need a break. "No, but thank you. I really do have a ton of laundry I need to catch up on. Besides that, my Kindle is calling my name."

"Next time then," he replies. "You ready?" he asks Nicole. She's looking up at his over six-foot frame and I'm suddenly afraid her face might crack if her smile grows any bigger. Her happiness is infectious and I find myself smiling as they walk out the door.

Deciding I need to tackle my mountain of laundry and get it over with, I head to my room and start sorting out piles. I know Brighton probably thinks laundry is an excuse; I should have shown him my room first.

After my first load is in, I grab my cell, Kindle, and a bottle of water and settle down on the couch. I pull the throw off the back and cover my legs to keep the chill of the air away. Just as I open my Kindle case, my cell beeps with a message alert.

Maxton: Laundry? Really? That's all you could come up with?

He thinks I'm making up excuses. I didn't make it up; however, I didn't necessarily have to do it today either. My closet is still busting with clean clothes. I decide to keep my answer short and sweet.

Me: True story!

He immediately replies.

Maxton: If you say so.

Me: I do. If you could see the piles, you would understand.

I wait for his reply and it never comes. After ten minutes of staring at my phone, I set it down beside me and pick my Kindle back up. As I'm scrolling through my list of books, trying to decide on my next book boyfriend, there is a knock on the door.

Not expecting company, but there are a lot of college kids who live in this building who often need to borrow things, like a cup of sugar. Seriously, that actually happened. We've also had a late–night knocker who was drunk off his ass asking if we had any condoms. Nicole felt sorry for him and gave him one. She's always the Girl Scout, always prepared. She doesn't sleep around, but says it helps to be ready in case the moment's right.

I look through the peephole and gasp at what I see. Maxton is standing outside my apartment door. What the hell is he doing here? I quickly scan my body. I'm in my yoga pants and tank, and my hair is in a knot on top of my head. No make-up. I start to panic having him see me like this. He knocks again.

"Kensington," he says through the door.

Shit! Maybe this is a good thing. I don't need to add to the chemistry or whatever in the hell it is that sparks between us. Maybe this look will turn him off and get him off my back. Taking a deep breath and slowly releasing it, I open the door.

16
Maxton

HOLY... FUCK ME! Kensington finally opens the damn door and the sight of her has me hard as a rock. Just like that, first look and I'm steel. I drop my eyes to her bare feet and bright pink toenails. I slowly scan my way up her legs, those hips, trim waist in that tight tank. I reach her breasts and I swear it takes effort to not swallow my damn tongue. Full. Firm. Mouthwatering. What I wouldn't give to feel their weight in my hands, to have my mouth on them, savoring her taste.

She clears her throat and reluctantly, I lift my gaze to find her smirking at me. "Maxton." My name rolls off her tongue. No one calls me Maxton, just Max. My mom is the only one who does and, well, I never talk to her she's no longer a part of my life. I used to hate being called by my full name for that very reason, but something about the way Kensington says it in her sexy voice. Yeah, I'm good with it.

"Kensi," I call her by the nickname that just came out last night. "I'm here for the visual," I tell her.

"Visual?" She tilts her head to the side to study me. "What are you talking about?"

I smile. I knew she wouldn't be expecting me. "Laundry."

Her mouth drops open in shock. "You drove over here to make sure I was really doing laundry?" she asks, incredulous.

I step toward her. I'm still standing in the doorway, and that just won't do. She doesn't know it yet, but she found herself a laundry buddy. I need to crack her defenses and get her under me. I'm not used to the chase, and it's fucking with me. This shit needs to happen, soon. "Yes, pretty girl, laundry," I say, tucking a loose hair behind her ear. I pull my hand away and walk past her to the couch.

"Please, come in," she says dryly.

"Thanks," I quip. I can play this game all day long.

I sit down on the couch and reach for her tablet or whatever it is. This gets her moving. She launches herself at me and pulls it out of my hands. I could have fought her, but I don't want her to kick me out, not yet anyway.

"Hands off the Kindle, buddy." She glares at me.

I throw my head back and laugh at her. She has the most serious look on her face. Her serious turns into a scowl and I quickly zip up my laughter. "What's the big deal?" I ask her. My voice is indifferent, but really, I would like to know.

"This is my life. I never leave home without it," she says, clutching it to her chest. "I love to read; it takes me away." She barely whispers the last part. Had I not been hanging on every word, I might have missed it.

"So what do you read?" I'm intrigued. I've never met anyone like her. Then again, I spend most of my time with chicks who are open to one-night stands and hang out in bars. Kensington is definitely a higher caliber than what I'm used to.

I watch as her neck goes pink and the color travels to her cheeks. Who knew a blush could be sexy? "You're holding out on me."

She closes her eyes. "Romance mostly," she says, eyes still shut.

I can't control my hand as it cups her cheek. "Open your eyes, Kensi." I wait until she's looking at me. "Don't ever be ashamed of who you are. This," I say, pointing at her chest where her Kindle is still clutched, "is a part of who you are. Never hide that. There's nothing wrong with reading." It's actually really nice that this is her passion. I'm used to chicks who's only passion is to seduce every man within a one hundred-mile radius. Women without depth and drive, their only worry is who is in their bed next. Kensington has both and so much more. I fight back a groan at the thought of what else she has. Her tight-ass tank causes her breast to play peek-a-boo as she leans over and sets the Kindle on the table.

Fighting back a groan, I change the subject. "So where is this mountain of laundry?"

She rolls her eyes playfully. "Come on, Mr. I-need-proof, let's get this over with." She stands from the couch and heads down the hall. I trail after her, watching the sway of her hips in those pants. We reach what I assume is her bedroom door. She opens the door and waves her arms. "Tada," she says with dramatic flair.

I chuckle as I survey what's in front of me. There are three piles sorted on the floor. One pile in particular catches my eye. Bras, barely-there panties, and thongs, this must be the intimates pile. As if my dick wasn't hard enough already at the sight of her. The chuckle dies on my lips as I stare at that pile of lace. I can't wait to be the one to peel every piece off her.

"Well?" Her voice breaks my stare of her piles of laundry—of that pile.

"Three loads, really? You turned down an afternoon with me and our best friends for three loads of laundry?"

"Four loads of laundry, smartass. I've already got a load in the washer," she fires back.

I step further into her room, walk around the piles, and sit on her bed. I immediately regret the action as her sweet scent surrounds me. Leaning back to rest my weight on my hands, I touch silk. Kensington is beside me in an instant reaching for this new treasure I've just discovered. I'm faster as I tighten my grip around the silk with one hand and catch her hand with the other.

I bring what appears to be a barely there nighty to my face and inhale. The feel of the soft silk against my skin infused with her scent has my dick fighting for release. She reaches for it again with her spare hand. I adjust my hold and wrap my arm around her waist, bringing her to stand between my legs. Her hands go to my shoulders to balance herself against the sudden change in position.

"Is this what you slept in last night?" I ask, my voice gruff.

The blush is back; light pink coats her skin. I watch as she swallows hard and slightly shakes her head yes.

Both of my hands are now on her hips, her tank has ridden up and my fingers gently caress her soft skin. Her chest is rising and falling with each deep breath she takes. I'm encouraged to know that I'm not the only one affected. My hands slowly lift her tank as the soft skin of her belly is exposed. I need to taste her. Leaning forward, I place a soft kiss right above her belly button. Her body quivers under my lips. Gently nipping at her skin with my teeth, I quickly soothe the site with my tongue. "Maxton..." she breathes. The sound my name on her lips, her voice laced with desire, has me ready to blow my load like a fucking fifteen-year-old.

My hands cup her ass cheeks as I bring her body closer to my mouth. It's my mission to have my lips on every part of her.

17

Kensington

I SQUEEZE MY eyes shut at the feel of his lips on my skin. He gently bites and immediately soothes the site with his tongue. My body trembles at the contact. I move my hands to his hair and run my fingers through his thick silk strands. This causes him to change the hold he has on me. His hands grip my ass and I find myself being pulled closer to him, to those lips that are driving me crazy.

The buzzer on the washer sounds, alerting me that my first load is done, and it's like a bucket of water has been thrown over my head. What in the hell am I doing? I remove my hands from his hair, lay them against his chest, and push myself away from him. He lifts his head to look at me, and the look in his eyes, the rapid rise and fall of his chest, has me almost launching myself back into his arms.

Almost.

The reality of the situation is that Maxton Cooper is the epitome of a sex god and I want nothing more than to let him have his wicked way with me. Want and need are two very different things. I need him and his sinful mouth to stay far away. Guys like Maxton remind me too much of Justin, and his brother. That is not what I need, not at all.

"Kensi?" he whispers my name. His voice is gruff and almost pained?

I take a step back as he reaches out for me. "Duty calls," I say, then turn and bolt from the room.

I take my time swapping the clothes from the washer to the dryer. I need to put in another load, but I don't want to go back to my room. I'm not even sure Maxton is still in there, on my bed.

"Kensington." His deep voice rumbles behind me. I close my eyes and focus on taking deep even breaths. His voice alone has me wanting to throw caution to the wind and drag him back to my bed. My body wants that, wants him. My head is telling me to keep my distance.

Stepping in the room, he stands behind me. I don't bother turning around; I can feel him. One hand goes to my hip and he laces our fingers together with the other. He tugs me so my back is resting against his firm chest. His lips trace the invisible lines of my neck. Just when I think I can't take any more, his lips are gone as he whispers in my ear. "I know I should apologize for what happened back there. I should tell you I'll never touch you like that again." His teeth graze my ear. "Something you should know about me, I will never apologize for going after what I want."

I say a silent prayer that he has an iron grip around my waist. Otherwise, I would be in a puddle on the floor. His words make my knees weak and my panties wet.

Maxton shifts to stand in front of me. Bending his knees so we are eye to eye, his hands cradle either side of my face. His thumbs are a soft caress to my cheeks. "I will not apologize for wanting you," falls from his lips as he leans in. I tense, preparing myself for the kiss that I don't have the power to fight. I'm shocked when his lips land on my forehead.

The kiss is brief, yet intimate, and just like that, his hands are gone from my face and he's walking out the door. I fight the urge to yell at him; for what, I'm not sure. I want to yell at him for using his playboy powers on me, and at the same time, I want to yell at him for leaving, for not finishing what he started. Instead, I lean back against the dryer and try to catch my breath. My heart is racing, my palms are sweaty, and the ache between my legs is a craving I've never known before. I've never felt this kind of chemistry. Just being in the same room as him lights me on fire, but damn if I'm going to fall for his seduction so he can carve out another notch on his bedpost. Not going to happen!

Once I finally get my heart rate to a normal rhythm, I set off to find Maxton. He's sitting on the couch, remote in hand. "Hey, what are you in the mood for?" he asks.

It takes me a few minutes to realize his question is not his normal sexual come on. I watch as he flips through the channels. His forehead crinkles when he gets to a channel that he has no interest in. "Kensi?"

"Uh, what are you doing?" Stupid question, I know. My head is all over the place right now. It's usually really easy to know what a player's intentions are. To get you in bed ASAP and move on to the next conquest. I expect that from Maxton. What I don't expect is for him to want to sit around in my apartment while I catch up on laundry and watch TV. He's a constant contradiction. How can I trust anything he says and does when he's all over the map?

Shrugging, he says, "Keeping you company while you do laundry."

His response is so... innocent. Not at all what I was expecting. "You don't have to keep me company, Maxton. I'm sure you have something else you'd rather be doing." Or someone else maybe.

"I don't do anything I don't want to do. I'm good." He pats the couch next to him.

I sit down on the couch, putting as much distance between us as possible. "I'm not real picky when it comes to movies. Anything is fine." I see no point in arguing with him. He has obviously made up his mind that he's hanging out with me today. I can't wait to hear what Nicole has to say about this.

18

Maxton

I HAD TO get out of there. I was two seconds from throwing her over my damn shoulder and carrying her back to her room. She's fighting it. I know she wants me; I can see it in her eyes, in the way her body responds to mine. Her chest is rapidly rising and falling with each breath. Her eyes are hooded with desire. I also see fear. She's hesitant, not willing to take what she so obviously wants. I want to know the cause of her fears, help take them away.

As bad as I want to sink inside of her, I never want her or any women to fear me. I'm not that kind of guy. I may steer clear of emotional attachments, but I never want to hurt them, hurt her. The girls I'm with know the score, as I'm sure Kensington does. There is a difference though. She turned me down and now here I sit, in her apartment, trying to get her to decide on what to watch.

I had every intention of leaving. I needed space to wrap my head around why I even ended up here today. As soon as I made it to the living room, the thought of leaving didn't sit well with me. I push that in the back of my mind. Not going there.

"*Armageddon?*" I ask as I stop on one of the movie channels.

"Hello, it has Ben Affleck in it."

"And?" I ask. I know where she's going with this, but I want her to say it. I need to get that easy banter back. My hope is that it will take over the thoughts of what just happened. Slim chance, but worth a shot.

"And he's hot!" she says as a slight blush covers her face.

"All right then." I reach down and slip off my boots and settle in, resting them on the coffee table. "You know what sounds good right now?" She doesn't answer, so I keep talking. "Popcorn." I turn my head to look at her. She's watching me.

The expression on her face tells me I'm acting as crazy as I feel. This isn't me. "You're right. I'll make some." She quickly hops off the couch and sprints to the kitchen.

I hit pause on the remote. I hear her banging around in the kitchen. The smell of freshly popped popcorn floats through the air. I wait a few more minutes and still no Kensington. Getting to my feet, my nose leads me to the kitchen. She's on her tippy toes reaching for a bowl. I move in behind her and place my hand on her hip while the other reaches over her head and grabs it.

I set the bowl in front of her on the counter, leaning down, placing my lips next to her ear. "You should have told me you needed me." My words have a double meaning and she knows it. She leans against me, which has me wrapping my arms around her waist. Instead of making a move and taking advantage of her, I just... hold her. She smells amazing and is a perfect fit for my arms.

Not liking where my thoughts are going, I release her and smack her on the ass for good measure. "Movie's waiting," I call over my shoulder as I flee to the living room.

I settle into the couch, leaning toward the middle on my elbow, feet again propped up on the table. Kensington walks in holding the bowl filled with popcorn and two bottles of water. She hands me a bottle and sets the bowl in between us on the couch. I wait until she is sitting before hitting play on the remote.

We sit in comfortable silence, eating popcorn and watching the movie. She's on one side and I'm on the other. I'm cautious to not reach for a handful at the same time as she does. My resolve is thin when it comes to touching her. I want her. My dick wants her. I will have her, just not today. I won't take her until I can no longer see that fear in her eyes.

She's timid, constantly fidgeting. She's moved the pillow on her lap at least twenty times. Her breathing is accelerated and her leg is bouncing up and down with nerves.

It's taking extreme effort to concentrate on the movie. We've almost made it to the end when I hear her sniff. At first, I don't think much of it, until it happens again. I turn to look at her and see tears rolling down her cheeks. Without thinking, I reach over and wipe the tears away with my thumb. She gives me a watery smile. "I forgot how it ended. I never would have agreed to watch it with you if I had remembered." She chuckles at herself.

Something in my chest tightens at seeing her tears. No man likes to see a woman cry in his presence, but this is different. I feel… protective of her. Like I could kick Ben and Bruce's ass for making her cry. Now I want to kick my own ass for even thinking it.

I watch as she offers me another smile through her tears. "Don't hold it against me," she says, chuckling.

I have something I would like to hold against her, in her, whatever.

I don't get the chance to respond as the door to her apartment flies open. In walks Nicole and Bright. Fuck! This is not what I need. This is going to go down one of two ways. He's going to be pissed that I pursued her or he's never going to let me live it down that she's gotten under my skin.

"Hey, you two," Nicole chirps as if seeing Kensington and I laying around watching television is an everyday occurrence.

"How was the movie?" Kens asks them.

"We didn't end up watching one. There wasn't anything we really wanted to see, so we grabbed some ice cream and went to the park."

I catch Bright's attention and raise my eyebrows at him in question. He shrugs and grins. He's so far gone for her.

Bright sits down on the loveseat and pulls Nicole down beside him. "What did you two get into?" he asks.

"Not much. I thought I would keep Kens company while she got caught up on her laundry." As if we needed the proof, the dryer buzzes. I smirk at Bright. I could tell he didn't believe me, as he shouldn't. That's not why I'm here. Well, it's not why I came here. Now… well, I'm not sure. All I know is that once I was here in her space, I couldn't make myself leave.

19

Kensington

"DUTY CALLS." I jump to my feet and head to the laundry room. Saved by the buzzer. I take my time folding and starting a new load. I even put the first load away, stalling as long as possible. Finally, with nothing left but to sit and wait, I join them back in the living room.

As I walk into the room, I hear Brighton ask Max what his plans are for the rest of the day. I take my seat on the couch beside him and he turns to look at me. "How much more laundry do you have to do?" he asks me.

"Uh, I just have one more load and I'm caught up," I say slowly. Why is he asking me that? Brighton asked him, not me.

I get my answer when he turns to Brighton. "Just gonna hang out here, man. You?"

What the…? Did I just hear him right? He's just going to spend the day here so I can get my laundry done. Seriously? Does he really think hanging around the house is going to get him access to my bed? Okay, yes, there was a moment earlier, but I came to my senses.

"You guys don't have to hang around on my account," I try to convince them. It doesn't really matter because my words fall on deaf ears.

"Let's order in. You all up for another movie?" This brilliant idea is from my best friend. What the hell is she doing? I try to give her the look, but I fail miserably. She just smiles at me as she pulls out her phone and orders a ton of pizza, breadsticks, and wings for delivery.

"I'm going to go get plates and stuff ready," I mumble, rising to my feet and fleeing to the kitchen. I'm gathering plates and napkins when Nicole walks in.

"So it sounds like you've had an interesting day." She cuts right to the chase.

"I guess so. He just showed up out of the blue."

"I would say having a guy who looks like Max show up to hang out so you could do laundry definitely qualifies for an interesting day," she quips.

"I'm not falling for it. He's trying to lure me into bed and it's not going to happen. The sooner he realizes the better."

Nicole studies me for a long time before answering. "He may want to sleep with you, but he can have anyone he wants. Yet, he's here with you. Think about that." She turns and walks out of the room.

I take a seat at the table and rest my head in my hands. I'm fighting an internal battle. I know if Nicole knew the entire story, she would understand why I am like I am. Why I fight so hard against trusting anyone with my heart.

As I battle with myself, I feel a warm hand on my back. I know it's Maxton without looking up. He kneels down next to me as he continues to stroke my back soothingly. "Kensi, are you all right?" he asks softly. I can hear the concern in his voice. This does nothing to confirm his image of the badass player that he tries to portray.

I lift my head and we're staring eye to eye. "I don't know," I tell him honestly. Neither one of us breaks eye contact. The pull he has on me is too strong. I can't look away.

Max tucks a loose piece of hair behind my ear, resting his hand on the back of my neck. "What's going on in that pretty head of yours?" he questions.

"Pizza's here!" Nicole yells. Maxton continues to hold onto me, waiting patiently.

"We better go eat," I whisper.

He nods and stands to his full height, pulling me up with him. His arms are around me in an instant and he's giving me a hug. He drops a kiss on the top of my head right before he releases me. I follow as he leads us back to our friends.

Just like that, Maxton Cooper has once again made me question who he really is. Is he this sweet tender guy that he has shown me so many times? Is he the playboy who will say and do anything to get into my bed? The more time I spend with him, the more I want to know. I want to piece his puzzle together until all the pieces are in their rightful place. I need to see the finished product. He's the first guy who has ever made me want to invest the effort to find out. There's just something about Maxton Cooper that reels me in.

We dig into the food like none of us have eaten for days. The guys more so, but what else could one expect from these two. They are both huge with muscled arms and defined abs. Their shirts look as though they are bursting at the seams. Brighton is slightly shorter than Maxton, but both are well over six-feet tall. Clean up is easy as we used paper plates and napkins. Nicole and I take care of that while the guys search Netflix for the movie. I'm prepared for Nicole to ask questions, but she doesn't. I'm relieved even though I know it won't last long. As soon as the guys leave, she will pounce. I know my best friend.

The guys have *Ocean's Eleven* pulled up and ask us if it's okay. Nicole blurts out, "Have you seen the cast? Yeah, we're good." She winks at me and I smile at her. One, because she's right, and two, because I know what she's doing. She's effectively getting under their skin. It's a macho thing.

"Come here, you," Brighton says, pulling Nicole onto his lap. I smile at his playfulness with her.

I take my seat on the couch and pull the blanket from the back. I watch in fascination as Maxton helps me cover my feet, tucking it around me. "Better?" he asks quietly, only for me.

I can't seem to find my voice, so I just nod. That earns me a smile. I can only assume it's because of the way he found me in the kitchen. He doesn't know how to deal with me. I push all thoughts out of my mind and settle in for the movie.

20

Maxton

I PUSH PLAY on the remote and try to keep my focus aimed at the television. I'm kicked back and leaning on my elbow in the center of the couch. The position has me closer to her. I don't know why, but that's where I want to be. Something is different; today changed things. I can't define what it is. I want her; but that's nothing new that's how this whole thing started. This crazy fucking spark that I feel around her. She turned me down and that fueled my pursuit. I refuse to tear it apart afraid of what I might find. I need to remember to look out for number one. That's the only way.

We are about twenty minutes into the movie and my hand is going numb. I shift positions, but instead of moving closer to my side of the couch, I'm in the middle of the two cushions. Kensington hasn't moved in a while and her breathing is deep and even. I have avoided looking at her, not wanting to give Bright any more ammunition than he already has. Of course, I doubt he's even paying attention to me right now with his girl curled up in his lap. I wouldn't be if I were him.

Shifting positions gives me the perfect reason to turn my head and glance at her. What I see takes my breath away. She's sleeping. Her head is leaned against the couch, the cover up to her neck. She's so fucking beautiful it almost hurts to look at her. Almost. I would regret if I let this moment pass me by, a chance to study her when she's peaceful, and the chance to look at her without the insecurity in her eyes. It's like she's always waiting for the other shoe to drop. I can see there is something there and I can admit that I want to know what it is. But it's an admission that I'm not ready to voice outside of my head.

A tendril of hair has fallen across her eyes and she bats at it with her hand. I reach over and gently tuck it behind her ear. I softy run my thumb across the dark circles under her eyes. How did I miss that?

"She doesn't sleep well sometimes." Nicole's whispered voice has me dropping my hand and turning to face her. "It's her story to tell; hell, I don't even know all of it. She hides it well, but it's there." She points to Kensington. "She doesn't have her guard up when she's sleeping."

I can see that. I turn back to Kensington, watching her sleep.

"I'm not sure what brought you here today," Nicole starts, but I don't turn back to face her, "but I know she can't take any more heartbreak. Please don't play games with her." Her voice is pleading.

"He doesn't play games, babe. Just because he doesn't do commitment doesn't mean he's out to hurt her," Brighton defends me.

Hearing her plea, asking me to never hurt Kensington, sparks something in me. Never. I would never do anything to hurt her. Turning to face them, I admit, "I won't hurt her. I could never." I shake my head. I don't know what this is, this feeling, but I want to protect her. The thought that someone has hurt her, or would hurt her, does not sit well with me. I turn back to Kensington, taking in her sleeping form and something inside my chest swells. I whisper the words, "She's different." They fall out of my mouth and I realize it's true.

"I can see that. Tread lightly, man," Brighton warns me. I know he's all in with Nicole and he doesn't want his girl upset. I get that, I do. However, it was me and him first; he knows me better than that.

I focus my gaze back on the movie. I'm not paying attention, but pretend to be. The conversation needed to end. I'm done talking about it, about her, about my feelings. She's different. I said the words and meant them, but fuck me if I know what it means.

When the credits roll, I'm ready to head home. There are so many things jumbled around in my head; I just need to clear my mind. Nicole yawns and Bright takes that as the cue that we need to head out. I look over at Kensington and her neck is bent at an awkward angle. She can't sleep like that all night.

Without another thought, I climb to my feet, lean down, and scoop her up in my arms. Her head rests against my shoulder and she burrows her face into my neck. "What the hell are you doing?" Nicole asks. Her voice is alarmed.

Brighton answers for me. He's knows me all too well. "Babe, she can't sleep like that all night. She looked uncomfortable as hell. Instead of waking her, he's taking her to her bed. You said yourself she doesn't sleep well."

She turns to look at me, Kensington in my arms. "It's the—" I turn toward the hall.

"I know," I whisper the words, not wanting to wake her up. I walk slowly down the hall to her room. Pushing the door open with my foot, I stalk to her bed and lay her down gently. She rolls to her side, facing me, and curls up into a ball. I, again, tuck her wayward curls behind her ear, pulling the cover up over her. Even though I know I shouldn't, I can't resist kissing her on the forehead. When I pull back, her eyes flutter open.

"Max," she whispers groggily. She never calls me Max. Always Maxton.

"Shh, go back to sleep. I just didn't want you to get a kink in your neck from the couch." I keep my voice soft and low.

"You scare me." Her voice is soft. I can tell she's still half asleep.

At her words, I drop to my knees beside the bed. I run my fingers over her hair. "I didn't mean to scare you."

"No, *you* scare me," she says again. Her eyes open and capture mine. They are full of sadness and I want to know why. I want to know what caused her pain.

I continue to run my fingers over her silky locks. "Why do I scare you, baby?" Her eyes are closed again. I watch her chest rise and fall. When it appears like she's really asleep this time, I lean in to kiss her forehead one last time.

As I go to stand, she mumbles, "I don't want to feel. You make me feel."

Her words stop me. I stop and stare at her. This beautiful girl is broken, and in this moment, I want nothing more than to make her whole again. I don't know why or what it means. I drop back to my knees and tuck that damn curl back behind her ear. I smile. I wanted her, want her, but now… I want her to feel whole again. Somehow she's weaseled her way past my cocky exterior that I use to guard my heart. She's worked her way past the barrier, and now all I want to do is help her propel over her own.

I hear a light tap on the door. I sigh and climb to my feet. Both Nicole and Brighton are standing there, watching me. "She's all tucked in." I try to keep my voice neutral. I don't want them to see how she is slowly crumbling the walls I erected long ago. I don't know what it means or how I even feel about it, and I sure as fuck don't want to go all Dr. Phil and talk about this shit. Not right now. Not sure that I ever will.

As I reach the door, they back away and allow me to pass by. I hear Brighton telling her goodbye, and then he's right behind me as we walk out the door. We walk in silence to the parking lot, climb in our trucks and drive away.

I pull into the drive behind him, but instead of going inside, I walk around back to sit on the lower deck. A few minutes later, he joins me, offering me a beer. I take it and take a long drink. We sit in silence for a long damn time, neither one of us wanting to talk about what's going on in each other's lives. We both know this shit is not us, not what we had planned. Hell, I was set out to seduce her and now all I want to do is make her smile. That shit is fucked up! So fucked up that I cannot even comprehend it.

After both of our beers have long been polished off, Bright finally speaks up. "First of all, before I say this, I don't want to hear any of your shit. Just let me get it out. I need to say it to see how it feels putting it out there, not just the thoughts jumping around in my head." He takes a deep breath. "I think I'm falling in love with her. The last few months spending the time to get to know her and now, after the time we've spent together, I'm… yeah…" His voice trails off.

I let his words sink in. He said think, but I pretty sure he already does love her. I think back and over the last three months; I've seen the subtle changes. Constantly on his phone, and he smiles more. He's content. I'm glad for him, I really am. Nicole seems like a great girl. Just because I've swore off commitment doesn't mean that he has to as well. "I'm happy for you, man." He grins. "Although," he groans and I chuckle, "I think you're fooling yourself. You already love that girl." I point out the obvious.

He breaks out in a huge grin. "Probably," he says, not really committing. I know this is something he struggles with as well. We were both confirmed bachelors for life. I guess that's how life is, nothing stays the same, you have to learn to live each day and roll with the punches.

He doesn't mention Kensington or my erratic behavior when it comes to her and I'm grateful. I wouldn't talk about it even if he did and he knows that. Knows me.

"All right, man, I'll see you in the morning." He climbs to his feet and head off toward the house.

I lean my head back and look up at the night sky. Six months ago, if Bright would have told me he was in love, I would have laughed at him. Tonight, watching him with her, watching them together, I see it. I may not understand it, but I can see it.

21

Kensington

THE FIRST WEEK of classes was busy. Getting my new schedule down and adjusting to a new routine. I only have three classes this semester, and then I tutor at the library. They tend to give those of us who are in our last year less hours. Most of us have internships and major projects due. Not me; however, I do have to find a small local company to volunteer eighty hours of time for. This is for future job applications. My major doesn't require it, however, my business professor does. She says that it's an opportunity to give back to the community as well as get some on-the-job training. Nothing better to prepare us for the real world. Her words not mine. I haven't even started looking, but I'm sure something will come up. Who doesn't want free help?

I haven't seen Maxton since the day he showed up to watch movies while I did laundry. I remember him carrying me to bed that night, but that's it. I had a dream that he was caressing my hair and calling me baby. This is not something I would admit aloud. Nicole didn't say much the next day. Her comment was that he insisted on carrying me to bed. She said he was sweet and attentive. I asked her if we were talking about the same person and she scowled at me. His sexy body and good looks have coaxed her to his team. She is most definitely Team Maxton as she continues to drop hints about how sweet he was to me. I don't remember it; therefore, it didn't happen. Besides that, Nicole is so wrapped up in Brighton; she wants everyone to be in the honeymoon phase right along with her.

She's seen Brighton every night this week. He's either at our apartment or she is at Cooper's bar with him. They invited me to go, but I declined. Maxton owns the bar, and I'm not ready to deal with him. Deal with how my body responds to him. I need to keep my distance for as long as possible, and I'm sure that once I do finally see him again, this crazy intensity will just be a vague memory.

Today is Friday and I don't have class. Tuesday's and Friday's are my free days. Nicole was grumbling this morning that she should have thought out her schedule a little better so she could always have a three day weekend. I took pity on her and made her breakfast. Well, I put her bagel in the toaster and filled her travel mug with coffee.

Now, I'm at the grocery store. It's been a few weeks since we've been, and with Brighton hanging out more, we need more than just fruit and yogurt. He claims he needs real food. We both laughed at him. I told Nic I would take care of the shopping today while she's at class.

By the time I reach the checkout, my cart is overflowing. I stand at my place in line waiting for my turn when I feel my phone vibrate in my pocket.

Nicole: How's grocery shopping?

Me: Uneventful. Standing in line to check out.

I snap a quick picture of my cart and text it to both Nicole and Brighton.

Me: Does this qualify as "real" food? ☺

Brighton: Yes! Finally, I was worried I would wither away. LOL

Nicole: Wow! I'll be home in 30 minutes to help put it away.

I slip my phone into my purse and start emptying my cart onto the belt. The cashier, God love her, is well into her seventies and her speed shows it. When I finally make it back to the apartment, Brighton is there waiting on me, and in the passenger seat is Maxton. I take a deep breath. I was hoping to be able to distance myself from him a little longer. Nicole pulls up on the other side of my car. I slowly climb out, grabbing my purse and popping the trunk as I do.

"After seeing that picture, I felt guilty, and since we were out and about, I thought we could stop by and help you pack it all in," Brighton explains. He must have seen the questioning look in my eyes.

Nicole skips over to him and he wraps his arms around her. I turn my head, giving them a private moment to say hello.

I reach into the trunk to start pulling out bags when I feel his hand on the small of my back. "We can get this. Go on in; we'll be right up," Maxton says. He's already reaching in and grabbing bags.

"I can handle a few bags of groceries, Maxton," I argue. I load up with bags and head into the apartment. I can hear him mumbling behind me as we go. The only words I can make out are stubborn and woman. I smile.

Brighton and Nicole follow him in, both loaded down with bags. "There are just a few more; we can get the rest," Brighton says. He kisses Nic on the cheek and walks back out the door. She's all smiles.

"He is so sweet," she gushes.

I agree. "Yes, he is. I was surprised to see them here."

"He does that, you know? Just kind of shows up. Yesterday, when I was leaving class, he was sitting in the parking lot. He knew I was done for the day, but he had to be at the bar. He just wanted to say hi. He also brought me a pumpkin spice latte from Starbucks."

"I'm impressed," I say as the guys walk in.

"About what?" Maxton asks. That man misses nothing.

"Oh, nothing. I was just telling her how Bright showed up after class yesterday." She wraps her arms around his waist.

Maxton just shakes his head and grins at his friend. He starts emptying bags. "Where does this go?" he asks, holding up a bag of sugar.

"I got this. Thank you both for helping, but I've got it from here."

"Kensington," he growls, "just tell me where you keep the damn sugar so I don't have to go digging through your cabinets."

"Hmpf," is my reply as I reach for the bag in his hands. He quickly moves it away. He's a good foot taller than me.

"Cabinet by the fridge, second shelf," Nicole spouts off.

I glare at her and she grins.

The four of us have the groceries put away in no time at all. I have to admit it was nice to have the extra hands.

"Babe, we need to get back to the bar. Why don't you two stop by tonight?" Brighton suggests.

Nicole looks at me. Her eyes are pleading. "Fine," I grumble.

She tells Brighton that we'll be by later as she walks him to the door.

"How was your week?" Maxton asks.

I shrug. "Good, first week of classes. Just trying to get my new routine down for this semester. You?" I decide I need to at least attempt to make small talk.

"Good, busy. Now that I have the renovation done on the bar, I need to get the rest of it in order. The books, ordering, staffing—Things like that."

"Sounds like you have your hands full."

He chuckles. "You could say that." Looking toward the door, he asks, "So I guess I'll see you tonight?"

Is he nervous? "Yeah, looks like it."

"Good." He walks over and kisses my temple. "Be safe," he says, then walks away.

What just happened? Sweet Maxton is not what I expected. Honestly, I don't know what I expected, but it wasn't him kissing me and telling me to be safe. This man confuses me; I don't get what his game is. He's all over the place and it makes it hard for me to pinpoint what he wants. Is he still trying to get me in his bed or does he want to be friends since our best friends are obviously in deep. I'm lost in thought, pondering the situation, when Nicole walks back in.

"Thanks for agreeing to go tonight. I really didn't want to go alone."

I wave my hand in the air as if it's no big deal. Normally it wouldn't be, but Maxton will be there. My only saving grace is that he will be working. Then again... he does own the place.

22

Maxton

I'M LOSING MY damn mind. From the moment she agreed to come to the bar tonight, I knew I was in trouble. When Bright suggested she come, I was sure she would turn down the offer. Then I saw the pleading look on Nicole's face and I knew she wouldn't say no. It was when she finally agreed that I felt my heart kick into overdrive. She was going to be there, on my turf. The excitement of being able to show her that I'm more than just the playboy she seems convinced that I am took hold. So much so that I found myself kissing her goodbye and telling her to be safe. Fuck! I'm glad Bright was in the other room. He would be riding my ass for that one. I couldn't seem to resist the pull.

Back at the bar, Bright and I rush around and make sure everything is stocked and ready to go. There's not much going on in town tonight, so it's sure to be busy. As the crowd slowly flows in, I catch Bright constantly watching the door. If he's not looking at the door, he's checking his phone. When he looks at the door this time, his face breaks out in a goofy-ass grin. He elbows me and tilts his head toward the door. "They're here."

I nod my head that I understand as I continue to serve the customer in front of me. We're fully staffed tonight, so technically, we don't need to be here. However, as owner and bar manager, we like to make our presence known. We usually do it on different nights, but when Kensington agreed to be here, I decided I had nothing better going on. Bright knows I wasn't planning to be here, but he didn't comment when I said otherwise. He and I usually alternate shifts, but we also schedule time off for us to just hang. Tomorrow is a good example. He and I are getting together with a group of guys and going riding. We both have four-wheelers and it's a blast when a group of us get together.

The crowd at the bar dies down. We have two servers out on the floor and two other bartenders behind the bar, which helps keep the customers spread out. It's also the reason that I'm not really needed tonight. Brighton isn't really either.

I watch as Brighton rushes to the door to greet the girls. He brings them to a table closest to the bar. I know it's so he can keep an eye on them. I would have done the same thing. I nod toward Brighton, letting my two guys behind the bar know that's where I'll be. With two swift nods in return, I head toward the table. Toward the girl I've tried not to think about for the past week, the girl who has consumed my thoughts since the day I met her.

Lance reaches their table the same time I do. I swallow back my irritation. He's a nice guy and we've been friends for years. Hell, he's going with us tomorrow. Even so, I don't like him sniffing around Kensington.

Lance stops behind Kensington and places his hand on her shoulder. I grit my teeth as I slide into the empty seat beside her. I know he was going for it, but there's no way in hell I'm letting that happen. "Hey, stranger," he says.

I watch her as she turns to see who it is. She smiles, stands up, and gives him a hug.

What. The. Fuck.

Since when are the two of them so chummy? They're standing there making small talk. Their conversation is swallowed up by the crowd, so I have no idea what they're saying. The blood is rushing through my ears as everything blurs except for the two of them. His arm slides around her shoulder and something I've not felt before bubbles up inside of me. The sound of her laugh brings me back in focus. "Sure, if you think you can keep up," she says.

"Oh, I can keep up all right." Lance winks at her. "I'm holding you to that dance," he says as he walks back toward a cute girl with brown hair. He's here with a fucking date and hitting on her. I never pegged Lance to be that guy.

"I didn't realize the two of you were so close?" I say, irritated as soon as she sits back down.

"We're not really. I met him that night we first met. He's a nice guy. We've texted a few times." She shrugs like it's nothing.

My guts twist at her admission. The thought of them together doesn't sit well with me. "Interesting. You seem pretty close to just have texted a few times," I accuse.

"His sister is in my finance class. He dropped her off the other day. When he picked her up, we all went for coffee," she explains.

I don't comment. I just stare over her head at where Lance is sitting. At this point, I'm not sure what pisses me off more, Lance being able to be close to her or my reaction to it.

"So what are you ladies drinking?" I need a change of subject.

They both say beer is fine. I head to the bar and grab four bottles and bring them back to the table. Bright raises his eyebrows at me, but doesn't comment. Usually I'm against him or me drinking here. It's hard to maintain authority when you're intoxicated. We need to remain professional for the staff. Tonight, well, tonight I don't give a fuck. My nerves are on high alert.

The four of us settle into easy conversation and the night flies by. After our one and only beer, Bright and I both switch to water. I want to say I did it to be responsible. In reality, it's because I need to be able to make sure she gets home safe. I'm sure Bright and I are on the same page with this.

Before I realize it, it's eleven o'clock. We've sat here for over two hours and it only seems like minutes. The four of us have a lot in common. The alcohol helps loosen Kens up a little and she's not as serious as she usually is. She's still guarded, just not as much. All is good until Lance steps up to the table.

"Ready for that dance?" He has both hands on her shoulders, looking over her. She tilts her head back and giggles. She fucking giggles at him. I love and hate the sound at the same time.

Kensington jumps out of her chair and stumbles. I reach out to catch her, but it's Lance who wraps his arm around her waist. She looks up at him and smiles. I want to murder him.

"It's just a dance, man." I hear Brighton trying to calm me down. He and I haven't talked about her. I've kept my mouth shut all week, trying to work it out in my mind. That doesn't matter; he knows me better than anyone and can read me like a fucking book. He knows I want her. I want her to be more than just under me, and it scares me to death.

My eyes never leave them. I watch every move he makes. The song turns slow and I'm out of my seat stalking toward them. No fucking way is he going to hold her.

23

Kensington

"MY TURN," I hear his deep voice rumble behind me.

Lance backs away with his hands up. He looks at me and winks. "Thanks for the dance, Kens."

I hear Maxton growl as he wraps his arms around my waist and turns me to face him, holding me tight against his chest. Words aren't necessary; he says everything with his eyes. Those gorgeous eyes are currently locked on mine. I slide my hands up around his neck, threading my fingers through his hair. He releases a heavy sigh as he tightens his grip on my waist and we start to move. I'm not sure you can even call what we're doing dancing. He's holding me so tight, it's more of a small sway back and forth. I've had a few drinks, more than I normally would. I don't know why, but something tells me it's okay to let loose a little with Maxton around. I definitely would not have fallen willingly into his arms if I were sober.

When the song comes to an end, Maxton leans his forehead against mine. "You're a perfect fit for my arms." His deep timber causes me to melt. Right there in the middle of the dance floor, I melt. Something about the way he says it, like he doesn't really want to but he can't help himself.

Standing to his full height he releases me, but not completely. He places his hand on the small of my back and leads me back to our table.

Maxton pulls out the seat that I occupied before Lance asked me to dance. I automatically sit, thankful, as my knees are still jelly from his words. Leaning in, he whispers, "What do you want to drink?" His hot breath sends a cold chill through my body.

I tilt my head up to give him my answer, and we're now close, too close. His face is not even an inch from mine. "Water," I whisper. The next thing I know, he closes the distance and places a soft kiss against the corner of my mouth. It happens so quick that it's over before I can process that he just kissed me. He kissed me in front of the entire bar.

I can feel the embarrassment heat my cheeks. Instead of turning to face our friends, and my embarrassment, I watch him go. Through the fuzziness in my brain, I know I'm playing with fire. I know flirting with him, allowing him to kiss me, is a mistake. He's going to take what he wants and forget he ever met me. I'm starting to wonder if that's really such a bad thing. Surrendering to what he wants, a night in bed with me, is bound to be a night to remember. He's already too close. Closer than any other has reached in a really long time.

I'm startled when the chair besides mine squeaks across the floor. Maxton settles his large frame into it, setting my water in front of me. I quickly grab the bottle, twist off the lid, and bring it to my lips. I tilt my head back and savor the cool liquid as it coats my throat. I down over half the bottle before I take a break. Realizing I didn't thank Maxton, I turn to do just that. The words get stuck in my throat. He's watching me. His eyes are on me. Eyes that are filled with want and desire. He takes my breath away. I can't tear my eyes off him. This is becoming a habit, and I know for sure with the alcohol running through my veins, I don't have the power to fight it. To control how I feel when he's around. I turn my body to face him; it's like a gravitational pull, this effect he has on me. I wish I could blame it on the alcohol, but I can't. The alcohol just makes me admit what it really is.

Attraction.

Lifting his hand, Maxton softly rubs his thumb across my lips. The rough pad of his thumb causes me to close my eyes and savor his touch. Keeping my eyes closed, I try to calm my heart, which is suddenly racing. I can feel the steady rise and fall of my chest. "Kensi." Maxton tries to get my attention. I squeeze my eyes closed tight and focus on deep even breaths. I feel his hand snake around my neck and pull me toward him. My forehead lands against his hard chest, which I notice has a rapid rise and fall like mine. One hand stays on my neck, his thumb stroking gently. The other wraps around my waist and I shiver at the contact.

"Kensi," his voice is low, next to my ear, "let's get you home, sweetheart."

Home. Yes, that's what I need. I need to go home, climb into my bed, sleep off my buzz, and never drink around Maxton again.

I manage to nod against his chest, still not willing to open my eyes. Even though I know it's wrong, I want to bask in his warmth for as long as I can.

"Kens." Nicole is trying to get my attention. I ignore her, wanting to stay in my Maxton bubble, oblivious to anything else. "Kens," she says again. This time she's closer. I feel her hand touch my arm. Turning my head, I blink open my eyes to look at her. "Hey, Brighton invited us to go riding with them tomorrow. What do you think?"

I can't think about tomorrow; I can only think about now. This moment with his strong arms wrapped around me, and his smell invading my senses.

"Kensington, are you even listening to me?" I can tell she's getting irritated.

"She's had too much to drink and obviously she's exhausted. I'm taking her home. I'll see you guys there," Maxton informs her.

"Wait! You mean you're taking her to our apartment, right?" Nicole, always my protector. "Kens, are you okay with him taking you home?"

Realizing she's not going to let me leave until I answer her, I reluctantly lift my head from his chest to address her. "Yes, he can take me home. I just want to go to sleep."

Nicole studies me before asking, "What about tomorrow, are you in?"

Releasing a heavy sigh, my forehead drops back to Maxton's chiseled chest. "Yes, fine, whatever. Can we go now?" I'm frustrated, not really with Nicole, but with myself. I know I should not be leaning on him like this, but I don't have the will power not to at this point.

"Great. We'll be right behind you," she chirps. Damn she's too fucking chipper.

Now that she's satisfied, I can finally go home. I lift my head to look at Maxton. He's already staring down at me. "Can we go home now?"

24

Maxton

HER WORDS CAUSE a tremor to run through my veins. I know what she meant, but it's the way it sounded. Her sweet voice asking if we can go home, together. I quickly shake off the thought of me and her as one unit. That's not what I'm about. Instead, I focus on her. She's clearly exhausted; mix that with the alcohol and she's dead on her feet. I realize she's waiting for my answer.

"Yeah, let's go home," I say against her ear. Just for her. I'm going to pretend I don't like how it sounds. Pretend like the thought of taking her home, to my home, to my bed, isn't the best fucking thought I've ever had. I don't take women into my bed. I'm always in theirs, or anywhere else. Never my bed; never let them get too close.

I place my arm around her shoulders and bring her as close to me as possible. My large frame causes people to move out of our path as we make our way outside. Once we reach my truck, I open her door, place my hands on her hips, and lift her into the passenger seat. She starts to giggle as soon as her feet leave the ground. That's the second time I've heard that sound tonight, and this time it's for me. I reach in to buckle her seat belt. Her head is already turned sideways; she's settled in for the drive home. I place a kiss on her temple, because I just can't fucking help myself.

The drive to her apartment is what most would call uneventful. I, however, cannot call it that, not at all. The cab of my truck smells like her. The sound of her breathing fills the air around us. This does nothing to dull the ache I have to be inside of her. The smell of her and the gentle sound of her sleeping peacefully will always be associated with this truck. I've never wanted someone, hell, anything, this bad. Ever!

Reaching our destination, I park and turn the truck off. I grasp the handle, and take one more look at Kensington before opening the door. The moonlight is filtering in through the window, casting a gentle glow. She's so fucking beautiful it takes my breath away. I'm frozen in place, just watching her sleep. I'm going to have to buy a new fucking truck because this night, her bathed in the moonlight, sleeping soundly, will forever be engrained in my memory.

Careful not to wake her, I quietly slip out of the truck. Bright pulls up next to me, so I wait for them to join me. "She's sound asleep. Can you unlock the door?" I ask this of Brighton. I know the girls come home by themselves all the time, but I would never forgive myself if we sent either one of them in alone and something were to happen while we were here. Bright holds his hand out for Nicole's keys and kisses her on the cheek.

"Would you mind closing the door quietly, once I have her out of the truck? I really hate to wake her." I sound like a pansy-ass, but I don't really care. She needs her rest.

Nicole salutes me with a smirk, but says nothing. Once I have Kensi in my arms, I carry her into the apartment and down the hall to her room. I don't bother turning on the light. I place her on the bed as gently as I can, trying hard not to wake her. As soon as her body hits the softness of her mattress, she curls up in a ball and sighs. The sight brings a smile to my face. Once she settles, I take a seat on the bed and slowly ease her shoes off her feet. I know she's going to have a killer headache in the morning. Nicole confirmed this as well. Kensington doesn't usually drink, so she'll definitely be feeling the effects tomorrow.

I stand to go search for some Ibuprofen and a glass of water. I want to have it ready in case she wakes up in the night. The sooner she takes it and starts to hydrate, the better she will be. I feel her hand wrap around mine, which stops me from leaving.

"Thank you," she whispers into the quiet room.

Not able to resist the pull, I sit back down on the bed. My hand automatically reaches for an errant curl that's hanging down over her eyes and tuck it behind her ear. "You're welcome. I'm going to get you some water and something to take for that headache."

"I don't have a headache," she mumbles.

"You will. I'll be right back." I stand to resume my search of headache meds and water. I want to kiss her, even just on the forehead. Anywhere my lips can make contact with her skin.

I pass Nicole and Brighton in the hallway. Bright tells me he's spending the night. Nicole asks about Kens and I assure her she will be fine, like I would let her be anything but. She directs me to the headache medicine, we say goodnight, and they disappear behind Nicole's bedroom door. It doesn't escape me that neither one of them asked if I was staying or heading home.

I quickly grab what I need and add the trashcan from the laundry room to the list. Just in case she gets sick. I don't think she's to that stage, but better safe than sorry. I find her right where I left her. Sitting the trashcan by the bed, I take a seat next to her. I rub my hand up and down her arm. "Kensi, wake up. You need to go ahead and take these." She can't be in too deep of a slumber; I was barely gone five minutes. Her eyes slowly flutter open. "The sooner you take this, the better you will feel in the morning." She reaches for my hand and I pull her to a sitting position.

She takes the Ibuprofen and sucks down the water without complaint. I throw the empty bottle into the trashcan and make a mental note to grab another before I leave.

"Can't sleep in this," she mumbles. She then lifts the hem of her sweater and tries to pull it over her head.

I avert my gaze, trying to offer her some privacy. It takes every ounce of will power I have. I want nothing more than to let my eyes roam over every inch of her body. I reach down and adjust myself as I have a sudden situation, which seems to happen a lot in the presence of Miss Kensington.

"A little help here," she huffs out.

Taking a deep breath, I turn to see what she needs. She has somehow gotten herself tangled up in her sweater and it's stuck over her head. I would laugh, but her bare belly and the bottom of what appears to be a black lace bra are mocking me.

"Maxton!" she whines.

This has me jumping into action. I reach for the hem of her shirt and tug upward. In one smooth motion, it's removed from her body. I toss it across the room into the chair in the corner. I don't bother looking away this time. I think it might kill me to try. Her plump, round breasts are swaddled in black lace, begging for me to touch, to taste, to savor them.

She ambles to her feet and begins to unbutton her jeans. Tearing my eyes away from her breasts, I'm a spectator as she shimmies her hips from side to side, trying to rid herself of the tight material. "Help."

Not needing to be asked twice, I fall to my knees and place my hands on her hips, stilling her little jig, which doesn't seem to be earning her the desired results. She places her hands on my shoulders to keep from falling over. Not able to help myself, I place a kiss right above her belly button. Her body quivers beneath my lips. I want her. I thought I wanted her before, but now seeing her like this, I've never seen anything more beautiful. I need to sink inside of her, like I need air to breathe… just not tonight. She's been drinking and I couldn't do that to her. I want her lucid when she makes that decision. I push back the thought of wanting her to want me, Maxton, just as much as I want her. I refuse to try and decipher what that even means.

Resting my forehead against her belly, I concentrate on taking deep even breaths. She removes her hands from my shoulders and begins running them through my hair. This simple act from each of us feels more intimate than any sexual encounter I've ever experienced. With one final deep breath, I grab onto either side of her jeans and begin to pull them off her. Steadying herself on my shoulders once again, she steps out one leg at a time.

"Ca-Can you hand me a shirt?" She points to the dresser. "Bottom drawer."

Without moving from my position, I reach out and pull open the drawer. I grab the first shirt I come to and hand it to her. Climbing to my feet, intending to give her privacy, I stop short at the sound of her next question. "Can you unhook me?" Her arms drop to her sides as if she doesn't have the strength to continue to try on her own.

Holy shit, but this girl is testing me. I'm so fucking hard right now I could break concrete. I have to remind myself it's the alcohol talking. No way would she be asking me to help her if she were sober. I know it's an asshole move, but I'm going to do it. No way in hell am I going to pass up a chance to see all of her. I just need to remain in control.

My index finger finds its way to the strap on her shoulder. I work my way underneath and slowly run my finger to where the strap ends just above her breast and back up to her shoulder. Knowing I'm playing with fire, I remove my finger from under the strap and pull her to stand in front of me. Once she has her balance, I turn her to face the bed. Gathering up her soft curls, I tuck all of them over one shoulder, exposing her back. I slowly unhook her. I want this moment to last as long as possible. I have no idea how long it will be before I'm with her like this again, or if ever. I need memories to carry me through.

Once she's unhooked, the straps slip from her shoulders. I close my eyes, fighting to gain control. I don't open them until my name falls from her lips. "Maxton."

My eyes pop open to see she has turned back around and is now facing me. Her hands are placed over her breasts, holding her bra in place. It takes extreme effort to not look below her face. "Kensington," I copy her.

With the sound of her name, she drops her hands and her bra goes with them. Standing before me, she's completely bare except for a tiny pair of black lace panties. The sight of her rips all the air from my lungs. My heart skips a beat and my mouth waters all at the same time. As I focus on breathing, my heart hammering in my chest, I stare at her. Yes, it's rude as hell, but what man would pass up a chance to look at perfection. She has her hand over the top of her right breast and I decide that just won't do. If this is the only time I'm ever going to witness her, I want it all.

Nothing in the way.

I reach for her wrist and she shakes her head no.

I trace above her left breast with my index finger, outlining its form. I try again to move her hand and she shakes her head no again. "Kensi, baby, I need to see all of you." I can't tell if it's fear in her eyes or just her non-trusting nature. I bring both hands to her face and cup her cheeks. Bending down so we are eye to eye, I promise her, "I will never do anything you are not ready for or don't want. All you have to do is say stop. This goes not farther than looking and maybe a soft caress, nothing more. I want you in my bed, Kens. Hell, I want you anywhere you will have me, but I want you sober." Leaving one hand on her face, the other goes to the hand covering her right breast. I have no idea what she's hiding, but I want to find out. I want to know every inch of her skin.

"May I?" I ask permission this time. Something I never do. If the girl doesn't want what I have to offer or want to take part in what I have planned, she can roll on. That is until Kensington. I can continue to try and hide it, deny it even. It doesn't make it any less true.

She's different.

I watch as she gives me a slight nod of her head. Reluctantly agreeing. "Use your voice, Kens. I need you to tell me it's okay." I need her to understand that she has the power. She says stop, I stop. It's just that simple.

"Yes." Her voice trembles.

Slowly, I pull her hand away from her breast. At first I don't notice anything. The overwhelming effect of seeing her, all of her, blinds me. It's when I study where her hand was that I see it. A faint scar about two inches long on her breast. Without thinking, I lean down and kiss the evidence of something that was obviously painful for her in more ways than one. Standing to my full height, she immediately wraps her trembling arms around my waist. I do the same with one arm and trace the swell of her breast with my free hand as I did the first time. I want her to see the scar does nothing to clamp my desire for her. It does nothing to take away from how beautiful she is. Something deep inside me needs her to know that, to believe it.

She nods once and I can tell it's going to take some convincing to get her to see herself the way I do. "Let's get you dressed." I reach for the shirt on the bed. I help her into it and pull the covers back. She climbs into bed.

"Stay, just until I fall asleep?" she asks. As if I would ever be able to tell this girl no. I climb in beside her and pull the covers up over us. She lays her head on my chest and I wrap my arm around her. Within a few minutes, her breathing has evened out and I know she's fallen asleep. I, however, do not. I was only supposed to stay until she fell asleep, that's what she asked for, but I can't seem to find the willpower to climb out of this bed, at least not with her in it. Instead, I run my fingers through her hair and watch as the shadows play on the ceiling. This is another first for me. I run the entire night over and over again in my head until the early morning sun starts to rise and casts its glow through the window. Reluctantly, I slowly slide out from underneath her, kiss her softly on the forehead, and leave her room.

25

Kensington

THERE'S A JACKHAMMER in my head. Rolling over, I force my eyes to open. The alarm clock reads nine o'clock. Right beside the clock is a bottle of water and something for the headache. God bless Nicole! I try to remember last night. It's not very often that I drink as much as I did. I remember dancing with Lance and Maxton interrupting us; after that, it's pretty fuzzy. Leaning up on my elbow, I toss back the Ibuprofen and take a few big gulps of water. I place the bottle back on the nightstand and fall back on my pillow. Maxton… I smell him. He seems to be everywhere.

I hear low voices in the kitchen. Nicole and Brighton must be up. Throwing the covers back, I slowly drop my feet to the floor and stand. I'm steady and the room's not spinning. This is a plus in my book. I step into my bathroom, take care of business and brush my teeth. Noticing I slept in just a t-shirt, I pull my robe from behind the door and slide my arms in. Grabbing a ponytail holder from the sink, I pull my hair into a knot on the back of my head and call it good. It's not like Brighton cares what I look like. He only has eyes for Nicole, as he should.

Opening my bedroom door, the sweet smell of cinnamon and bacon hits me. Nicole isn't much for cooking breakfast, so it must be Brighton my stomach needs to thank him. As I get closer to the kitchen, I can hear a deep timbre along with Nicole's ever-chipper voice. It's not until I turn the corner do I hear another voice, one I will never be able to forget. "Maxton." His name slips off my tongue without thought.

All three of them turn to face me. "Hey, sleepy head, how ya feeling?" Nicole chirps. I swear that girl can drink double what I did and wake up the same happy, chipper Nicole. Then again, she's had a lot of practice.

I don't acknowledge her. Instead, I walk to the other side of the table. I can feel Maxton's eyes on me and it's making me self-conscious. I pull my robe tighter around my waist. I drop into the chair, rest my elbows on the table, and bury my face in my hands.

"That good, huh?" Nicole laughs. I groan at her words and still don't bother to reply.

I don't bother looking up until I see and smell a plate being placed under my face. I feel him place his hand on my shoulder. Leaning down, he whispers, "Eat, you'll feel better." He is so close that his scent overrides the breakfast he has laid before me. His hot breath on my ear sends goose bumps down my back.

I lift my head and remove my arms from the table. The French toast and bacon smells amazing and, luckily, my stomach is not trying to revolt.

I take a sip of the glass of orange juice that must have appeared at the same time as the plate of food. Maxton sits down beside me with a plate filled as well. I look across the table to see Brighton and Nicole are already digging into their plates. "You cooked?" I say to Maxton.

He shrugs. "Yeah, it's not a big deal. My dad loved to cook and he taught me. Mom didn't ever, so he and I did most of it." He forks a huge bite of French toast into his mouth.

I feel like I've entered another universe waking up with both of them here. Did he sleep here? Did he come over just to make us breakfast? My stomach grumbles, so I push the unanswered questions out of my mind and pick up my fork. Just as I'm about to take my first bite, Maxton leans in and whispers in my ear, "Did you take the headache medicine I left for you?"

What? Maxton left that there? My mind starts to race as I flip through foggy memories of last night. Did I sleep with him? Shit! I finally gave into this temptation that has been plaguing me since we met and I can't even remember it.

Just my luck.

Maxton reaches under the table and places his hand on my thigh, which is now bare since my robe has fallen to the side. His touch causes me to shiver, not because his hands are cold, it's the exact opposite. The heat of his hand is searing my skin. "Hey, you okay?" he asks. His thumb is gently tracing my thigh.

I nod because I can't seem to form words. This is surreal.

"Eat up. We need to leave in an hour," Nicole says as she stuffs the last bite of French toast into her mouth.

What the hell is she talking about? "Where are we going?" I ask before taking another bite.

"I'm not surprised you don't remember." Nicole laughs. Suddenly, my best friend is getting on my last damn nerve. Maybe this is a dream. I reach down to pinch myself and yelp at the pain.

Maxton's hand immediately goes to my leg as he gently rubs my thigh trying to ease the ache He watches me intently.

"I thought I was dreaming," I mutter as an explanation.

Nicole and Brighton leave the room. I assume they're going to get ready for wherever it is we are supposed to be leaving for in an hour. Make that fifty minutes.

"You're definitely awake, pretty girl." Maxton's deep voice rumbles in the quiet room. The hand that was on my thigh, soothing the pain from my self-induced pinch, raises to tuck a strand of loose hair behind my ear. "I like you like this," he says softly.

"Like what?" is the smartest thing I can come up with. His touch has me reeling.

"Like this," his hand slides behind my neck, "just Kensi."

I don't really understand what he means? I'm always just me. Instead of asking for further explanation, I go with what's really bothering me. "Where am I going?"

Maxton smiles and my heart skips a beat at the sight "We," he motions between the two of us, "along with those two," he points down the hall, "are going riding today. You agreed to come with last night," he says.

"Riding?"

"Yeah. Bright and I get together with a group of guys and take the four-wheelers out as much as we can. Last night, one of the guys stopped and said he was bringing his girlfriend. Bright asked Nic to come and she said she would if you tagged along. You said yes and we leave in," he turns to look at the clock on the microwave, "forty-five minutes."

"Why are you here?" I blurt out. I know I'm being rude, but last night is fuzzy and I need answers.

His hand on my neck begins a soothing massage. "You were really wasted, so I brought you home. Nic and Bright were in their own little world and I wanted to make sure you were okay. I helped you into your room, gave you some water and headache medicine, and helped you into bed."

I look down at my now gaping robe. "Did you help me change?"

I watch as he swallows hard. "I did. I've never seen anything so beautiful." His voice is wistful as if he is remembering it plain as day.

"Did we…?" I trail off, not able to ask the question. I can see from the look on his face he knows what I'm trying to ask.

"No, we didn't. I helped you change and put you into bed. You asked me to stay, just until you fell asleep. I climbed in beside you and you buried your head in my chest. You were out within fifteen minutes."

"So, you came back early just to make breakfast?" I sound like an idiot, but I need details. I can't trust my brain to fill in the missing pieces, so I have to rely on Maxton, something I am not entirely sure I should be doing.

He turns to face me so that his legs straddle my chair. "No, I didn't."

He doesn't elaborate, which irritates me. He knows where I'm going with this. Why won't he just tell me?

"Did you sleep on the couch?" I pry for more information.

Leaning in close, he whispers, "No, sweets, I didn't sleep on the couch. I held you. I stayed awake all damn night, holding you in my arms. You unnerve me, Kensington." He sits back in his chair, his hand still on the back of my neck. It takes all of my willpower not to moan as he works my sore neck muscles.

I tilt my head forward and let him work out the kinks in my neck. His hand feels amazing.

"That was a first," he says quietly.

"What was a first?"

"Last night, that was a first for me. I've never spent an entire night in bed with a woman. It's too intimate, too permanent. That's never what I've been about." He rests his other hand on top of mine on my thigh, lacing his fingers through mine. "I held you the entire night. I went back and forth from watching you to watching the shadows play out on the ceiling." His voice trails off, so I turn to face him. "I didn't want to leave you, to let you go. I can't explain it and I sure as hell don't understand it." He brings our entwined hands to his lips. "I'm not even sure I want to." He kisses my knuckles.

"You were gone when I woke up."

He nods. "I wasn't sure how you would react waking up with me, so I slipped out around sunrise. I sat on the couch until Bright and Nic woke up. They think I slept on the couch."

"It was a first for me too. I wish I could remember it," I admit. The thought that I spent the entire night in his arms and can't remember it is depressing. I wonder if I'll ever have that chance again. If I do, would I take it?

26

Maxton

THANK FUCK I'M sitting down; otherwise, her admission would have brought me to my knees. I want to pick her up and carry her ass back to her bed. I want to slide under the covers and hold her next to me. Leaning in, I place a kiss on her temple. "Anytime. Anytime you want me in your bed, no matter what the reason, you let me know."

I should be appalled at my words, but I'm not. I meant every fucking word and I don't know what to do with that information.

"Go get ready so we can run to the house and pack up the quads," I tell her.

She hesitates. "I promise it'll be a good time. You need to get out more." I bump my shoulder into hers, trying to lighten the mood.

Releasing a heavy sigh, she climbs to her feet and picks up her plate. I take it from her hands. "I got this; you go worry about you." With a nod, she turns and heads toward her room.

I busy myself loading the dishwasher and cleaning up from breakfast. This is how Bright finds me.

"Nic's almost ready," he says, leaning against the counter. "Kens still going?"

"Yeah, she doesn't remember saying she would go, but she's getting ready now."

"Good. Nicole really wanted her to go. I was afraid she would back out, and then I'd miss out on spending the day with my girl."

He says it so casually, yet it's still odd hearing him say things like that. He's never claimed having a girl before, and now he's ready to yell it from the rooftops. It's hard to get used to.

"Well, you can relax." I, on the other hand, cannot. Lance is going to be there. I don't know what his intentions are toward Kensington. She said he's her friend's brother, is there more to it?

Nicole comes bouncing out of her room. She stops next to Bright and he doesn't even hesitate to wrap his arms around her and pull her into his chest. I pretend to be wiping off the counter to avoid starting at them. A few minutes later, Kensington enters the room. Even if Nicole wouldn't have started talking to her, I would have known she was there.

"You ready for a day of outdoor fun?" Nicole asks her.

Kensington smiles and nods. "Let's get this show on the road," she quips. I can't help the smile that tries to break free. She's taking this like a champ, going with the flow. I'm impressed.

"All right, ladies, let's do this." Brighton puts his arm around each girl's shoulders and leads them to the front door. I want to protest and tell him to keep his hands to himself; then I realize I have no say so. She isn't mine. Bright turns to look over his shoulder and smirks at me. Fucker! He's trying to wind me up. I swallow back the irritation and act as if his hands on her doesn't faze me.

In the parking lot, we load up in my truck and head to the house to get our bikes. Bright climbs in the back with Nicole, which leaves Kensington to sit up front with me. I like it, more than I should. I have the urge to reach over and place my hand on her thigh to feel her smooth skin against my fingertips. Instead, I grip the wheel with both hands and drive. By the time we reach the house, my knuckles are stiff and white. I quickly jump out of the truck and leave the others to follow behind. I need a minute to get my shit together. This girl is alarming my senses. She has me wanting to break the rules. I'm struggling with that, with her and what she makes me feel. Can I trust that feeling? I think about my dad and how he trusted my mother. She crushed his soul, can I take that risk?

"Hey, man, where's the fire?" Bright yells as he enters the house. I don't bother to answer. I continue on to my room and change my clothes, brush my teeth, and grab a hoodie. It's early fall and a seasonably warm day. Chances are slim to none I'll need it, but she might. I almost leave it behind, but I like her in my clothes. Being able to take care of her wins out and I shove it under my arm.

I march out the front door, not bothering to address the girls who are waiting patiently in the foyer. I hop back in my truck and throw the hoodie in the seat. I back the truck up to the front of the trailer. I've done this a million times and never need anyone to guide me. Hopping out of the truck, I work on fastening the hitch to the truck. Once I'm done, I open up the ramp gate in the back so we can easily load the bikes. Brighton joins me and it takes no time for both of our four-wheelers and gear to be loaded in the trailer. Bright loads up the cooler. Josh is supposed to be bringing the grill. We'll stop on the way to get ice, drinks, and chips; that's our contribution. We also need to get the girls helmets. No way are they getting on the back of a bike on those trails and not be protected.

"I think that's it," Brighton says as he loads the toolbox. We always take it just in case.

"Looks like it."

"Hey, man, I know we have to stop off to get the supplies, you think we can make another stop?" he asks.

"Where? We need to stop at the bike shop and get the girls a helmet." It's not up for debate, not that I think he will fight me on it. Nicole means a lot to him and I know he would want her safe.

"You read my fucking mind. That's what I wanted to do. No way is she going on those trails with all those other idiots without a helmet. We need to keep our girls safe from those asshats," he quips, pats me on the shoulder, and walks off in their direction.

Our girls.

Kensington.

My girl.

Shit just got real.

27

Kensington

AFTER THE GUYS get the trailer loaded, we hit the road. I'm still not completely sure what I'm getting myself into, but Nicole is happy and that's what matters. So many times she has sacrificed for me; this is the least I can do. Maxton pulls into a strip mall that has a grocery store, a bike shop, and a salon. I assume we're here to get the supplies I overheard him and Brighton talking about earlier.

I watch as Maxton hops out of the truck, walks around the front, and to my door. He opens the door and holds his hand out for me. Brighton opens the back door, and he climbs out with Nic right behind him. I place my hand in Maxton's and he helps me down. Not that I needed it, but it was another chance to touch him and have a good reason for it, so I took it.

Instead of heading toward the grocery store, like I assumed, he leads me to the bike shop. I guess we need more than just food for the trip.

Brighton opens the door for Nicole and leads her inside. Maxton catches the door, places his hand on the small of my back and guides me to follow them. A big burly guy behind the counter greets the guys by name. "What can I do for you?" he asks.

Brighton speaks up first. "These lovely ladies need helmets. We're going riding today."

Nicole smiles at him sweetly, soaking up his need to take care of her. I, on the other hand, feel awkward and out of place. Maxton probably feels obligated to insist I have a helmet as well.

"All right, you two, follow me," burly guy says. Nicole dutifully follows him to the back of the store, while I stand still holding my position.

I feel Maxton grab my hand as he begins walking to the back of the store. I'm no match for his strength, which leaves me no choice but to follow along. Nicole already has a helmet on her head. Big burly guy and Brighton are checking to make sure it's the right fit for her. Maxton, still holding my hand, stops in front of a shelf and studies it. He chooses a helmet, releases my hand, and offers it to me. "Here, try this on," he demands.

I shake my head no. "Maxton, this isn't necessary. I don't need this. I might not even ride. I can just stay back and cook or something." I don't know what exactly the protocol is for bringing a girl riding, but I can only assume it will mean I am riding with him, or another guy. I fight back the panic of the unknown.

Maxton studies me, looking for what, I don't know. He sets the helmet on a stack of boxes beside us and cups my face with his big hands, his eyes boring into mine. "I'm only going to say this once. Understand?" I nod my agreement. "I need for you to be safe. There is no way I would let anything happen to you, and you wearing this helmet is a part of that. Please don't argue, and try the damn thing on." His voice is pleading.

I blindly reach over and grab the helmet from the stack of boxes. He takes it from my hands. With his free hand, Maxton pushes my hair back behind my shoulders. He then lifts the helmet and places it on my head. Once in place, he fastens the chinstrap, making sure it's tight. He then turns my head in all kinds of different angles to ensure the proper fit.

"Perfect."

"I couldn't agree more," burly guy says from behind Maxton. He

116

walks over and places his hand on my shoulder while the other goes through the motions Maxton just went though. Satisfied, he loosens the strap and slides the helmet from my head. Leaning in, placing his hand on my hip, he whispers in my ear, "Looks real good, doll."

I don't get time to respond before Maxton is jerking the guy back by his shoulder. He twirls around to stand in front of me, facing off with burly guy. "Don't ever fucking touch her again," he seethes.

I place my hands flush against his back. I can feel his ridged muscles underneath his shirt.

Burly guy throws his hands in the air. "Didn't realize she was yours. I wasn't about to let a beauty like her slip away," he smarts off. Maxton growls and I feel him start to take a step forward. Instinctively, I wrap my arms around his waist and bury my face in his back. He stops in his tracks. I feel him take in a deep breath and slowly exhale. His large hands slide over top of mine, which are still clinging to his stomach.

"Consider yourself warned. You don't touch her, don't even fucking breathe in her direction. You see her on the street, you turn around and walk the other direction." His voice is filled with anger.

"I would listen to the man, Marty." Brighton's voice comes from behind me. Seems burly guy does have an actual name. "Ring these up so we can be on our way," he tells him.

Marty makes it a point to bump his shoulder into Maxton's as he walks by. I feel the contact and wrap my arms tighter around his waist. I don't want him to go at it with this guy over me. That's when it hits me. Maxton protected me. Not once did memories of the past surface at Marty's closeness. His sleazy come on and his hand on my hip normally would have sent me back to that night. I don't do well with these types of situations. Uninvited touching is off limits. Sometimes, even dancing with a stranger can cause panic to swell in my chest. Instead, my thoughts were solely on Maxton, on keeping him from beating the shit out of the guy.

I wasn't afraid of Marty. I knew Maxton and Brighton were there. Later, when I'm not plastered to his back with my hands planted firm against the hard ripple of his abs, I'll figure out when I placed that kind of trust in him. I knew deep down I was safe. He'd protect me.

28

Maxton

I'M RELIEVED WHEN Brighton steps in. He's saying something, but I don't know what. As soon as he starts talking Marty fucking shoulder checks me and I am about to lose my shit on him, until she tightens her grip. Kensington is holding me like her life depends on it. I close my eyes and focus on taking deep even breaths.

I overreacted.

What Marty did wasn't that bad. If it had been any other girl, I wouldn't have thought twice about it. The hand he placed on her hip was in a respectable position. He didn't pull her into him. He simply lightly touched her and leaned in to tell her how good she looked in her helmet. What Marty didn't realize was it wasn't just any girl... it was Kensington. *My girl.*

As soon as he touched her, I saw red. Jealous rage plain and simple. I'm losing my shit over this girl.

"Max?" Her soft voice brings me out of my head. It doesn't escape me that she calls me Max. It's always Maxton, formal. Not this time.

I grip her arm and give it a gentle tug to guide her in front of me. I want him behind us, where he can't even see her. Irrational, but it is what it is. As soon as she's standing in front of me, I wrap my arms around her waist and pull her against my chest. She doesn't fight me as her hands land on my hips.

"I'm sorry," I finally say. "He should have never touched you."

She looks up and our eyes meet. I fight against the urge to press my lips against hers, to taste her. She smiles and my heart skips a beat. "I thought you were taking me riding?"

Just like that, the anger is gone. It's as if just being around her grounds me. It's bizarre yet comforting at the same time. It's also scary as hell.

"Let's get the hell out of here." Bright's voice grumbles behind us. I couldn't agree more. Reluctantly, I release her from my grip, place my hand on the small of her back, and lead her out of the store. We drop the helmets off at the truck and venture into the grocery store. I'm more than ready to get the rest of this day started, putting the incident at the bike shop behind me. I don't have time to analyze my actions; besides that, I've already concluded I overreacted. However, I couldn't control my response.

Luckily, the grocery store is uneventful and we're back on the road in no time. The drive to the trails we are riding today is about an hour away. I settle into my seat and try to avoid the pull of the gorgeous girl who is once again riding shotgun.

The four of us make small talk. Nicole and Kens asking questions about the trails and what it's like. They both seem genuinely interested and that's a rarity. These two, they're in a league all their own. A league I'm not sure I'm ready to be a part of. I'm used to girls who just want to hang on your arm and get into your bed. I've never brought a girl on any of our guys' trips. Technically, she's not with me, but I think I want her to be.

We arrive in what seems like no time. Kensington and Nicole start unloading the truck with our purchases while Bright and I unload the quads. By the time we're done, Nicole and Kensington have the cooler stocked and are waiting for instruction on where to put the food. "We generally put a few folding tables together in the center of all of our trucks and everyone helps themselves," Brighton explains.

Nicole points over her shoulder. "There?"

"Yep," Brighton chirps. Yes, he fucking chirped his reply. He's in deep.

Without saying another word, they gather the rest of the food and carry it over to the table. I turn away from them, working on getting our gear unpacked. I start with Kensington's helmet. I take all the tags off and sit it on the rack of my bike.

"Shit!" I hear Brighton curse beside me.

Turning around to see what the deal is, I freeze. Lance and a guy I've only met one other time, so I cannot even remember his fucking name, are standing close to the girls, talking... flirting.

I feel a hand clamp down on my shoulder. "Chill, man. You look like you're ready to murder him."

I realize my hands are at my sides in tight fists. I shove them in my pockets, trying to calm myself down. "Why in the hell does he always seek her out?" I grit out.

"So far, it's harmless. Just wait."

Brighton tightens his grip on my shoulder. We're both watching them, waiting to see what happens. A gust of wind blows through and Kensington's hair falls in her eyes. Lance raises his hand to push it out of her face. "He needs to keep his hands to himself," I growl. My hands, which were tucked into my pockets, come out and are once again balled into fists.

"You willing to fight for her?" Bright questions.

Am I willing to fight for her? Her sweet smell, her soft lips, her smooth skin. That smile that makes my world shine brighter? Fuck! "Yes," I growl. Breaking away from his hold, I head toward the girls.

Kensington looks up and sees me coming. She takes a step back from Lance. Good girl.

Never breaking my stride, I don't stop until I'm standing behind her. I place my hands on her hips and pull her back against my chest. She doesn't protest and my chest swells at the realization. "Babe, your helmet's all ready to go." The words leave my mouth before I realize what I've said. *Babe?* I wait for panic to take me at my blatant display of affection toward her. Nothing happens. No panic. Just increased heart rate due to her body being aligned with mine.

Kensington looks over her shoulder at me. "Thank you." She doesn't scold me or give me the look— the one telling me I'm a possessive asshole and need to back off. She doesn't tell me I have no claim to her. None of that, a simple thank you with a smile is what I get. It's with that smile that another layer to the walls I have constructed around my heart falls away.

29

Kensington

I COULD TELL by the look in his eyes as he stalked toward me that he was not happy. I expected more of what happened in the bike shop earlier. That's why I stepped away from Lance, hoping to diffuse the situation. What I didn't expect was for Maxton to claim me. At least, that's what it feels like. His hands are on my hips, his solid grip letting me know I'm where he wants me. My back flush against his chest. I want to wiggle my hips to see what kind of reaction I get out of him, but I don't want to poke an angry bear.

Today he's different, protective. His eyes in the bike shop when he apologized were caring. It's obvious there is a spark there. I feel it and so does he. My problem is, I don't know what to do with it.

I wasn't expecting sweet Maxton from the look on his face, but that's exactly what he gave me. Calling me babe.

"Lance," Maxton says in greeting.

"Hey, glad you all could make it." Lance darts his eyes toward me. I can only assume he's trying to gauge my reaction to Maxton the bear. Lance is a great guy. He knows it's hard for me to trust; I told him that much. I offer him a smile, letting him know I am, indeed, okay. He seems to relax at my gesture.

"You ladies ready to hit the trails?" Lance asks.

"Spending the day wrapped around Bright, uh, hell yeah I am." Nicole laughs. I would have laughed right along with her, except I just stopped breathing. Am I going to be riding with Maxton? I guess I never thought too much about it. Just the thought causes me to squeeze my legs together to stifle the desire I feel for him. He affects me like no one ever has. He never says or does what I expect and he seems to keep coming back. Sure it's only been a few weeks, but that hasn't stopped him. He's been very vocal about wanting me in his bed, yet he doesn't push the issue, letting me come to terms with it in my own time. At this point, I feel like it's inevitable. I was trying to avoid a messy situation because I know how Nicole feels about Brighton, but resisting him is getting harder and harder.

I'm not sure I want to resist him anymore. The thought of being wrapped in his strong arms while he... I need to think about something else.

"And you?" Lance directs the question at me.

"Will be riding with me," Maxton answers before I have a chance.

Well, all right then; that answers my question.

"We're going to go suit up," I hear Brighton tell Lance. I didn't even know he was there.

"Sounds good. I'll spread the word we should be ready to head out in about fifteen or so." Lance winks at me, and saunters off.

Maxton growls behind me. I can't help but smile at his reaction. It causes butterflies in my stomach. I've never allowed myself to spend enough time with a guy to feel this way. To feel wanted and protected, it's a heady feeling, one that's starting to really grow on me. Is it possible Maxton could be the one to stick around? Do I want him to be?

"Ready, beautiful?" Maxton's hot breath hits my neck as he buries his face there. It's only mere seconds that he allows the contact before he's pulling away from me. He places his hand on the small of my back, a move I'm finding out I love, and leads me back to his truck.

Nicole already has her helmet on, raring to go. I pick mine up from the bike and slide it over my head. I'm struggling to tighten the chinstrap when I hear his voice. "Let me." His hands take over and he has the helmet secured in no time. He checks it over, testing to see if it's tight enough before releasing me. "You're perfect." His deep voice croons as he steps away. He immediately turns his back and slips his own helmet over his head.

I stand frozen in place, his words repeating over and over in my mind. "You're perfect." Once again, Maxton Cooper has altered my original perception of him.

Maxton turns to face me. "Make sure you hold onto me. I'll take it easy. If there is anything you're not comfortable with, you let me know."

I nod my understanding. Satisfied, he climbs on the four-wheeler and leans up toward the handlebars, allowing me space to climb on behind him. Once I'm on, I scoot back on the seat and rest my hands on my thighs. Brighton and Nicole pull up beside us; as expected, she's clinging tight to Bright.

"Ready?" Bright asks.

Maxton doesn't say anything; instead, he reaches behind him and places his hands behind my knees. He pulls me against his back. My hands automatically wrap around him to hold on. He guides me to link my fingers together, and places them against his ripped abs. Good Lord, his body is sinful. "Don't let go." He raises his voice over the engine. Turning back to Bright and Nicole, he says, "Now we are. Lead the way."

I do as he says and keep my grip tight. About a mile or so into the trail, I relax and let my body lean into his back. The views from the trails are beautiful with the changing of the leaves. Fall is such a beautiful time of year.

Maxton hits a bump and my ass raises off the seat. When I land, it feels like I'm even closer to him than before. My hands are now also gripping his stomach, no longer clasped together. "Hold tight," he says over his shoulder, preparing me for an upcoming bump in the trail. One hand clutches his shirt, causing it to rise while the other lands on his bare skin. My fingers rake against his hard abs. *Holy shit!* His body feels amazing. Not thinking of anything but how good it feels to run my hands all over him, that's exactly what I do. My hand that was clutching his shirt releases the hold and slides underneath as well. Holding myself to him with one hand, I explore him with the other. Gently tracing the ripple of his stomach, I mentally count an eight pack! Softly running my fingers across his skin, tracing patterns, I'm lost in the feel of him. My legs are wrapped tight around him, my chest pressed tight against his back. I feel his muscles twitch and it spurs my exploring fingers to linger a little longer.

Maxton has me mesmerized. I don't realize we've stopped moving until I feel his hands roam up and down my thighs. I instantly freeze, embarrassed at my actions and even more so at getting caught. Lifting my head, I take in our surroundings and see we're alone. I swallow back the desire running through my veins. Maxton removes his helmet. As he does, I release my iron grip and remove mine as well, sitting it on the rack behind me. Maxton reaches back for my hands one at a time and places them back on his stomach, under his shirt.

At first I don't move. My hands remain where he placed them. I'm not sure what's going on, but I'm about to explode with desire for this man. "Please," he inhales deeply, "not yet, don't let go," his strangled voice whispers as he holds me tighter.

He wants me to touch him. Hesitant at first, I trace circles with my index finger. Maxton releases a deep breath and rests his head back against my shoulder. Growing more confident by his actions, I resume my previous exploration. When my name falls from his lips, "Kensi," I bury my head in his neck. Overwhelmed by his warm body under my fingers, his smell all around me, I lightly press my lips against his neck. My tongue only takes a quick taste of his skin. His entire body shudders at my bold move.

I should be worrying about where the others are, worrying someone might drive up on us and know we are up to no good, but I'm not. All I can think about is how good he feels, how good he tastes, and how I want more. I want so much more.

30

Maxton

IT'S OFFICIAL. KENSINGTON James is going to be the death of me. Her soft hands exploring my body have me barely hanging on. Just when I think I'm getting myself under control, her lips touch my neck and her tongue darts out as if she's dying to taste my skin. I know the feeling. I'm dying to taste her, every single fucking delectable inch of her. I want my tongue to be there. She makes this noise, so soft I would have missed it if her mouth were not right by my ear, and it sends me over the edge. I climb off the bike, hold my hand out to her silently, asking her to join me. She hesitates, worry in her eyes. She thinks I'm pissed off... I'm not. I'm so fucking turned on I feel like I'm going to blow any second now.

I need more.

She places her hand in mine and allows me to help her off the quad. Giving her hand a gentle squeeze, I climb back on, never letting go. This time, I pull her next to the bike. "Climb back on; I need you to face me." Yes, I sound like a greedy bastard, but I don't care. All I care about is getting closer to her, to taste her, to explore her body like she was mine. She's been driving me wild with her hands.

I watch as she blushes but does what I ask. She steps onto the footrest and throws her leg over. She's now standing in front of me, straddling the bike. Not able to wait another second without physically touching her, I rest my forehead against her stomach and place my hands on the back of her thighs. Her hands grip my shoulders, catching her balance. Her fingers run through my hair, the simple gesture warming something inside of me. It's like she knows I'm trying to reel this in. This need I have for her, it's like nothing else I've ever felt. If I was asked to explain it, I couldn't. There are no words for this moment.

My hands start to roam, taking off on a journey all their own. They end up underneath her shirt, softly stroking her spine, my hand hitting the strap of her bra. I want nothing more than to flip the clasp and strip her bare, but not here. Not where Lance or any of the other guys can drive up on us and see her. That's not a risk I'm willing to take. Instead, I focus on the softness of her skin and the way her body trembles beneath my touch. She tightens her grip as her legs tremble. Placing my hands on her waist, I guide her to sit on my lap. She's now straddling me on my quad and I've never in my entire life seen anything more beautiful. She's sexy as hell, flushed cheeks, eyes filled with desire.

Now sitting face to face, I brace my arm around her, holding her close. I can't seem to get her close enough. Sliding my hand behind her neck, I gently stroke her cheek with my thumb. Our eyes are locked, never straying. I wait to see if she's okay with this. I don't ever want to push her into something she's not ready for. Waiting for Kensington James is a torture I'm willing to endure. Her eyes leave mine and settle on my lips. She licks her own, causing my already rock-hard erection to grow even more. Her hips rock into mine, just slightly and only once, but it's all the invitation I need to move things further. Her lips are mine.

I take hungry possession of her mouth, my tongue tracing over her puckered lips, dipping between the seam. Taking what I want, her, Kensington. I want to be surrounded by her, consumed. If the whimper she releases is an indication, she and I are finally on the same page.

The sound of quads passing on a nearby trail brings me back to reality. I want nothing more than to sink deep inside of her and stay there, but I can't. Won't, not here. I slow the kiss as I nibble on her lips. Needing to slow this down, I kiss the tip of her nose, her eyes, and her cheeks. Burying my face in her neck, I can feel the blood pounding through my veins, my heart thundering against my chest. Breaking the connection, I cup her face in my hands. That's when I notice the trembling. At first, I thought it was her, but it's not; it's me.

The reality of the situation crashes into me. She's slowly chipped away at the walls erected around my heart. My motto: the only way to have truth in any relationship is to stay true to yourself, slaps me in the face. My truth is no matter how hard I fight it, or deny it, it's there. I feel something for her that I've never felt. She's softened my hardened heart to the point that all I see is her. In the back of my mind, I know this is what my dad meant when he said when you found the one you would just know. That nothing would be able to keep me from her. I feel that, now with Kensi. Is she "the one"? I'm not ready to dive into that just yet, but she is the one "for right now," and that's a first for me. For the first time in my life, I want a relationship. I want to get to know her, explore her luscious body.

The game has changed; I still want her in my bed, but now I also want her. I refuse to share her. Having someone like Lance swooping in and catching her attention is not something I'm okay with. I need to tread lightly and feel her out. I need to convince her to give this, to give being with only me, a shot. We can learn together, and maybe, down the road, she will be "the one."

The thought of her really being mine, it humbles me. This girl is amazing and… yeah, I need to make that happen.

"You're shaking." Her voice is reverent.

"That's all you. You wreck me, Kensi." No truer words have been spoken.

"Max," she whispers, and just as I'm about to capture her lips again, I hear them coming back. Not able to prevent it, I place a chaste kiss on her forehead and help her off the quad. I remain sitting; otherwise, they will all know what we've been up to, or at least what I'm up to.

31

Kensington

I QUICKLY HOP off his lap and stand beside the four-wheeler. I stretch my arms above my head, pretending to be stretching, when all I really need to do is pull air into my lungs. He leaves me breathless.

Bright and Nicole pull up beside us. Bright shuts off the bike and they both take off their helmets. "What happened to you two?" she asks.

"I just wanted to stretch my legs. I was so nervous; I was gripping Max too tight." As soon as the words leave my mouth, I'm blushing. They sound crude and suggestive and fit into what was happening between us just minutes ago. Thankfully, my best friend laughs it off. She would never believe what just happened. I'm the girl who shy's away from guys, especially guys like Maxton. I don't get close enough for events like today's to occur. I keep to myself and live in the past. I now understand what Dad was trying to tell me. This is what he wants for me, well, maybe not groping a ridiculously hot guy in the middle of the woods, but living. He was trying to tell me that he and Mom had this and he wants that for me, that she would want that for me.

I feel tears well up behind my eyes. I bend over, pretending to be messing with my shoelaces, until I can fight them off.

"We're heading back to fire up the grill," Bright chimes in.

"Sounds good, man. We're right behind you," Max agrees.

Within no time, their helmets are back on and they are speeding off toward the truck. Max climbs off his four-wheeler and stands next to me. His hands rest on my shoulders. Bending his knees, he makes himself eye level with me. "You okay?" His voice is concerned.

"Yeah, I'm good. We better head back before they come looking for us."

Maxton exhales, stands to his full height, and wraps me in a hug. I feel a light kiss on the top of my head, then the loss of his warmth. He climbs back on the four-wheeler, holding out his hand to help me climb on. Placing our helmets back on our heads, we head back to the lot.

Nicole and I take over setting up the food. There are two grills going, both operated by guys we don't know. Two other girls are here as well, but they're sitting around with the guys, vying for their attention. Nicole and I have everything set up by the time the grilling is done. Several of the guys comment on how nice it was for us to take care of set up. A few of the guys throw us winks, but nothing inappropriate. Bright and Max are the last two in line. Bright carries Nicole's plate to the trailer; they have a table set up and a small heater. Apparently, they brought it for us. It's a little chilly, but not terrible. Max and I make our plates, and he takes mine as we join our friends.

The food is great; of course, we're all starving. None of us have eaten since Maxton's breakfast this morning. A few of the guys come over, and we are introduced. Everyone seems friendly and I find myself having a good time. This morning I was dreading it, now I'm more than glad I came.

Just as we finish eating, Lance stops by to tell us one of the guys has a flat, but as soon as it's fixed, we'll be ready to go out again.

"I think we're going to head up the north trail," Brighton informs him. He looks at Max for approval.

"Yeah, I think the girls will like the overlook," Max agrees.

Lance nods, tells us he'll catch up with us later, and heads back to the group.

"You don't have to change for us," Nicole speaks up.

"Yeah, if you think it's too much, we can just hang out here," I chime in.

"Not gonna happen, Nic," Brighton says. "Besides, it has nothing to do with you not being able to handle the trail." If I'm not mistaken, there is a slight blush to his cheeks. "I just wanted to be away from the group." She seems to finally get what he's saying, because she lays a loud kiss on his lips. His smile widens.

We spend the next twenty minutes, for lack of a better term, shooting the shit. Bright and Max entertain us with stories about their childhood and growing up together.

The guys decide, since we're not going on the same trail as the others, we can go ahead and head out. I take my place behind Max and hold on. He places his hand over mine and laces our fingers together. He doesn't let go until we reach the trail and are able to pick up speed. I relax against him and watch the fall colors roll by.

Maxton stops beside Bright and they discuss which way to go next. Apparently, there is an overlook that has a great view they are trying to remember how to get to. I'm not paying too much attention because as soon as we stopped, Max once again placed his hand over mine and laced our fingers together. He's melting my resolve one touch at a time.

The guys finally decide on which way to go and we're off. Feeling brave from his affections, I slip my hands underneath his shirt and clasp my hands back together. Every once in a while, I draw a lazy pattern with my thumbs, but for the most part, I just hold on, skin to skin. I hold on tight.

32

Maxton

WHEN WE REACH the lookout, I'm disappointed. She seems to relax when we're riding, so much so that she tortured me with those hands of hers. Not that I'm complaining.

Reluctantly, we climb off the quad and remove our helmets. Bright and Nicole are already at the edge taking in the view. "Kens, you're missing out," Nicole yells over her shoulder. Kensington reaches for my hand; her face is lit up with a smile as she drags me to the edge.

I take in her beauty while as she takes in our surroundings. In this moment, there are no shadows that follow her. She's blissfully happy. Powerful affection grips my heart in the realization I did that for her. I brought her here, to peace.

"It's beautiful," she breathes

"I couldn't agree more," I reply. Although, I'm not looking at the scenery; I'm only looking at her.

She turns to face me and I can see in her eyes she knows I'm talking about her.

A gust of wind passes through and she shivers. I don't hesitate. I step in behind her and wrap her in my arms. Her body relaxes against mine, and the peace I saw in her just minutes before washes through me.

The four of us remain quiet on top of the mountain, looking out over the horizon. The sun is starting to set and we couldn't have timed this better if we tried. Then again, knowing Bright, this is exactly what he had in mind.

As the sun sets further into the horizon, I will it to slow down. I don't want to leave this moment. I could stay here with her in my arms for hours. I know we need to head back soon; the quads have headlights, but the trails can be difficult to navigate in the dark of night.

I hear Bright tell Nicole it's time to go. I want to stomp my foot and throw a fit; I'm not ready to go. Instead, I gather her hair and place it over one shoulder. I lightly kiss her neck, trailing up to her cheek. "It's time to go, pretty girl." My voice is soft. She sighs, relaxing further against me. I squeeze her tightly, letting her know I feel the same way.

We climb back on the quad and wait for Bright and Nicole. I rest my elbows on her knees as my hands roam her calves. This day turned out a hell of a lot better than I expected it to.

When we're finally ready to hit the trail, I lift my shirt and place her hands against my skin. I try to tell myself it will help keep her warm, and it will. However, that's not my motivation. I need the physical contact with her; it's a craving that's all new to me.

We're the last ones back from the trails. Most of the guys have already loaded and are ready to go. As soon as we get to the truck, I hop off and grab my hoodie. Instead of handing it to her, I slip it over her head, helping her put it on. I watch in fascination as she lifts the collar to her nose and breathes in deep. "It smells like you," is her explanation, along with a beautiful smile.

In the desperate attempt to resist her, I drop a kiss to her temple and leave her standing. I focus on loading up the quads and cleaning up our site. Walking around the trailer to where the girls are, I'm stopped in my tracks. Lance is with them, laughing and smiling. Will this guy ever leave her alone? "You gonna put him in his place?" Bright asks.

"Hmpf. I thought I already had." This guy is really pissing me off.

"Kill 'em with kindness my, man." Bright slaps me on the shoulder and walks on.

I watch as Lance starts flipping Keni's hair and she swats back at him, laughing. He does it again; this time she takes off chasing him. Her laughter rings through the night air. I watch her, playful, having fun... until she isn't. Out of nowhere, she falls to the ground with a yelp.

I'm running.

She's only about a hundred feet away, but it seems like miles before I reach her. Lance has his hands on her ankle. I grab his wrist and squeeze. "Don't fucking touch her," I grit out.

Holding his hands in the air, he backs away. Sitting on the ground next to her, I tuck her hair behind her ear. I need to be able to see her face. She winces in pain as she adjusts her position. I hold her face in my hands as I ask, "What hurts?" I focus on keeping my voice gentle. I can't let her see how pissed off I am at Lance for fucking with her. I mask the worry that has settled around me at seeing her in pain.

"Just my ankle. I just landed wrong." She winces again.

Leaning in, I kiss her forehead, quickly releasing her so I can assess her ankle. I run my hands over her leg until I reach my destination. It's a little swollen, but nothing too terrible. "Can you move it?"

She nods and twirls her ankle in a circle, her face showing her obvious discomfort.

"I think you're right about landing wrong. I don't think it's broken; I think it's strained from the odd way you landed. We've got a first-aid kit in the trailer; it has an ice pack. Let's get you settled in the truck with that and get you home."

"Kensington, are you okay with that?" Lance asks her.

He can't be fucking serious. He's really testing my patience. I'm just about to go off on this fuck-stick when she speaks up.

"Of course, I'm okay with that. Maxton will get me home safely." Her voice holds conviction.

It's with her declaration, those words of trust, which I know is not something that comes easy for her, that I give a piece of my heart to this girl. I've been teetering on the edge, fighting it, not wanting to be like my dad. Fighting what I know to be the truth.

Kensington James is a smart, funny, beautiful, incredibly sexy woman who owns a piece of me. It's with that realization I also recognize I was never strong enough to fight this connection we have. Day one, she got under my skin.

Not even bothering to address Lance and his off-the-wall accusations, I stand to my full height, lift her into my arms, and carry her to my truck. Nicole holds the passenger door open while Bright grabs the first-aid kit. I set her in the passenger seat, make sure she's in, and close her door. I run around to the driver's side, pull open the door, and slide in behind the wheel. I lift the center console and gently lift her leg to rest on the seat.

Bright appears at my door with the ice pack wrapped in a clean shop towel. "Thanks." I place it on her ankle and hold still. "Are we good to go?" I ask Bright.

"Yep, last thing to load is us," he says as he and Nicole climb into the back seat. I reach out and pull my door closed, settle in behind the wheel, then lift her foot to rest on my thigh.

"Max, you're driving. I can hold that." She reaches for the ice pack at the same time, trying to lift her leg from mine.

"I'm good. You just strap yourself in and let me do this for you."

She doesn't argue further; instead, she does as I asked and fastens her seat belt.

33

Kensington

ABOUT FIFTEEN MINUTES into the drive, Max removes the ice pack. I assume he's tired of holding it. I lift my leg to move it, but can't. His hand is now on my thigh holding me in place. He's driving, so he doesn't turn to face me. Instead, he tenderly strokes my thigh. I settle back into the seat and enjoy his affection.

By the time we make it to the apartment, my ankle barely hurts. It's tender but no major pain. I try to convince Max I can walk, but he has no part of it. Instead, he whispers in my ear, "Let me take care of you." Needless to say, I zipped up the complaints and let him have his way.

He carries me to my room and places me on the bed. Dropping to his knees, he starts removing my other shoe. I study him; he looks haggard. That's when I remember he didn't sleep last night. He held me instead. I reach for him, placing my hand on his jaw. The dark shadow of stubble roughened his jawline. It's sexy as hell. I trace his jaw with my thumb. "I'm sorry you're tired."

His eyes, although exhausted, smile at me. "Never be sorry for letting me hold you. Given the chance, I wouldn't take it back. I was exactly where I wanted to be." His words cause my heart to stumble, before finding its rhythm once again.

Surprisingly, his words echo my thoughts. Although I wish I could remember it, spending the night in his arms is something I one day hope I might get to do again. Clarity washes over me as I realize I trust his words. In the depth of my soul, I know Maxton is being honest with me. The harder I try to ignore the truth, the more real it becomes. Not knowing what to do with this new information, I need to be alone, need a minute to organize my thoughts. Standing, I timidly put weight on my ankle. "Careful," Maxton urges.

It's tender but no searing pain. "I'm good. No pain, just tender."

"I can get you whatever you need."

Sweet Maxton. "I'm just going to use the restroom. I'm fine, I promise." To further prove my point, I stand on my tiptoes and place a kiss on his cheek. "Be right back."

Taking my time in the bathroom, I brush my teeth and wash my face. I wish I would have brought pajamas to change into. Realizing I'm stalling, I dry my hands and open the door. The soft glow of the bathroom light filters into my room and what I see knocks the breath from my lungs. Maxton is lying in my bed, arm slung over his eyes, sound asleep. Not wanting to wake him, I quickly turn off the bathroom light and let my eyes adjust. The moonlight filters in through the window as I take in his sleeping form.

Maxton with his broad shoulders and muscular arms, standing well over six feet tall, and his massive self-confidence is intimidating. Maxton lying in my bed against my lavender sheets, he's… adorable.

I've never been able to give myself completely to any man. I've had physical relationships, but none of which ignited an ounce of the passion that Maxton can pour into me with just one look.

Knowing how exhausted he is, I don't have the heart to wake him. To be honest, I want him right where he is. There is a peace that settles inside of me when Maxton is around. Decision made, I grab a t-shirt and shorts and quickly change into them in the darkness of the bathroom, not willing to take the risk of waking him with the light. Walking through the darkness, I slowly climb into bed with the least amount of movement at possible, sliding under the covers. Even though there is a good foot between us, I swear I can feel his warmth. I want it wrapped around me. I still feel shortchanged about last night. He held me the entire night and I don't remember any of it. I have no one to blame but myself, and my alcohol consumption.

Lesson learned.

Rolling on my side, I watch him sleep. I take in the quiet rise and fall of his chest, the corded muscles in his arms, to his hands long fingered and strong. The memory of what the rough pads felt like against my skin. Realizing my intense examination is doing me more harm than good, I roll over, placing my back to him. The ever-present desire when in his presence hits me full force. Laying this close to him, I fight the urge to "take care of things" on my own.

Squeezing my eyes shut, I try to distract myself. I think about school and my internship that I need to start working on. I need to find a local business I can assist for six weeks before winter quarter begins. The distraction helps as I slowly start to drift off to sleep.

Feeling the bed move pulls me out of my almost slumber. I say a silent prayer that he doesn't leave. That's when I feel him. His large frame scoots in next to me, his arm drops over my waist, and he tugs me close. I freeze, not knowing what he's going to do next. His face is buried in my neck and he's breathing deeply.

He's still asleep.

I relax against him, relishing the fact I'm in his arms. He may not realize it, but as his warmth seeps into me, I decide it doesn't matter. I still feel safe and protected and… I just want to enjoy it while I can.

Lying next to him, I focus on his breathing. Soon, not only are our bodies aligned, but so is our breathing. However, it doesn't last long when Maxton hugs me tighter, if that's even possible, sighs with contentment, and mumbles in his sleep, "My girl."

My heart flutters in my chest at his subconscious admission, and then plummets when I realize there have been a lot of "girls" for Maxton.

Chances are slim he's thinking about me. Deciding to pretend otherwise, I let the echo of his words wrap me in a silk cocoon of peace as I drift off to sleep.

34

Maxton

KENSINGTON. I SMELL her. As I start to wake, that's the first thing I realize. I can smell her sweet scent. I can feel her. I don't want to wake up from this dream, ever. Even though I fight it, my body still pulls me to consciousness. I feel a hand on my cheek and I swear if feels real, like she's here with me. I feel a soft puff of breath in my face, which causes my eyes to flutter open. I blink several times to make sure the sight before me is real. Make sure she is real.

"Morning." Her voice is husky from sleep, but her smile, her smile lights me up inside.

I take a minute to survey the situation. One of her legs is between mine. My arms are around her waist holding her close. It's not a dream. I held her for the second night in a row. This time, I'm the one who missed it.

Her soft hands reach up and caress my jaw. "You were exhausted," she informs me.

Resting my hand on the rounded curve of her hip, my heart pounds in my chest and blood rushed through my veins. I slip my thumb under her t-shirt and stroke her bare skin. Her breath coming in tiny pants fuels me. I slide my hand to her back and stroke her spine.

"Morning, beautiful," I finally address her. Her face lights up and a smile tips her lips.

"I remember it this time." Her voice is musical.

My hand continues its journey, learning her curves. Reaching her hip again, I slide my hand underneath the waist of her shorts and trace her soft skin. "Remember what?" I ask, fighting to not let myself get lost in her.

"You holding me."

"I thought I was dreaming. When I woke up, I could smell you, feel you. I thought I was dreaming." My eyes lock on hers. My hand ventures over her flat belly, up further until I feel the swell of her breast. She closes her eyes and takes a deep breath. I trace underneath the swell with my index finger. "I was wrong, you are so very real." My voice is deep and filled with my desire for her.

Opening her eyes, she finds me still staring, trying to gauge her reaction. All I see is longing and desire, no hesitation, no regret. "Kiss me," she pleads. Not one to disappoint, I lower my mouth to hers.

I trace the soft fullness of her lips with my tongue. Parting her lips, she raises her head off the pillow to get closer to me. Her tongue tentatively duels with mine. I drink in her taste, taking every bit of what she's offering.

Lost in the kiss, my hand cups her breast. I run the rough pad of my thumb over the swollen peaks. She shudders, but doesn't pull away. Her hands grip my arms, holding me to her. Fumbling through my craving for her, I tug on her shirt until her breasts are bared before me. Once again, I seal my lips over hers, nipping with my teeth, soothing with my tongue "Maxton," she breathes my name and I've never heard words more sweet. Making sure I lavish both peaks, I let one nipple slip from my grasp then capture the other. My hand finds its way back to the waistband of her shorts. This time I don't stop. I slip my hand underneath, seeking her delicate softness, making her hips buck forward.

"Please," she pleads. Her hands now clutch tightly in my hair.

I'm sure I know what she's asking for, but I need to be positive. I need her to tell me. "Please what, sweetheart? Tell me what you want."

"You, Max, I want you," she pants.

Not good enough. "Where? How? What do you want me to do to you?" I need to hear the words.

Her hand drops from my hair and slowly follows the path mine just took. She slips her hand underneath her waistband and places it over mine. "Here, Maxton. I want you here. Touch me, please."

My chest swells with an emotion I can't name. I'm humbled that this gorgeous girl wants me to touch her. I've thought about this moment since I first laid eyes on her. I've wanted her every second since then, fantasized about what it would be like. Never did the fantasy include me needing her to breathe. That's how I feel, like I need to touch her, kiss her, and just be with her in order to breathe.

"Maxton."

No time to think about what it all means. My fingers seek her entrance. I find her bare and, as I slip between her folds, wet. Hot, wet, and fucking sexy as hell. My lips return to lavish her breasts while I gently stroke one finger then two inside of her. Her breathing accelerates and I know she's close. I add the ministration of my thumb while I nip and suck each peak. I feel her start to pulse around my fingers. Releasing her hard nipple, I capture her lips with mine just as her release hits her, swallowing her cries.

I continue to run my fingers through her folds, enjoying the feel of her release, silky smooth against my fingers. Kensington breaks our kiss and lays back on the pillow. Her face is flushed, her hair a mess, her chest rapidly rising, trying to recover from her release. I've never seen anything more beautiful than her in this moment on the heels of the hottest fucking sexual experience of my life.

My girl.

35

Kensington

"I HAVEN'T SEEN much of you this week," Nicole states. It's Friday night and she's getting ready to head to the bar to see Bright.

"I've been busy. I need to find a local business for my externship." It's not a complete lie. I do need to find a local business and I did look, sort of. I also spent a ton of time in the library avoiding this very conversation and others. When Max and I walked out of my room on Sunday, Nic and Bright were already up. They both regarded us, but neither said anything. Bright convinced Nicole to go back to their place, so I was given a pass.

I wouldn't say things were awkward necessarily with Max, just off. I'm embarrassed at how I threw myself at him, begging for him to touch me. I go back and forth from thinking it was totally worth the end result to being ashamed of my actions. He's texted me every day this week. Always friendly, asking about my day, sending funny one-liners, but saying nothing about what happened between us. I'm surprised he's texting at all. Max isn't really the type of guy to stick around.

"Kens! Are you even listening to me right now?" Nicole accuses.

Shit! "Sorry, what were you saying?"

"What happened last weekend? I've been dying to talk to you about it all damn week but you've been MIA," she scolds me.

Double shit! "You and Bright seem to be getting along well," I deflect.

"Yes and don't change the subject."

I throw myself down on her bed and take a deep breath. Taking the plunge, I start talking. I tell her about my run-ins with Max, doing laundry, the night they brought us home from the bar. She was shocked to find out Max slept with me that night, well, held me, yet nothing happened. I told her about trail riding and the night after. I told her about Sunday and how he set my body on fire. By the time I finish, she has abandoned her make-up bag and is sitting on the bed next to me, hanging on every word.

"Wow. That's a lot to take in. Why haven't you said anything?"

"I don't know, because I was fighting it. He's not at all what I expected." As if he knows I'm talking about him, my phone chirps with a text.

Maxton: Hey! Are you coming with Nicole tonight?

"Is that him?" Nicole leans over to see the screen.

"Yeah. He wants to know if I'm coming with you tonight."

Me: No, staying in. I have homework to catch up on.

Still reading over my shoulder, she says, "How could you possibly have homework to catch up on?" She's onto me.

"I have a business plan to finish for my admin class." I do have to finish it, but it's not due for another month. I leave that part out. My phone chirps.

Maxton: I miss you

My eyes are glued to the screen. I blink a few times to make sure I read his words correctly. He misses me? I thought... well, I'm not sure

146

exactly. Yes he's texted all week talking about being up to his neck in paperwork, but I figured it was just an excuse. He misses me.

"He's into you. Bright even says so. Says he's never seen him act the way he does around you," Nicole informs me.

"What do you mean?"

"Bright says Max doesn't spend the night with anyone, never has. He also couldn't care less if another guy talked to a girl he was with. That's so not the case when it comes to you."

"He's just being nice. Besides, he didn't really seal the deal so to speak. It's all a part of the game." I cringe as I say the words, I don't really believe that. The way he looks at me and touches me… that's not a game.

"Right," Nicole laughs. "You just keep telling yourself that." She climbs off the bed. "I have to finish getting ready. I told Bright I would be there at eight. You sure you don't want to come with me?"

"Positive. Tell them I said hi." I leave her to finish getting ready. I set up camp in the living room, my laptop and books spread around me on the couch. I might as well make good use of my time. Grabbing my phone, I read his last message sent twelve minutes ago.

I miss you.

Me: I miss you, too

I type out the message and hit send before I can talk myself out of it.

"All right, I'm heading out. I'll be back in a little while."

"Have fun, tell everyone I said hello." She waves and walks out the door. I check my phone to see if there is a reply from Max. Nothing. Forcing him out of my mind, I open my laptop and begin working on my business plan.

My grumbling stomach alerts me that I missed dinner. I check the time on my laptop and see I've been at it for almost two hours.

Time for a break.

As I head into the kitchen, there's a knock at the door. I'm not expecting company. Ever cautious of who could be waiting on the other side, I peer through the peephole before answering. Maxton. He raises his hand to knock again, but I open the door before he has the chance.

He grins at me. "I brought dinner," he motions to the pizza box in his hand, "and work." He motions to his side where a messenger bag hangs. "I figured since you had work to do and I've been up to my eyeballs all week, then at least we could have dinner together and just… be together while we work."

Is that a blush I see? Could it be possible? Maxton Cooper blushing? Who would have thought? More so, how can I send him away when he looks like that? My stomach growls and he smiles.

"Come on in." I step back, letting him through the door. "We might as well sit in here. I'll grab some plates and drinks." I clear off the coffee table then head to the kitchen. I grab paper plates, napkins, and two bottles of beer.

Max is sitting on the floor leaning against the couch. I hand him the plates and he works on serving us while I open our beers. "Thank you for dinner," I say before taking my first bite of the cheesy pepperoni goodness.

"You're welcome. So what are you working on?" He motions behind him to my laptop and stack of books.

I finish chewing the huge bite I just took and wipe my mouth. "I have a business plan as a final project that's due at the end of the semester." I realize my mistake. I'm sure he's going to ask me what business and I'm going to be busted.

"Wow, what's your business."

I knew it. Grabbing my beer, I take a long slow drink. "A bar," I mumble before taking another big bite, hoping he will leave it alone. It's wishful thinking on my part.

"Seriously? That's awesome. Can I see it?" He genuinely sounds interested.

Shrugging, I feign indifference. "Sure, if you want." He seems satisfied with my answer and continues to eat. Turnabout is fair play and all that. I spy the messenger bag he brought in. "What's had you so busy this week?" I inquire.

I watch as his shoulders slump; he looks defeated. "The books. Dad wasn't a great bookkeeper and I'm not the best either. I've spent so much of my time worrying about the remodel that the books sort of took a back burner. I'm afraid if I let it get worse, then I will never be able to dig myself out of the hole." He reaches up and tucks my bangs, which have fallen in my eyes, behind my ear. "I'm sorry it took me away from you this week. I wasn't even sure you wanted to see me." He drops his hand back to his lap. "I missed you, Kensi."

I swallow hard. "I missed you, too." Not sure what to say or do, I pick up my beer and finish it off. "I can help you, if you want. My degree is in Business Administration with a minor in finance." He's quiet so I backpedal. Maybe he doesn't want me involved in his business. "Or not, it's fine either way; I just thought I would offer."

"Thank you." He scoots closer to me. His hand comes around the back of my neck and he rests his forehead against mine. "I would really appreciate any help I can get. First, though, I want to kiss you. It's been five days, Kensi. Five fucking days since I last tasted you." Then his lips are over mine, demanding yet soft. All too soon, he's pulling away.

"I'll grab us another beer and throw this trash away." I stand on wobbly legs and carry our trash to the kitchen, grabbing us both another beer. Max is sitting on the couch with his laptop open. I take a seat beside him and he begins to explain what we're looking at. That's how Bright and Nicole find us four hours later.

36

Maxton

BEAUTIFUL AND SMART. In the last couple of hours, Kensington has taught me more about my own fucking business than I could have imagined. She knows her stuff.

"So you see, if you scan your receipts, you can attach them to the line item. This allows for you to go paperless and still have all required documentation for the IRS." She's explaining when Bright and Nicole walk in.

"Hey, you two, what's up?" Nicole bops into the apartment, Bright hot on her heels.

"Maxton brought pizza. We were just going over some books for the bar," Kensi explains.

"Kens! That's awesome. Why didn't we think of that sooner?" Nicole says.

I turn to look at Kensi. "What's she talking about?"

"Her externship. She's been looking for a local business to extern for during winter quarter and you've been under her nose the entire time."

My eyes are still on Kensington. "Why didn't you tell me?"

She waves her hand in the air, dismissing me. "I didn't want you to feel obligated."

I consider her words. Would I have felt obligated to her? No. Would I have jumped at the chance to spend time with her? Abso-fucking-lutely!

"So it's settled," I say. "You can do your extern at the bar. Just let me know what you need and it's done."

"Max, no, you don't—" I place my fingers over her lips.

"It's done. No arguments. That's the least I can do for all that you helped me with tonight."

"Right, well, kids, we're off to bed. See you in the morning." Nicole pulls Bright from the chair, and he waves goodnight.

Holding my hand in the air, I wave to them, but my eyes never leave hers. I need to make sure she understands that I want her there. The thought of her being around the bar for six weeks excites me. Hell, normally I avoid this kind of shit like the plague; this time it's different. I'd be lying to myself if I said otherwise.

"Thank you. I won't be in the way. I can even do more of what I was showing you tonight, help you get everything set up and make sure—"

I place my fingers to her lips. "I want you there." The words roll of my tongue with no regret. I mean every word. I can think of nothing I would like more than to have time with her. If Dad could hear me now.

I almost leaned in to kiss her again. Not wanting to push my luck, I stand to leave. "It's getting late. Let me help clean this up before I go." I grab for the pizza box and make my way to the kitchen.

Kensington stops me when she says, "I could have gotten that."

After situating the pizza in the fridge, I turn to face her. She's leaning against the doorframe, legs and arms crossed. I want to grab her, sit her on the counter, and devour her. Yep, definitely time to go.

"You've been drinking."

"I've only had two, and that was hours ago, I'm good," I reassure her.

She shakes her head, letting me know she disagrees. "I don't like the thought of you driving after drinking two beers or ten."

My heart skips a beat as yet another protective layer tumbles to the ground? Knowing she cares enough to be concerned crumbles my resolve. In two long strides, I'm standing in front of her. I hold my arms open and she settles into her place, right against my chest. I rest my chin on the top of her head. I hold her tight and soak up the feel of her in my arms. Realizing it's time to go, even though leaving her is the last thing I want to do, I change my plans for her. "I can call a cab, and then Bright can bring my truck home tomorrow."

Lifting her head, she says, "I think you should stay."

Stay? I want nothing more. However, I'm sure my version of staying over and hers is completely different. I see myself in her bed; I'm sure she sees me on the couch. Regardless, I say, "If that would make you feel better, I'll stay." If it makes her happy, keeps her from worrying, I'll do it.

Her face lights up with a smile. Pulling away from me, I watch as she makes sure the front door is locked and turns out all the lights except for the lamp beside the couch. I sit down on the couch and bend over to take off my shoes. Her hand appears in my line of vision. Looking up, she's holding it out for me. "Kensi?" My heart is racing. I hope she wants me in her bed and I get the chance to wake up next to her again.

She doesn't say anything. Instead, she reaches for my hand, laces our fingers together, and pulls me from the couch. Leaning down, she turns off the lamp. I follow her blindly down the hallway. Once we reach her room, it's lit from the moonlight shining through the window. When we reach the bed, she lets go of my hand. I sit on the edge because my knees are weak just knowing I get to hold her again. All. Night. Long.

It's a good thing I'm sitting down. Kensington pulls her shirt over her head and drops it to the floor. I have to remind myself to breathe. I watch as she reaches behind her back and unclasps her bra, slowly sliding each strap down her shoulders before letting it fall to the floor. I ball my hands into fists against the quilt on her bed. I want to reach out and touch her so fucking bad it hurts. Next comes her pants, she shimmies her hips to wiggle free, kicking them to the side. She steps close in between my legs; I swallow hard, fighting against what is featured before me. Pure.

Fucking. Perfection. Nothing else could ever describe her.

Even in my aroused state, it doesn't escape me that she no longer hides her scar from me. She trusts me. It's that trust that is keeping me from throwing her on the bed and having my wicked way with her. All good things come to those who wait and all that. At least, that is what I keep repeating in my head, trying to convince myself.

Her hands grip the hem of my shirt and lifts. Instinctively, I raise my arms in the air, letting her take control. I watch as she takes my discarded shirt and brings it close to her face and inhales. She's fucking smelling me. My dick is so hard right now; I need to touch her. "Kensi," I croak. My voice sounds like a pubescent boy, but holy hell, this girl affects me like no other.

She doesn't answer; instead, she slides my shirt over her head. I watch as the material glides over her naked body. Mine. The first thing that pops in my head at the sight of her in my shirt is mine. I want her to be mine. I want that claim. I want her in my arms every night. Kensington James has just officially turned my world upside down.

Her soft hands graze my abs as she works to unbutton my jeans. Placing one arm around her back to steady her, I stand and allow them to fall to the floor. Kicking them to the side to join her discarded clothing, I wait for her next move. It's barely a heartbeat before she's wrapping her arms around my waist and resting her cheek against my bare chest. Not one to let opportunity pass me by, I wrap my other arm around her and hold on tight.

37

Kensington

PROTECTED. THAT'S WHAT it feels like to be in Maxton's arms. It's a feeling I crave. I really was worried about him driving, but it wasn't until I asked him to stay that I was able to admit to myself what I really wanted. Taking a deep breath, I decide to take the plunge and ask for what I want. It's risky because my heart beats faster any time he's near, and I think about him all the time. I've gotten to know several sides of Max and I still don't know if I can trust who my heart tells me he is.

"Hold me." My voice is soft yet loud enough in the quiet darkness of the room.

"Anytime, anywhere," he replies. Sweet Max is still here. It seems like he's the one I see more often than not.

Reluctantly, I break our connection. Pulling the quilt back on the bed, I climb in. I hold it up in invitation and he takes no time sliding in next to me. He immediately aligns his body with mine and holds me against him. Relaxing into him, I let his warmth and scent surround me.

Max scoots closer, if that's even possible, and buries his face in my neck. His hot breath sends goose bumps across my skin. We lay like this, not saying a word, just enjoying the moment, at least I am. It's not until I hear him release a satisfied sigh that I know we're on the same page.

Kissing my neck, he whispers into the darkness, "Goodnight, pretty girl." It's with those words and the protection of his arms that I drift off to sleep.

Waking up with Maxton draped around me is something I can definitely get used to. Nicole peeked her head in about ten minutes ago to tell me she and Bright were headed out to breakfast. They wanted to know if I wanted to join them. Imagine her surprise when she found Maxton curled up beside me.

I'm glad Nicole bursting into the room didn't wake him up. It gives me time to study him, to enjoy the feel of his warmth swathed around me. I watch as he slowly opens his eyes and grins. "A guy could get used to this," he says, tightening his hold on me. He runs his stubble covered chin against my jaw and a giggle escapes my lips.

"I love that."

"What?" I question. He's obviously still half asleep.

"You, the sound of you giggling and happy, in my arms. Waking up with you. All of the above."

Wow! He just... wow. My heart is fluttering in my chest and the butterflies are working overtime in my belly. I open my mouth to speak but the words won't come. I lay my palm against his cheek. Max takes that as an invitation as he leans down and softly presses his lips to mine.

Breaking the kiss way too soon for my liking, he asks, "What are we doing today, beautiful?"

He wants to spend the day with me. Giddy excitement takes over as a smile spreads across my face. "First, I'm going to make you breakfast. Nic and Bright left about twenty minutes ago."

Shit. I forgot to tell him Nicole walked in on us. Not that we were doing anything, but we were tangled up in each other.

Max places his thumb on my bottom lip, which causes me to release it from my teeth. "What's wrong, Kensi?" His voice is gentle. This big bear of a man is always so tender with me. I have not seen Asshole Max since that first night. It almost makes me think sweet Max is here to stay.

Could I be that lucky?

"Um, Nicole kind of walked in this morning thinking it was just me. She wanted to see if I wanted to go to breakfast with them." I'm staring at his jaw, not wanting to see the look in his eyes if he's pissed off.

Max lifts my chin with his index finger. "What's wrong with that?" he asks.

"Well, I know this," I point between the two of us, "is not something you do. I'm not sure how you feel about Nic and Bright knowing you spent the night with me, again." I rush through the words.

"Baby, I'm right where I want to be." He tucks a wayward curl behind my ear. "I don't care who knows you spent the night in my arms." He kisses my forehead. "Kensi, I don't know what this is between us, but I know I can't seem to spend enough time with you. I know being with you changes something in here." He lays his hand against his chest above his heart. "I'm not a believer, at least I wasn't. Now, I'm not so sure. What I can tell you is no one else even enters my mind, not since the night I met you. I know I want to give us both time to see what this means."

"Max, it's hard for me... to trust. My past is something that shadows me every single day." His face falls a little and I'm eager to tell him the rest so that look will disappear. "Even so, I feel different with you, protected. I know it sounds crazy, but it's true nonetheless. I find myself opening up to you more and more, and it scares the hell out of me." I watch his face as my words sink in and a slight smile tilts his lips. "Six months ago, I couldn't see myself allowing a guy to stay over, to become so entwined in my world." I laugh aloud. "Hell, six weeks ago, the night we met, I would have bet my life that you wouldn't be." I run my fingers through his hair. "That all changed when sweet Max showed up; sweet Max changed the rules." I lean up and kiss his cheek.

"Sweet Max?" he questions, a smile crossing his face.

I scoot closer, if that's even possible, my lips mere inches from his. "Yes, sweet Max. The one who's okay with holding me." Kiss. "The one who's okay with sneaking a few of these." Kiss. "The one who protects me." Kiss. "The one who's slowing reviving me."

He crashes his lips with mine. Urgently, his tongue slides against mine. This isn't slow and sensual. No, it's sloppy and intense… hot! Pulling away, his lips brush against mine one last time. "That's not sweet Max, sweetheart; that's me. That's me falling so far out of my comfort zone that sometimes it's hard to breathe. That's just you and me; that's us together, pretty girl."

38

Maxton

I PRETTY MUCH just laid my cards out on the table. I have no filter when I'm this close to her. Fuck, waking up with her in my arms is something I could do forever. Believe it or not, it's not the thought of forever that induces panic. It's the thought that it might never happen again.

"So, breakfast first, then what?" I need to change the subject. I can't let myself think about forever, about not being in this exact moment ever again. Nope, pushing that out of my mind and focusing on spending the day with her.

Kensington smiles and all is right in the world. "Let's start with breakfast. Besides, I'm sure you have better things to do than hang out with me all day." She sits up to get out of bed. I immediately miss the warmth of her in my arms.

"Stop!" She turns to look at me. "Don't do that. Don't act like I'm doing you a favor by spending time with you." Cupping my hand behind her neck and bringing her closer, I whisper, "I can't get enough of you, Kensi." My lips lightly press against hers then skim over her jaw, her neck. I can feel the rise and fall of her chest.

"Breakfast," she croaks out.

Reluctantly, I pull away, even though I want to keep going. I want my lips on every inch of her creamy skin. "Breakfast," I whisper.

Kensington hops out of bed and dashes out of the room. I wait a few minutes to think about puppies and unicorns and shit.

When I finally get myself under control, I find her in the kitchen. She has music playing while she sways back and forth to the beat at the stove. I've heard the song, something about players and shaking it off. It plays a lot at the bar. I focus my lust filled gaze on her hips as they shimmy from side to side. I want her next to me.

In three long strides, my hands are on her hips and we are rocking to the beat. She looks over her shoulder at me and smiles, never stopping the sensual assault that her hips are playing on me. I reach around her and pull the pan she was preparing for omelets off the burner, turning the burner off. The heat between us is enough; we don't need to burn down the apartment.

Kensington turns in my arms and places her hands around my neck, clasping her fingers together. I'm so much taller than her; I automatically drop my head, just to feel closer to her. She stands on her tiptoes and our lips meet. Our hips thrust in a steady rhythm, bringing me closer to my breaking point. I don't stop. I can't. The feel of her in my arms as she's moving against me. Not stopping.

The song changes to a slower one. Kensi starts to pull away and I want no part of it. I lock my arms around her and pull her against my chest, where she belongs. It only takes a few beats before she's softly singing the words. This song, it's perfect. I glance over at her iPod— Cole Swindell - "I just want you." I make a mental note to download this song.

As I listen to the lyrics, I feel it deep in my soul. I just want her. Any way I can get her, I want her. I've never been more sure of anything in my entire life. I smile, thinking how Dad was right. I get it now. I understand how he dealt with all the bullshit for years, how he could give her all of him and let her do the things she did. It's in this moment that I can admit Kensington James owns me and I'm good with it. Now I just have to work on her, slow and steady. I need to give her time to get where I am;

then I can make her mine. In my heart, she already is. I just need for her to catch up.

The apartment door opens just as the song ends. I don't pay attention to what comes on next; my attention is on her. I remember her words this morning. How she was afraid I would be upset that Nicole saw us together. With my recent revelation, I couldn't care less. I'm all in. Kensi places her hands on my chest and tries to pull away with weak effort. I can tell she doesn't want to, but she thinks it's what I would want. She thinks it's what she should be doing. I hold tight and slightly shake my head no. Leaning down so my lips are next to her ear, I whisper, "I just want you." I then hug her tight. That's how Nicole and Bright find us, in a tight embrace with my fucking heart on my sleeve.

"Hey, you two," Nicole says brightly. I can't help but chuckle as I turn to face them. Instead of letting go of Kensi, I pull her to stand in front of me and wrap my arms around her waist. I'm going to have a hard time not claiming her as mine.

"Hey, how was breakfast?" Bright grins at my question.

"Good, but not as good as yours," he says.

My face hurts from the grin I'm sporting. "Kensi was making omelets; then we got distracted and, well… yeah." What else could I say? That her sexy swaying ass turned me rock-hard and I had to have her next to me? That a single country song opened my eyes to years of not understanding my dad and that I… I just want her? Yeah, I doubt Kens would appreciate the honesty. Besides, she doesn't know all the details yet.

"I see," Nicole quips. "So what are the two of you getting into today?"

"Breakfast," Kens says, tearing out of my arms and facing the stove.

"Not sure yet. We've haven't really got that far," I answer.

"I'm taking Nic to the house. Thought we could hang out there for a while," Bright says.

"Yeah, I need to check in at the bar. Technically, it's my night to be there," I mumble this last part. I'm so wrapped up in her that I forgot about the bar.

"Why don't the two of you come too? You need to go home to change and Kens can just hang out with us until you get back?"

I'm mentally high fiving my best friend right now. He's a fucking genius. I turn to face the stove and place my hand on the small of Kensi's back. I lean in so only she can hear me. "Babe, do you like that idea? Coming to my place and hanging out while I check in on things at Cooper's? You could even come with me, if you want to." I like the thought of that even better, but I'll let her decide. I hope she doesn't come up with a third option on her own, one that does not end with the two of us in the same place at the end of the night.

"Maxton." Her soft voice pleads. "You don't have to worry about me. Go do what you need to do."

Crazy girl. "I want to spend time with you, Kens. Does this plan work for you? If not, we can figure something else out."

She flips the omelet and turns to face me. "I can go with you, if that's okay?" she hesitatingly replies.

YES! "That sounds good to me, beautiful." I kiss her cheek and turn back to Bright.

"Kens is going to come to the bar with me. It'll give her a chance to get familiar with the place before she starts her extern." That's not why, but I know the excuse will help her handle the situation a little better. She can avoid what's obviously happening between us a little longer, well, at least to them. She can't avoid me; I won't let her.

"Sounds good, man." Bright turns to Nicole. "Baby, go grab some clothes and we'll head out." She stands to kiss his cheek and walks out of the kitchen. His eyes finding me again, he motions his head to the living room.

"Kens, I'm going to go wait with Bright in the living room. I'll be back in a few. You need me to do anything first?" I ask.

That earns me one of her soft smiles. "No, I'm good here. Breakfast should be ready in about five minutes." She turns to focus on the skillet.

I find Bright in the living room sitting on the arm of the couch. "Look, man, I don't want to get in your business, but please don't be fucking with her," he blurts out.

What. The. Fuck. I ball my hands into fists. "I am not fucking with her," I grit through my teeth.

"I know you might not think you are, it's fun right now, but, really, she's—"

He doesn't get to finish because my anger takes over. I grab him by the collar and pull him up from the couch. "It's not just fucking fun, asshole. I'm fucking falling in love with her." I freeze as soon as the words leave my lips.

Bright is grinning. I release him from my grip and slouch against the couch. "I know," he informs me. "I can see it. I see the way you are with her, the way you look at her. I know. I just wasn't sure you did."

I don't say anything as I let the words I just spoke settle inside me. I'm falling in love with her. "She's different." My voice is tight. I'm trying to fight back the emotion of my revelation.

"I'm right there with you, man."

"Have you told her?" I ask him.

"No. I'm scared as hell that she's not with me yet. I don't know if I could handle her not saying it back. I've never said it, you know? When I do, I want to know that the other person feels the same. She's getting there, I hope," he laughs.

I understand. I know exactly how he feels. Hell, just today I was able to finally admit to myself that I want her, only her. I've known for a while, but have been too damn afraid to admit it, even just to myself. However, in the heat of the moment, my heart spoke for me and it speaks the truth.

Truth... five letters, one word.

My heart knows the truth. The truth is that I'm already in love with her.

39

Kensington

As I'm setting breakfast on the island, Nicole walks in. "Hey, so I guess I'll see you a little later," she says.

"Yeah, I'm going to go to the bar with Max, take a look at what he'll have me doing. Last night I was helping show him how to better organize the books. I assume that's what I will be doing for him," I ramble on.

"Kens, I'm so happy for you. I can see how much you like him and he adores you. It's cute to watch the two of you."

"We're just… I have no damn clue what we are," I tell her honestly.

"What do you want to be?" she questions.

"I'm not sure. I know he surprises me daily. He's sweet as hell and he holds me all night long, never asking or pushing for more."

Nicole smiles. "Girl, he's got it bad for you. I would say just as bad as you've got it for him. Just take it day by day. Learn to trust each other."

There it is that word—trust. Five letters, one word summing up the existence of my love life, or should I say, non-existence of my love life. I've never been able to let myself trust anyone to get as close as I've let Max. I trust him. With everything in me I know I can trust him. Justin's brother, he took that away from me, until now. Dread fills me when I realize Max has no idea. He knows about the scar and I said one day I would tell him about it. I have yet to do that. I can't. Nicole must see the panic in my eyes.

"Hey. Breathe. It's okay. Max adores you, take it slow." She soothingly rubs my back. Nicole has been my rock for the last four years.

"He doesn't know," I whisper.

She nods in understanding. "I know that too. I know that when you're ready to tell us, you will. Just know that you're not alone. You have people who love you."

"What's wrong?" Max strides into the kitchen and stops at my side at the island where I'm sitting. He drops to his knees. He places a gentle hand on my thigh. "Kens, what's wrong, sweetheart?"

My heart aches at his concern for me. Nicole's words just minutes ago filter through my mind and I can see it. He cares; Max really cares about me. The thought is humbling and scary and exciting all at the same time. Placing my palm against his cheek, I admit, "I was just thinking about the past." My other hand goes to my chest, right over the scar. His eyes show recognition.

"No one," he grits out, "no one is ever going to hurt you again. I don't know the details, and I don't need to, not until you're ready to tell me, but I can promise you no one will ever lay a hand on you again without going through me."

He scoots in close and wraps his arms around my waist, burying his head in my chest. "Do you hear me, Kens? I mean it. You are safe; with me you will always be safe." His voice is pleading.

I look up to gauge Nicole's reaction to the scene before her and tears are streaming down her face. "He loves you," she mouths.

Her words shock me. I don't have time to process them before Max is rising to his feet, dropping a kiss to the top of my head, and pulling our plates to the edge of the island. "Eat before it gets cold," he says. There we are—his arms still around me as he stands beside me on the stool as we eat our breakfast. It's situations like this one that help push the bad memories away. I don't even want to think about how bad they will be once Max decides he's done with whatever this is between us.

"All right, you two, we're heading out," Bright says, joining us in the kitchen. He has no idea what just happened. I'm sure Nicole will fill him in.

"I think we'll head on over to the bar so I can do what I need to do and then head back to the house," Max tells him.

"You're not staying all night?" Bright questions.

Max looks down at me, his eyes filled with emotion. "Nope, just going to go over last night's register, check in with the staff, and head out," he replies, never taking his eyes off me.

We finish our breakfast, which is now cold, in silence. Max takes our plates, rinses them, and places them in the dishwasher.

"I guess I'll hop in the shower real quick, if we have time."

He turns to face me. "We have time. I'll just finish cleaning up." He reaches out his long arms and grabs me by the waist, pulling me against him. He hugs me against his chest, kisses my temple, and releases me. Taking that as my cue, I head toward the bedroom.

I close my bedroom door and head to my bathroom, taking off my clothes as I go, dropping them on the floor. I reach in and turn the shower on, letting the water warm up. Getting the temperature where I want it, I step under the hot spray. Tilting my head back, I close my eyes and get my hair wet. When I lift my head and open my eyes, he's there. Max. He's standing in the doorway staring though the glass door of the shower.

I watch as he pulls off his shirt and kicks his jeans and underwear off to the side. He's now standing before me, all of him. My breath catches at the sight of him. His strong muscular body is a work of art. I could stare at him all day. Although right now, I want to do more than stare. I want to touch him... everywhere.

Max doesn't move closer. He just stands there in all his naked glory. His chest is heaving with each breath he takes. I want to touch him. Hell, the truth is, I want all of him, now. I watch as he takes himself into the palm of his hand and lightly strokes. That image will be with my until the day I die. I need him now.

I slide open the door, which causes him to suck in a sharp breath. If not for the look on his eyes, I might have been offended. I'm not. His eyes tell me he wants me, which is convenient because I plan to hand myself over for the taking.

I hold my hand out to him. I'm dripping water all over the floor and he's just staring at me. Did I read him wrong? I thought he wanted this, wanted me. "Maxton," I whisper his name. I'm surprised he heard it over the spray of the water.

He blinks a few times, and with his free hand, reaches out to take my hand. He laces his fingers through mine and walks toward me. He stops right outside the shower door. My gaze trickles down his hard abs and stops. I watch as he slowly pumps himself a few more times then stops. He lifts my chin so he can look into my eyes. "Kensi," he breathes. Leaning down, his lips assault my neck. "Do you want this? Tell me what we're doing here. I... I'm sorry I walked in on you, but I came in to grab my shoes and saw your clothes on the floor and..." He swallows hard as his voice trails off.

"I want this; I want you," I tell him honestly. My words spur him into action. He reaches in and turns the shower off. "What are you—" He shushes me as he helps me step out of the shower and wraps a towel around me. He takes another and runs it over my hair.

"As hot as the idea is, I'm not going to have you in the shower the first time I get to be inside of you. I need you in a bed. I need you under me," he says as his lips return to my neck. The next thing I know, the towel that's draped around me drops to the floor and I'm in his arms. He carries me to the bed and releases me. I immediately slide over and make room for him. He climbs in, pulls the cover over us, and gathers me in his arms.

40

Maxton

I SLIDE INTO bed beside her and the feel of her skin against mine has me ready to blow. I feel like the fucking fifteen-year-old me. Kensington affects me like no one else ever has. I guess love will do that to you. Looking at her beautiful face, I want to tell her. I want to tell her how much she means to me, how I've fallen head over heels in love with her and sink in balls deep. And stay there. I know this is going to be an experience like no other. I've never slept with anyone I cared about before, and well… I more than care for her.

I smooth her still damp hair back from her face and cup her cheeks in the palm of my hands. "I've never made love before." The words slip off my tongue. Way to go, jackass!

I'm expecting her to freak out, but she doesn't. Instead she says, "Neither have I." My heart does fucking summersaults at her admission. It's not an exact declaration of love, but the way she said it tells me she's about to. Today we're both making love for the first time.

Gently, I rub the pad of my thumb over her nipple. "Max," she says on a sigh. I love how I can do that to her. With one touch, she's wanting more of me with her.

"What?" I ask her. My cocky side rearing its ugly head just from the way she reacts to my touch.

This girl's mine. I'm going to need for her to confirm that minor detail before this goes much further.

"Tell me what you want, love."

The corner of her mouth lifts. "I want you, Maxton Cooper." She smiles at me. "Inside of me," she adds with a wink. She's fucking flirting with me and I just fell even more in love with her. I've never had this, fun with the person I'm in bed with. Then again, I've never been with Kensi, not yet. Running her fingers through my hair, she asks, "Tell me what you want, love," she throws my words back at me.

Without hesitation, I answer, "I want to make you levitate. I want to be so far inside of you that we can't tell where you end and I begin. I want you to tell me that you're mine."

Her eyes are wide like my words surprised her. "Yours?" she asks; her voice is soft.

"Yes, baby. Mine. Before I'm inside of you, I need to hear you say it. I need to know that no one else gets to be where I am. I need you to tell me you're mine," I lay it out for her.

A slow lazy smile crosses her face. Her hands are clasped behind my neck. "Are you mine, Maxton Cooper?"

"Irrevocably."

"Then, yes, Maxton, I'm yours." She pulls me to her for a kiss. We both get lost in the kiss. Her lips on mine is an addiction I never want to be free of. "Make me levitate, Max," she whispers against my lips.

My fucking pleasure!

I climb on top of her and settle in between her legs. She opens wide for me. I can feel her heat and all I want to do is thrust forward and bury myself inside of her. I don't. Not this time. I need this time to be different; she's not just some hook up. I place my arms on either side of her head and prop myself up.

"You're trembling," she informs me.

Yep. My arms are shaking. This is a big deal. I've never felt this way and I know, deep in my gut, I know that once I'm inside of her, all bets are off. I'm going to be a changed man, and I'm good with that, as long as I have her. I'm good with it.

"This is… you mean a lot to me." There I go with word vomit. I can't seem to help myself where she's concerned.

"Glad to know I'm not alone," she replies. "It's just us. Kensington and Maxton. I want this; I want you. Nothing else matters."

Leaning down, I capture a nipple between my teeth. I nip and lick one then the other. Kens is running her hands through my hair, tugging me closer to her chest. "Maxton," she moans my name and it's the sexiest fucking thing I have ever heard in my entire life.

My lips trail down her stomach. I nip and soothe with my tongue, taking my time savoring the taste of her. I can smell how much she wants me as I get closer. I place a wet sloppy kiss right below her belly button and she giggles. "Maxton, stop teasing," she scolds me through her giggles. I love the sound. I love how we can be this way with each other— open, free to feel and be who we are. No expectations, just Max and Kens.

I look up and see she's staring at me. "No one's ever…" She trails off and my heart fucking swells. I get to be a first for her. I'm going where no one has ever gone before. She's chewing on her bottom lip. She's worried. "Kens, sweetheart, I promise you're going to want me here," I lick just above her folds, "as much as possible. But if you don't like it, tell me and we stop. We'll never do anything you don't want, okay?"

She releases her lip from her teeth, takes a deep breath, and lies back on the pillow. That's my green light. I tap on the inside of her thighs, letting her know to spread open for me. She doesn't hesitate. Placing my hands under her ass, I tilt her up for better access. I start slow, just a short quick swipe of my tongue. She gasps at the contact. I smile against her thigh as I kiss her, drawing patterns with my tongue. She tastes so fucking sweet; I could spend hours right here, but I won't. I need to be inside of her. Next time, I promise myself. I smile at the fact that there will be a next time. She said she was mine, and I'm fucking ecstatic.

Her hands grip the sheets. I hover my mouth over her, breathing against her skin, letting her anticipate my next move. Leaning in, I make a few slow swipes with my tongue. She moans my name, "Max..." I continue to use slow strokes of my tongue, just to get her used to me being all up in her business.

I reach up and lightly pinch her sensitive nipples, causing her to release a deep, throaty moan. Heat surges through me as she bucks her hips, causing my tongue to go even deeper. I slide my fingers through her silk and increase the pressure of my tongue. "Max!" she cries out my name and it fuels me to drive her over the edge. She's writhing beneath me. I lift her legs and place them over my shoulders. She locks them behind my neck, which keeps me locked right where she wants me.

I work my tongue up to her clit. I need for her to tumble over the edge so I can bury myself deep inside of her. Fingers and tongue in simultaneous rhythm, I go no holds barred. Kens lifts her hips, bucking into me. I lay my hand on her belly to help keep her still. "Maxton... Max... Fuck!" she screams as her body shudders against my tongue and my finger are both laced with the silk of her release.

Lifting my head, I slide her legs from my shoulders and look up at her. She's lying there with her eyes closed, panting, her chest heaving from her climax. The sight before me has me sucking in air. She literally steals the breath from my lungs. The vision of her like this will be forever ingrained in my memory. This entire experience will never leave me. It's never been this way, tasted as good. I've never wanted to please someone so bad. Truth is... love changes everything.

41

Kensington

WHAT THE HELL was that? Keeping my eyes closed, I try to focus on breathing, deep breath in and out. I didn't realize what I've been missing. I've only slept with a few guys, and usually it's when one or both of us are a little intoxicated. Not too much that I don't know what I'm doing, just enough to take the edge off, to relax long enough to complete the task and move on.

I feel Max's fingers lightly trailing back and forth over my abdomen. I can't bring myself to open my eyes yet and face him. My emotions are all over the place and I'm afraid he'll be able to see right through me. I tried humor earlier and a little flirting so he wouldn't be able to see how nervous I was. Now, now I'm afraid he'll be able to see how much he means to me. That he'll be able to see I've opened my heart to him, given him two things that I've not been able to do since I was seventeen. Not only does he have my heart, he has my trust. I don't want to scare him away.

His lips graze my nipple and my eyes pop open. "Hey, pretty girl." He softly kisses my lips. I can taste myself, and as much as I always thought that would turn me off, it doesn't. Not after how those lips made me feel.

"Hi." I turn my head away so he doesn't see me blush.

Cupping my face in the palm of his hand, he turns me to face him. "Don't hide from me, Kens. Not now." His voice is pleading.

"I'm sorry, I just… I'm embarrassed at how I acted." I feel the heat flood my cheeks. "I got lost there for a few minutes," I push the words out.

The corner of his lips tilts up until he is full on grinning. "You let go with me. You have no idea how sexy you are, how sexy you were in that moment, hearing you cry out my name, writhing against me. Never apologize for enjoying our time together." He leans down and kisses my nose. "This isn't a one-time thing, Kens. You said you were mine, and I'm holding you to that. I want to see you come undone from what I do to you. I fucking love the fact that I'm the only one."

"Just you," I whisper the words, not really sure I want him to hear me. He does.

"Just us," he says as he drops his head, bringing his mouth to my sensitive nipple. I run my fingers through his hair while he feasts on one then the other.

"Max." I try to get his attention, but he doesn't stop. "Maxton." I try again. This time I tug a little on his hair.

His head rises and eyes blazing with passion are staring back at me. I'm in awe of how much this man means to me. How he snuck his way in, and now, I don't ever want to think about what life might be without him in it. However, once he knows, he may not feel the same. He may not want to be with the "broken girl" when he can have anyone he wants. I need to seize every minute, every memory I can and lock them away for when that happens. "Make love to me."

On trembling arms, Max places himself on top of me. I open my legs and he settles between them. Slowly, he eases his body onto mine, careful not to crush me. Then, he nestles his face in the crook of my neck. I can feel the rapid rise and fall of his chest, the quick pants of breath against my skin. I run my hands up and down his back in a soothing manner, the hard planes of his muscles under my fingertips. He's so big, yet gentle.

We lay like this for several minutes and I'm starting to get worried. "Maxton, we don't…" My words die in my throat as he lifts his head and locks his gaze on me.

"You're everything I never knew I wanted. I want to stay in this moment forever. I need for you to understand what this means to me, that you're giving me this… this gift of you. I will forever cherish you, Kens." He wipes my cheek capturing the tear that has just fallen with his thumb.

I need him. I need him as close as possible. I lock my arms and legs around him, which brings him where I need him. Our eyes lock as he slowly pushes inside of me. "Fuck, Kensi." He stills above me, inside of me.

"Max." I wiggle my hips. I need him to move.

He chuckles. "What, babe?" he asks as he starts to rotate his hips. I make a noise between a sigh and a moan, really I have no idea what kind of sound it is and I don't care. He feels so good. "You feel amazing," he whispers in my ear, his lips traveling down my neck.

Propping himself on one elbow, his other hand travels over my body. If it's within his reach, his hands are there, caressing, driving me crazy.

"You're so fucking beautiful," he says, peppering kisses across my chest.

"Maxton, please," I beg him. This slow onslaught that he's doing is great, really, but I need him.

"Tell me what you need, Kensi," he whispers against my lips.

"I need for you to fuck me." I cry out as he thrust deep. Finally! I move my arms under his and grip his back, holding on to him. He's relentless as he thrusts over and over. I watch as his eyes are closed tight, his breathing rough. Feeling my gaze, his eyes open and lock on mine.

He moves his hand to rub my clit. "Kensi, babe, I'm close. Are you ready?" he asks, never losing the rhythm of his hips or his thumb. "I need you to go with me, babe."

"Yes," I pant, "I'm there, Max." His lips crash to mine, swallowing back my cries as we both fall over the edge of pure bliss. "I've never… j-j-just never been like that," I stutter the words.

Max moves to lie beside me. He wraps his strong arms around me and holds tight. "Kensington," he breathes.

My head is resting on his chest; the thunderous beat of his heart is right below my ear. We lay still as we both catch our breath and come down from the high we just experienced. I have no doubt he is just as affected as I am.

Kissing the top of my head, he says, "Pack a bag for tonight. I want you in my bed."

I'm quiet while I let his words sink in. "Kens, I just want you in my space so I can hold you like this." The rough pads of his fingers trace my spine.

"Okay," I finally say as I move to sit up. He tightens his hold on me.

"Where do you think you're going?" he asks. His voice is husky.

"To finish my shower." He reluctantly releases me and I stand. I feel the evidence of our passion and freeze. "Shit," I breathe.

Max is standing beside me in an instant. "What's wrong?" His big hands are holding my face, his gaze locked with mine.

"Condom," I croak out.

Max furrows his brow. "That's never happened before. I've never forgotten. Never." Sitting on the edge of the bed, he pulls me onto his lap. "I'm sorry, Kens. It's my responsibility and I just… I was so lost in you that it didn't even cross my mind." He kisses my shoulder.

I mentally count the days in my head. "I think we're okay," I tell him.

With his index finger, he turns my head so he can look into my eyes. "Of course we'll be okay. Whatever happens, we'll figure it out. Either way, however this turns out, we'll be fine." His voice is a little shaky.

Trust. I nod my head that I heard him, kiss his cheek, and head for the shower.

42

Maxton

I WATCH HER as she walks away from me. I can't believe I forgot to suit up. That's never happened to me. No wonder she felt so fucking incredible. I wanted to crawl inside of her and never leave. What if she's pregnant? Holy shit, what was I thinking? Obviously, I wasn't but... fuck! I know better. If making love to her results in a baby, then I'll do right by her, but we are so not ready for that. I'm not ready for that. I hear the water turn on in the shower and it hits me that my girl is naked and wet in the next room... without me.

I jump to my feet and cover the distance until I'm standing in the bathroom door. I watch her for a few minutes until she notices me. Déjà vu. She smiles when she sees me and opens the door. In one stride, I'm stepping in to join her. Closing the door behind me, I pull her into my arms and just hold her. I know she's worried, I am too, but regardless of the fear, I would never abandon my baby.

She finally relaxes against me. I grab her loofa and lather it with body wash. I take my time washing every inch of her skin. I move to her hair and she moans as I massage her scalp. Once I'm finished, she returns the favor. I've taken showers with women before, but it's always been about the sex. This is intimate and tender—two things I could never imagined me being a part of until Kens.

We finish in the shower and I remind Kens to pack a bag. I want her in my bed, in my arms. Yeah, that's so happening. We head to my place so I can change clothes before heading to the bar. Walking in, the house is quiet. I assume Bright and Nicole are in his room. With Kensi's bag on my shoulder and her hand tightly gripped in mine, I lead her down the hall to my room. Once we're inside and the door is shut, I release her hand. I set her bag in the bottom of my closet. I find Kensi sitting on the edge of my bed, her hand smoothing over the comforter.

All kinds of sappy shit is running through my head. I smile because it's something that only happens in regards to her. "You look good there," I tell her.

"You're place is beautiful, Max," she says with a smile.

I sit on the bed next to her. "It was my folks. My dad passed away a few years ago and left it all to me. He and my mom were divorced."

"I'm sorry." She laces her fingers with mine. "Do you still see your mom?" she asks.

"No." It comes out harsh and she flinches. I run my thumb over her knuckles, hoping it soothes her. "Sorry, no, I don't talk to her. She's not my favorite person. My dad gave her everything. He worked his ass off to provide for her and all she did was tear him down day in and day out. He tried his best to give her the world and it was never enough. She cheated on him and they divorced about six years ago."

She doesn't say anything, but her grip on my hand tightens. "How long has it been?" Her voice is soft.

"Over a year. I have no desire to see her." I don't talk about this shit with anyone. Bright is the only person who knows everything, how I feel, how what she did affected my father. I find that I want to tell Kensington. Just as I'm about to tell her everything, there's a knock at the door.

"Come in," I yell. Bright pokes his head in the door.

"Hey, I'm going to order some food, you guys hungry?" he asks.

I look at Kens, silently asking what she wants. "If we're going to the bar, we can just pick something up on the way," she states.

"We're good, man," I tell Bright. He taps the door and shuts it behind him.

"I guess we should go. I don't need to stay long. I just want to verify the drawer from last night and make sure everyone shows up," I explain.

She shrugs. "Either way is fine. Are you supposed to be there all night?"

"Usually Bright or I one are there on weekend nights. My staff is capable; I just like to be a part of it. Let them know I'm around." I tuck a loose curl behind her ear. "Tonight I have something more important. I need you in my arms, in this bed. Preferably sooner rather than later."

"We have all night," she quips.

"I know and I plan to have you in my arms every second if it," I fire back. I stand and pull her to her feet. I lead her back out to my truck to the driver's side door. Opening the door, I reach in and lift the center console, really loving the fact I don't have bucket seats. Stepping back, I motion for Kens to climb in. She raises her eyebrows in question, but climbs in anyway. I follow close behind her and place my hand on her leg when she starts to scoot to the passenger side. "Here," I say and she stops. "I just want you close." More sappy word vomit, but I can't seem to stop.

I place one hand on her thigh and one on the wheel and we're off. We end up going through a drive thru and grabbing sandwiches and fries. We eat them on the way to the bar, finishing up in the parking lot when we arrive. Kens gathers our trash and follows me into the bar. I have her hand clasped tightly in mine. This is a first for me. I don't bring girls here. I've hooked up with a few after closing but never bring them here. The crowd is light; it's late afternoon, so this is normal for a Saturday. I wave to a few of the regulars and watch as their eyes widen when they see my hand linked with hers.

My chest swells with pride that she's mine. Another first. I wave to the two guys behind the bar and lead Kens down the hall to my office. Closing the door behind us, I take a seat behind my desk. "Hopefully, this won't take long," I tell her.

"Why don't you let me do that? You can go out and check on the staff," she suggests.

"Kens, you don't have to do that."

"I know, but I want to. It will help me get my feet wet for the externship. I technically don't need to start my hours until winter quarter, but as long as you sign off that I put my hours in, it will be fine." She walks around the desk and places her hands on my shoulders and kneads at my muscles. "Let me help you, Max."

Looking over my shoulder, I wink at her. "Gets you in my bed that much faster, I'm in."

She giggles. "If that's your motivation, then yes, it gets me in your bed that much faster."

She steps to the side as I scoot back in the chair and allow her to take my place. Leaning down, I capture her lips with mine. "I'll be quick," I promise her, then walk out the door.

Mike and Andy are working the bar tonight. They've both worked here a long time, as far back as when Dad was alive. I know the place will be in good hands.

"Who the hell is that?" Andy asks, tilting his head toward my office.

I growl at the look in his eyes. "Mine," I grit out.

He holds his hands in the air and backs up a few steps. "Dude, no offense, I've just never seen her before," he explains.

"I've never seen you bring anyone here," Mike adds.

I don't bother with a reply. They both know what it means; they're just giving me shit. I take note of the inventory and write down a few things I need to order. I like to order on Sundays so the shipment is here on Tuesday. It's what Dad did and I figure if it's not broke, why fix it? The door opens and I see Lance and another guy we ride with, Steve, walk in. They throw their hands up in greeting and cordially I wave back. I'm glad Kens is in the back so I don't have to deal with him hitting on my girl. I'm going to have to talk to him about that.

"Hey, babe, I'm finished. Anything else you need help with?" she says from behind me.

I'm momentarily frozen at the sound of her calling me babe. I like it way more than I should. Turning to face her, I smile. "No. Thank you for helping with that." My arm snakes around her waist and I kiss her temple. "I'm almost finished here and then we can go."

She waves me off. "Take your time." She grabs a rag and starts wiping down the bar. She fits here, with me.

I turn back to the liquor shelf to finish the inventory, trying to finish what I need to do so we can get the hell out of here. I freeze when I hear his voice.

"Hey, stranger, you working here now?" Lance asks Kensington.

"Hey, Lance. No, I'm not working here. Max and I stopped by so he could do a few things."

I stand still with my back to them, smiling. My girl worked me right into the conversation.

"Max?" I hear the question in his voice. "You two seem to be spending a lot of time together."

I grit my teeth and fight the urge to slam my fist into his face. Why the fuck does he care? Taking a deep breath, I force myself to finish the last shelf. I turn around and walk to where she's standing. I slide my arm around her waist and bring my lips to her ear. "Ready, beautiful?" I whisper.

I know Kens would be pissed if I hit him, so I decide to make it known that she's mine. Kens laughs when I nip at her neck and pushes away from me. "If you are," she says, still laughing.

Tearing my gaze from her, I turn and see Lance watching us. "Hey, Lance. How are you, man?" I ask. I purposely smile and kill him with kindness. His eyes travel to my hand that's gripping her waist.

"Hey," he finally responds. "What are you two getting into tonight?" he inquires. He tries to make it sound like casual conversation, but I can tell it grates on him that she's with me.

I look down at Kens. "Just hanging out." I wink, letting her know what we are doing is so much more than just hanging out.

"Cool, you should join us for a beer," he says.

"Actually, Max promised me a night in tonight. Maybe another time," Kensington tells him.

My fucking heart soars! Instead of shying away from us, she jumped in feet first. I know she considers Lance a friend, especially since she has classes with his little sister. I lean down and capture her lips with mine, because in this minute there is nothing else I want more. "Ready when you are, beautiful," I say breaking the kiss.

"All right, well, I guess I'll see you around," Lance says. His eyes are on Kens. He watches her for what seems like an eternity before grabbing his beer and walking away.

Taking a deep breath, I turn my attention to my girl. "Let's get out of here."

43

Kensington

"JUST IN TIME," Nicole says as we walk into Max's house. "We're getting ready to watch a movie."

"Kens?" Max questions. He's leaving the decision up to me. It's only six o'clock, so I nod in agreement.

Max plops down in the recliner and pulls me onto his lap, wrapping me in his arms. My legs are hanging over the side of the chair. "Right where I want you," he whispers.

Bright gets up to turn off the lights and the room is lit from the glow of the television—the very large television, which looks a hell of a lot bigger in the dark.

I settle against Max, resting my head on his shoulder. He sighs and kisses the top of my head and I feel… content. It's not a feeling I'm used to, at least not when a guy is involved. Max changes… everything.

Warm in his embrace, I find myself dozing off not ten minutes into the movie. I couldn't resist.

I wake to Max setting me on his bed. "Hey." My voice is thick with sleep. "Sorry I fell asleep on you."

Max bends down so he's looking up at me. "I loved every minute of it. You were in my arms, Kens. That's all I want."

He stands to his full height, walks back to the door, shuts it and turns the lock. He turns off the light and walks back to the bed. The bathroom light is on, which cast a glow across the room. "Your bag is in the closet."

"Thank you." I slide off the bed and walk toward the bathroom. Going through the motions of brushing my teeth and washing my face, I stare in the mirror at my reflection. My thoughts go back to earlier today lying in bed with him. Skin to skin. That's what I want. I strip out of my clothes and fold them into a neat pile, placing them on the floor in the closet. I turn off the light before opening the door. I need the courage of the dark.

"Kens," Maxton says into the darkness.

I stop beside the bed and crawl in. He reaches for me and sucks in a breath when he feels nothing but bare skin. "I wanted that feeling back. The one from earlier when we were skin to skin. If you'd rather—" My words are cut off from Maxton literally hopping out of bed and stripping off his boxer briefs and t-shirt. He quickly slides underneath the covers and reaches for me again. This time, I'm the one who sighs at the contact. "Thank you." My voice is soft.

He chuckles. "Sweetheart, any damn time you want to feel my skin next to yours, just say the word."

I nuzzle in closer, working myself deeper into his embrace. This is perfect. No expectations, no worry of an awkward walk of shame. I know when I close my eyes, when they open again, he will be there.

"My dad... he loved my mom. I always wondered why he put up with her shit. She would constantly nag at him and nothing was ever good enough. He worked his ass off to give her everything she could ever want. She didn't even work." He pauses and I wait patiently, letting him process his thoughts. "She cheated on him. It crushed his world. Even then, he was willing to forgive her. He said she was the light of his life. He used to tell me one day I would find the one and I would understand where he was coming from." He pauses again. My fingers trace patters on his chest. I remain silent, not wanting to interrupt his thoughts. "She refused to take him back and made him feel like her cheating was his fault. Six months later, he took his own life."

I wrap my arms around him and hold tight. I don't have the words. "I worked construction at the time, me and Bright. I was driving home one day and decided to take a different route than I normally would. I don't know what possessed me to do it, but something in my gut was telling me to, so I did. Just as I was crossing the Marathon Bridge, I spotted a truck that looked like his. I slowed down as I passed. I noticed the Cooper's lanyard hanging from the rear-view mirror. I immediately slammed on my brakes and pulled off to the side of the bridge. Cars were honking; I'm sure I was flipped off a time or two. I didn't care. I knew, deep in my gut, I knew something was wrong. As I walked toward his truck, I pulled out my cell to call him; it went straight to voicemail. I tried to convince myself that he just had car trouble and a friend picked him up. I almost had myself believing it, until I reached the truck. There was a note on the dash."

The last words are choked out. "You don't have to tell me," I murmur into the darkness. He tightens his arms around me almost painfully.

"I want to. I want you to know all of me, Kens. This is a huge part of who I am. Why I always believed what I did. There was a note on the dash addressed to the police. It was written to the effect for them to call me when they found the truck and to tell me and my mom that he would always love us. He jumped." I can hear the pain in his voice.

"Oh, Max, I'm so sorry," I say the words even though I know they won't help. Nothing can help. I know from personal experience. I've had so many people say the exact same thing to me and it never helps. Never.

"He loved her. She was his world and I never understood. I couldn't begin to understand why he would put up with it all." He's quiet for several minutes. "I see it now. I see how you can care so much for one person that nothing in your world matters without them in it."

Max pulls me onto his chest, holding my face in the palm of his hands. "I can see it because of you. I'm falling... so hard. I'm falling and

183

you are quickly becoming all that matters." His lips caress mine.

I mold my lips to his, hoping he can tell I feel the same way. I want to tell him, but I... can't. It's too soon. My heart feels it. With every touch, every look, every word we share, I feel it deep inside me. I'm just not brave enough to tell him. It's a big step for me and I just... can't.

Instead, I deepen our kiss, putting my feelings into actions. Placing my hands on his waist, I slowly glide them over his muscled back. It's only been a few hours, but I want him again. It's usually once for me and then not again for months. I'm taking full advantage of having Max and his body at my disposal. Wrapping my legs around his waist, I pull him into me. I can feel him at my entrance, I squeeze my legs tighter, but he fights it, holding himself back.

"Kens, we don't have to. I just want you here," he kisses my nose, "in my bed. I didn't ask you to stay for this," he tells me.

"I know that. That makes me want to even more. I can't seem to get enough of you." My voice is soft at my admission.

"Kensi—" I place my index finger over his lips.

"Kiss me."

Max does as he's told, and as he deepens the kiss, I tug him with my legs while lifting my hips. He slides into me. Finally.

"You feel so fucking good," he rasps. He begins to thrust slowly at first, but with each push into me, he picks up rhythm. "You okay?" he pants.

Is he serious right now? Am I okay? "Harder." I bury my nails into his back and hold on tight.

44

Maxton

AT HER REQUEST, I don't hold back. I get lost in her. All too soon, I've worked myself to barely hanging on. "Kensi, sweetheart, are you with me?" I pant.

God, I hope she's close. Talk about embarrassing, our second time together and I blow without her. I feel her tighten around me and cry out my name. I follow right behind her. Slumping against her, I try to get my breathing under control. After several minutes, I move behind her and wrap my arms around her. I bury my face in her neck and simply breathe her in.

It still amazes me how every moment with her is different. She makes me want to be better. She makes me better. I'm man enough to admit that. This, what I have with her, was not what I ever would have signed up for willingly. However, Kensington, she got to me and now she has me. Every fractured piece of my heart, my soul, she owns. Someday I'll get the nerve to tell her. Not yet, I don't want this to end.

"I could get used to this."

"What?" She tilts her head up to look at me.

I squeeze her tight. "This, you in my bed. I like it way more than I ever thought I would."

"You act like there's never been a girl in your bed before." She laughs.

I let her finish her laughing spell. Partly because I need to make sure I have her attention and partly because I love the sight and sound of seeing her happy. Finally I say, "Never, I don't bring women here. It's always their place. Sometimes my truck or... the bar," I finally admit.

Rolling over, she blinks a few times before a slow beautiful smile spreads across her face. "You trying to tell me you like me, Cooper?" she teases.

Like her? If she only knew the thoughts and feelings that are swirling inside me when it comes to her. "I more than like you, sweetheart. You're different. Please don't ever forget that. You're special to me, Kensi."

"Ditto," the soft reply leaves her lips as she buries her face into my chest. I hold her tight and kiss the top of her head and drift off into what turns out to be one of the best nights of sleep I have ever had.

Feeling the bed move, my eyes pop open. Kensington is trying to remove my hand from around her waist. I pull her back against me. "Don't go."

Her low chuckle gives me hope she wasn't trying to sneak away. "Max, I have to pee," she informs me.

"Promise you'll come right back?" I want her in my bed as long as possible. I don't think this is a one-time thing, not the way things between us have been going, but regardless, I want to capture every minute of it.

She sighs. "I'm not going anywhere, Maxton." Something about the way she says it has by heart leaping in my chest. I kiss her shoulder and reluctantly release her. I force my eyes open again to watch her walk across my room. I like her here, in my space. I like waking up with her just as much as I liked seeing her in my bed for the first time.

I watch the bathroom door, waiting for her to come back out. When she finally emerges, I can tell she's brushed her hair. She walks back to bed in all of her naked glory. She's perfect, scar and all. I want to ask her about it, again. Now that we are... what we are, I'm not exactly sure how to define it. I want to know all of her. Someone hurt her and I want to know who, how, and why. I want to make sure that she knows I will never let anyone hurt her again. She climbs back into bed and burrows into my side, just where I want her.

"What are we doing today?" she asks.

We. "Anything you want. I have to order supplies for the bar, but I do that online and will take about thirty minutes tops. I'm yours the rest of the day." I'm yours for as long as you'll have me. Forever. I can't ever see myself getting over her, over this feeling of being with her.

"Anything I can do to help?"

No whining about me having to work, just acceptance and support. I hit the fucking jackpot with this girl. Never do I ever remember my mother asking that of my father, her husband.

"No, but thank you for offering. That means a lot to me. She would never have asked that, my mother. She was always whining and bitching at Dad for working, yet she had no problem blowing through the money he brought in."

She's quiet for a few minutes before she asks, "What's the weather supposed to be today?"

Thankful for the change in subject, we had enough heavy yesterday, I reach for my phone on the nightstand. Swiping the screen, I see that I missed a text from my buddy JT. Making a mental note to read it later, I pull up the weather. "Rain all day."

"Hmmm..." She's quiet for a few minutes before she says, "Maybe Bright and Nic want to go bowling?"

"I haven't bowled in years."

"Me either. Me and my... parents used to go a lot when I was younger, before Mom..." she trails off and I can hear the pain in her words.

"Sounds like a plan; let's see what they say." I hit Bright's number on my phone and she chuckles. I don't miss the way she swipes her thumb across the bottom of her eye, catching the moisture. I wish I could take the pain away from her. I wish I knew what hurt her, who hurt her.

"Maxton?" I hear the question in his voice when he answers.

"Hey, man, Kens and I thought it would be fun to go bowling today. Are you guys in?" I make it sound like both of our ideas, hoping her thoughts will stay with me, and not the pain I saw just moments ago in her eyes. I hate seeing it.

"Did you guys go back to Kensi's place last night," Bright asks.

"No."

"Then why in the hell are you calling me when we are in the same damn house?" he asks.

I laugh. "Well, I am currently in my nice warm bed with my girl lying on my chest. I would much rather call you than leave this bed at the moment. I assumed you were in a similar situation," I explain.

"Good point, hold on." I hear him talking to Nicole, asking her if she wants to go. He comes back on the line. "We're in, what time?"

"Babe, when did you want to go?" I ask Kens.

"Well, you need to work, so let's get that done first, showers, food... let's just say one. Gives more time for this," she says as she snuggles into my chest.

My heart swells. "Later, man, around one sound good?"

"Perfect." Bright hangs up, or at least I hope he did because I hit the end button, tossed my phone on the nightstand, and put my arms back around my girl. More time for this is exactly what I need.

45

Kensington

THE LAST FEW months have flown by and it's hard to believe it's Thanksgiving. Apparently, Max and Bright always do a big dinner and it's just the two of them, so this year, it's going to be the four of us, plus one, my dad. Max doesn't speak to his mother, and his grandparents and dad are gone. I don't know the details of Bright's family, just that he has nothing to do with them and he too is an only child. Nicole's parents are on a cruise. She, being an only child as well, assured them she would be fine for the holiday without them.

That leaves my dad. I'm nervous as hell for him to meet Max. I've talked to him several times, but I tried to downplay what he means to me. "He's just a friend, Dad." "He's fun to hang out with." "He and Nic's boyfriend, Bright, are trustworthy." All lines I've used. Never, "He makes my heart beat again." "He makes me feel like nothing in the world matters but me." "He looks at me like I'm a rare gift." "I love him so deeply that my heart beats for him." Nope, didn't say any of that and now I kind of wish I would have.

Just like he said he would be, Max was there through the 'Could we be pregnant?' scare. Turned out all is well and I'm now on daily birth

189

control. There was no need to even take a test as Mother Nature answered our silent plea. We were both relieved, and yet, I was also a little disappointed. Did I tell him that? No, but the sound of being a mom, giving to my kid what my mother gave to me, it's not a scary thing for me. I had accepted the fact that I was pregnant. Think the worst and hope for the best. Somewhere along the line, the idea settled inside of me. I wouldn't be crushed if it happened. Hopefully, in a few years, but I wouldn't consider it a hindrance no matter if or when it happens.

Max refused to let us help with dinner. He and Bright both are really good cooks, so I'm not worried. Dad didn't seem to be either. He accepted the invitation without hesitation and here we are, two weeks later, getting ready to have Thanksgiving dinner at his house. Nicole is already there; she spent the night last night. We both did actually. I drove home to meet Dad at the apartment. Not that he would care, but it's my dad and, well, you know.

I tried waiting on the couch, but my damn leg kept bouncing up and down, so now I'm pacing the living room. Dad is always punctual, so he'll be here any minute. The knock on the door stops me in my tracks. Taking in a deep calming breath, I open for him. My dad immediately engulfs me in a hug, squeezing tight. "I missed you, Kensi," he says.

"Can't breathe," I gasp.

Dad laughs and releases me. "It's been too long," he scolds me.

"I know; things have been busy. I'm glad you're here. Let me grab my keys and we can go."

"I can drive us." He raises his hand and dangles his keys in the air.

Nodding in agreement, I grab my phone and wristlet and lock the door.

On the way there, Dad doesn't drill me with questions about Max. We talk about school, and I find myself telling him about some of our adventures. Riding four-wheelers and, just last week, Nic and I let Max and Bright talk us into playing paintball. A guy they know owns the park, so he turned the pressure on the guns down for us. We had the entire place to ourselves for two hours. "Shockingly, it was a really good time," I tell him.

"Wow, you have been busy," he replies with a smile.

"Make a left up here," I tell him as we turn on Max's road. "Second house on the left." I wipe my sweaty palms on my jeans.

Dad parks the car and rests his hand over top of mine. "Kensington, you like this guy?" He waits for an answer, so I nod yes. "Is he good to you, treats you like you are the moon and the stars?"

"Better," I confess.

"Good, that's all I care about. Let's go see if this Max of yours can cook a bird." He climbs out of the car and I do the same. We meet in front of his car, and he throws his arm around my shoulders and we walk to the door.

I don't bother knocking. I just walk on in. I spend more time here than our apartment, so does Nicole.

I lead Dad to the kitchen. Max, who is carving the turkey, looks up and his face lights up. "Hey, beautiful," he greets me. He moves his gaze to my father. "Mr. James, welcome." He holds up the knife. "I hope you're hungry." He grins and it's infectious.

"Smells delicious," Dad replies.

"Well, Dad, this is Maxton, and, Max, this is my dad, Tom."

"Pleasure, sir. Kensi, there are drinks in the fridge, help yourselves and go relax; it will be ready in ten," he says.

"Can I—" he cuts me off.

"Nope, you just enjoy today. Nicole is already in the living room, doing just that on Bright's orders." He winks at me.

Bright comes in carrying a bag of ice. "The ice maker decided to quit on us this morning," he says in greeting.

"Bright, this is my dad, Tom. Dad, this is Bright, Nicole's boyfriend and Max's best friend and roommate," I introduce them.

Bright reaches out and shakes Dad's hand. "Happy Thanksgiving. Make yourself at home."

"Well, what would you like to drink?" I name off everything in the fridge without looking. We all went to the store together. Dad either doesn't notice, or doesn't let me know that he does. "Water is fine," he says.

I walk around the island and grab two bottles of water from the fridge. As I shut the door, Max says, "Kensi." I turn to look at him and he motions me over with his head. Stepping next to him, he leans over and kisses my temple. "Missed you," he says softly. I feel my cheeks warm at his obvious display of affection in front of my father. My eyes find Dad and he's smiling. It's then I realize that he heard him. He nods in approval and I release the breath I didn't even realize I was holding.

Dinner is amazing; the food is delicious and my dad seems to get along well with both Bright and Max. They are currently in the living room watching football. Nic and I insisted on cleaning up since the guys would not let us help cook. They both fought us until my dad finally said, "Boys, let the ladies help. We can watch some football." Reluctantly, they agreed and retreated to the living room, where they are hooting and hollering at the television.

"They seem to hit it off well," Nicole comments.

"Yeah, I'm glad. I was nervous about it," I confess.

"Kens, your dad is amazing; he wants to see you happy. It's obvious Max does that for you. That alone is enough to win him over. Not to mention how he treats you and let's not forget this kick-ass meal our guys just whipped up." She grabs a piece of turkey from the platter and shoves it in her mouth. "I'm stuffed, but I can't resist," she says, grinning.

We find the guys in the living room on the edge of their sets. Bright is in the chair; Nicole plops herself right on his lap. Dad and Max are sitting on the couch. All three of them are caught up in the game, that is, until he sees me. His eyes lock with mine and I can't help but notice how his sparkle. As I reach them, he holds his hand out for me. I place mine in his and he guides me to sit next to him. If Dad were not here, he would have had me on his lap. I'm actually surprised he didn't anyway. He hasn't held back even though my father is here.

I sit next to him and his arm comes around me, pulling me closer to him. I don't fight it; I can't. Even if my body would resist him, I wouldn't want to. We spend the next two hours like this. Me in his arms, Nic on Bright's lap, and the three of them yelling and cheering at the television.

When the game's over, Dad stands and stretches. He looks down at us and I blush. "Give your old man a hug; it's time for my nap." He chuckles.

I feel Max kiss the top of my head before he removes his arm from around my shoulders. I chance a glimpse at my dad and his face is all smiles.

Standing up, I walk into his outstretched arms. "You need a ride home?" he asks me.

Pulling back from the hug, I glance over my shoulder at Max. "No, Max will make sure I get home safe."

"I have no doubt that he will." He looks over my head at Max. "You take care of my little girl," he says, his voice more stern.

"With my life," Maxton says as he stands. He walks to us and stands behind me. His hands go to my hips and I lean my back against his chest. I can't fight it no matter who's in the room with us.

"All right, kids, Max, Bright, thank you both for having me. Girls, you don't wait so long before calling an old man." He taps a finger to my nose and turns for the door. Max laces his fingers through mine and pulls me to follow my dad. We walk him to the door. Releasing Max, I give him one more hug and a kiss on the cheek. We stand on the front porch, Max cradling me in his arms, and watch him pull away.

"He's a great guy."

"Yes, he is. I seem to be surrounded by those lately."

"It's you, sweets. You make us better," he says, placing his hand on the small of my back and leading me back into the house. "You make me better, Kens," he says, once inside.

I turn to see him watching me. This man has slid into my world and is now the most important part of it. I have no words for the fact that he thinks I make him better, when inside, I know he's the one who healed me.

"Thank you for today, for inviting him. He likes you."

"It was nice to have it be more than just me and Bright. I like your dad. He reminds me a lot of mine."

"It was nice to have a group together. I've missed it." I slide my arms around his waist and look up at him. "Thank you."

Leaning down, he softly touches his lips with mine. "Anything for you, Kensi. Anything for you."

46

Maxton

BRIGHT AND NICOLE are still curled up on the chair when we get back in the house. I take my place on the couch and pull Kens down on my lap. It's what I wanted to do earlier, but I decided to tone it down a little with her dad sitting right beside us. A little was all I could do and that was a struggle.

"So what are we—" My phone rings in my pocket. Pulling it out, I look at the display. "Shit," I say.

"What?" all three of them ask in unison.

"It's JT. He's texted me a few times and I read them with the intentions of reply and keep forgetting." I swipe my thumb across the screen and place the phone to my ear. "Hey, man," I greet

"He's alive," JT retorts. "Finally decide to stop dodging me?" he asks.

"Not dodging. Just been busy," I say as I drop a kiss on Kensington's temple.

"All right, I hear ya." He laughs. "Listen, the reason I've been trying to get ahold of you is next weekend we are getting a group together out at the farm. I haven't been there in years and it's been forever since I've seen you. I have Mark and his girl Tabby, Rick and his girl, I don't know her name, it's a new one each week, and me and this girl Angie I've been seeing. You and Bright should come," he says.

Kensi settles against my chest. I run my fingers though her hair. "Yeah, man, let me check with Bright and our girls and see what they say."

"Girls? You've both been caught?" he asks, shocked.

"More than caught, but yes, we both have girlfriends. Besides, you're one to talk. It's been what, high school since you've had a serious relationship?" I ask him. JT was dating a girl he seemed to really like, but then his brother got into some shit and went to jail. JT was never quite the same after that. I never knew the specifics and figured it was none of my business unless he wanted it to be.

"Yeah, well, when shit went down with Joe, it was a while before I was willing to dive into anything more than casual. Angie's a great girl."

"You deserve to be happy, man. Listen, the girls are here, so let me talk to them and I'll send you a text tonight and let you know if we're in or not. Sound good?"

"Sounds like a plan. Hope you all can make it. It's been forever since we've gotten together and I want to meet this girl."

I laugh. "Sounds good, happy Thanksgiving, man." He says goodbye and I end the call.

"JT?" Bright asks.

"Yeah, he said a group is getting together out at his parents' farm; he invited us up." Kens sits up to look at me. "JT is a friend from way back. Our parents were friends back in the day and we would vacation together when I was younger. It stopped once I got into high school. By then, Mom was already cheating on Dad and the vacations stopped. She said he worked too much and there still wasn't enough money. In reality, she would take weekend girls' trips and meet with her lover." It's not until the words are out that I realize that Nicole just heard the story. Bright knows and Kens knows a little, and, well, now Nic knows. It's not like it's some big secret. I just hate thinking or talking about it. However, that's really the exact opposite when Kens is around. Words fall out of my mouth and I feel lighter, better. Just like I told her, she makes me better.

"His parents own a farm about two hours away. It's about a hundred acres or so. No one lives there, but they keep the place because JT and his brother loved it. We go there and spend the weekend, take the quads. It's a good time." I turn to Bright. "He said Mark and Rick are going. All three of them are bringing dates."

"What do you think, Nic? You up for a weekend trip?" Bright asks. I don't hear her reply because all my focus is on Kens.

She's snuggled back into my chest, her head resting on my shoulder. My fingers find their way through her silky soft hair. "You up for a trip, baby girl?" I ask her.

Without missing a beat, she replies, "If you're there, that's where I want to be."

It's on the tip of my fucking tongue. I love you. I want to tell her. I want to shout it from the fucking rooftops. Every damn day this girl burrows her way further inside my heart. I don't want it to be a blurted confession. I want it to be something she will always remember. She deserves nothing but the best.

"We're in if you are." Bright's booming voice catches my attention.

"Kensi, babe, are you sure?"

She raises her head and smiles. "A weekend away with my three favorite people? Count me in. Besides, I can sleep anywhere in your arms."

She does too. Every damn night I make sure we are in the same bed. I don't care who's but she needs to be beside me. It's been that way since the beginning. I want it that way forever.

"We're in," I tell him.

"I have class Friday until one," Nicole groans.

"Why don't you guys leave Friday morning and Nic and I will come Friday afternoon. It'll give you time to catch up before we get there," Kens suggests.

"No, we can wait," I tell her.

"Dude, it's not a bad idea. It will still be daylight when they get there, so they won't be traveling at night," Bright chimes in.

"Really, it's a two hour drive, that's what you said. We'll be there by five for sure," Kens says.

"All right," I sigh. Kens wraps her arms around my neck and hugs me. I hold her tight against my chest. "Babe, you better not change your mind. I can't sleep without you," I whisper in her ear. "If you decide you don't want to go, call me and I'll come to you. You're what matters, Kensington," I tell her.

I don't know why, but I just feel like I need for her to ride with me. Irrational I know, but it's just a feeling I have. Like I need to stay close to her.

"I won't back out on you. I don't sleep without you wrapped around me, Cooper." She winks at me. It does little to alleviate my concern. I can't shake this feeling.

"It's settled. I'm excited for a weekend away. Then a week to study for finals and we're out of classes until January," Nicole says. I feel Kens slightly stiffen in my arms at Nicole's words. I chalk it up to me being panicked for some unknown reason. I need to relax.

Needing a distraction, I tickle her ribs. She squeals with laughter and all is right in the world. She wiggles around and ends up straddling my hips. Her hands are clasped behind my neck and my arms are around her waist, holding her against me. "You want to go take a nap?" I ask, low enough for her only to hear. She rests her forehead against mine.

"Yes."

I stand with her still in my lap. She immediately wraps her legs around my waist. Her hands cup my cheeks and she presses her lips to mine. Never breaking the kiss, I carry her to my room. Luckily, neither one of us are injured in the process.

Being in a serious relationship is the shit. So is birth control. I slowly undress her and make sweet love to my girl. Bare, nothing between us. Making love is something that we both enjoy, that's obvious. Loving her, being in love with her that's all me. I have to tell her soon. If I don't, I'm going to end up blurting it out. I drift off to sleep thinking about how Dad was right. I wish he were here to meet her.

47

Kensington

"MAX, GO. IT'S fine. Nicole's class lets out at one and we're leaving right after." I've told him this at least ten times since last night.

"Okay. Promise you will text me as soon as you leave. I can't shake this feeling, Kens," he tells me.

I take his face into the palms of my hands. "Maxton Cooper, I'm fine; look at me. I'm okay. Nicole is fine. If something does happen, you can be back in two hours tops. Go, catch up with your friends and we will see you this afternoon," I try to reassure him.

He pulls me into his chest and holds me. "I hate this feeling. I can't explain it; all I know is that nothing can happen to you. I need you in my life, Kens," he says. His voice is sincere and I can tell how serious he is.

"Hey, it's me and you, right? I agreed to be yours a long time ago, Maxton."

"It's not that; I know we're solid. I just can't shake this feeling that I need to stay with you. Please be alert and lock your doors, fill up the tank before you leave, and make sure you take your car charger for your cell. You are taking your car, right? I looked it over, changed the oil, and checked the tires earlier this week," he says.

I smile at his worry over me. "Yes, we are taking my car. I already have my bags packed. I cleaned out the fridge at the apartment and I'm going to do that here at your place once you leave to drop Nic off at school. Then I'm going to pick her up and drive straight to you."

"Maxton!" Nicole yells down the hall. "This train's leaving. My class starts in a half hour. Let's roll." I hear Bright laughing at her.

"I miss you already," he tells me.

"I'll see you by five o'clock. I have the directions you saved into the GPS in my phone. The charger is there. My bags are packed, so are Nic's. Go, be safe, have fun. I l... I'll see you soon."

Shit! I just about told him I loved him. He studies me then leans in and kisses me slow and sweet. All the while, Bright and Nic are yelling that they will meet him in the car. "I'll see you soon, beautiful." He kisses my forehead, letting his lips linger. "Be safe, Kensi." One more chaste kiss on the lips and he turns and walks away.

I take my time cleaning out the fridge. We're only going to be gone two days, but coming back to spoiled milk is not something I enjoy. I spend just as much time here, more actually, than I do my apartment. I throw in a load of Max's laundry and run the sweeper. By the time it's done, folded, and put away, it's time to pick up Nicole.

I turn off all the lights and lock the door. As soon as I get in the car, my phone chimes.

Maxton: Babe, be safe. I'll see you soon.

Me: Always. I miss you, Max.

Maxton: You have no idea. I can't wait to show you how much.

Me: Promise

Maxton: With everything that I am

Me: <3 See you soon

I wait to see if he's going to reply before placing my phone in the cup holder and starting out on my journey.

Nicole is in the parking lot talking to a group of people. I recognize a few of them. She spots me, waves to the group, and heads my way. "Hey! Are we ready for a weekend of fun?" she asks.

I laugh at her. "Yes, and, hopefully, when we get there, Max will chill. He's been telling me all week that he has this feeling that he needs to stay with me today. I had to keep reassuring him that I'm fine," I tell her.

"Bright mentioned something about that. He thought maybe Max was just being over protective. He wanted to make sure I knew that he didn't love me any less than Maxton does you because he wasn't making a big deal about it." She shrugs. "He said we are grown women and driving two hours in broad daylight. He didn't think we weren't safe," she rambles on.

There was so much information in that rambled cluster that I don't know where to start. I decide I would start with what stands out first. "What makes him think Max loves me? And since when are the two of you telling each other 'I love you'." I end up rambling just like she did.

"Well, for your information, he told me on Thanksgiving. I haven't really seen you much this week. Max has kept you occupied. As for Max being in love with you, anyone can see it. Anyone who sees how he looks at you, or watches how he touches you, just how he acts around you in general. You love him too, have you not told him?"

"I… no, I haven't told him. We haven't said anything like that. He tells me how important I am and how much he needs me in his life, but love… not yet."

"Why not? I know you love him. What are you afraid of?"

I let her words sink in and think about that question. What are you afraid of? "Honestly, in the beginning, I was afraid to trust him. To trust that he wasn't out to ultimately hurt me."

"Kens, I know as well as anyone that you have trust issues. I don't know the details, but as your best friend, I have lived your pain with you. You can tell me, you know?" she says.

She's right. I can tell her and I need to. "Soon. I promise. Let's get through this weekend. I don't want to spoil the fun. I don't want to think about it," I tell her.

"It's coming up," she says, her voice low.

Yes, it is. The anniversary of my mother's death is fast approaching. One week from today to be exact. Two weeks before Christmas. "Yeah. I want to tell you. It's not that I don't trust you, Nic. I do. It's just hard to talk about it, to think about it. It's easier to bury it and lock it away."

"I understand that, but at the same time, me knowing and Max knowing, we can help shoulder that pain, Kens. We love you and we want to help you. It would be easier for us if we knew the details. Does Max even know that next week..." Her voice trails off. She knows it's the anniversary of my mother's death but not my involvement.

"When we get back, I promise you and I are having a girls' night with lots of alcohol and I will tell you the entire story. Bring tissues," I say as a side note.

Nicole reaches over and places her hand over mine. "You got this, Kens. The four of us are our own little family. We will always be there for you," she tells me.

I don't know why, but I start talking. "My high school boyfriend, Justin," I swallow hard, "it was his brother. His brother killed my mother. He was coming for me. He was a gang member. Justin was, apparently, trying to join as well. The letter he wrote me said he always looked up to his older brother and wanted to be just like him. Anyway, Justin wanted to be a part of the gang. His initiation was to seduce a girl who was chosen for him. He was supposed to..." I swallow again, fighting back the emotion. "He was supposed to rape me and film it. He had to provide proof that he did it. They gave him six months to finish the job. Our six-month anniversary, he was supposed to pick me up from work. I worked at a local pizza joint. He called right before my shift ended to tell me something came up and he wouldn't be there. He sounded nervous. I asked if he was okay, and he said he just wasn't feeling well and didn't want to risk me getting sick. I didn't think too much of it, told him I hoped he felt better and ended the call. A co-worker drove me home. The house was dark when I got home. Dad was working late again, and Mom I assumed was at the grocery store. She said Friday nights were never busy and the best time to go."

I take a break to take the tissue that she hands me from the glove box and wipe my tears. "Kens, you don't have to," she says, her voice worried.

"No, this is good. I can't run away and I don't have to look at you. Better chance of getting through it," I admit.

"Just as I'm putting my key in the door, I hear a deep voice say hello. Startled, I spin around and see Justin's brother standing there. I always felt uncomfortable around him, the way he was always staring at me. I immediately am on alert, telling him that Justin wasn't feeling well and stayed home. He moved in closer and I started to freak out. He slapped me and told me to… to shut the fuck up. He was calling me names. Said I brainwashed his brother, turned him against him and I had to pay. I tried to fight him, but he was so much b-bigger than me." I pause to collect myself. The tears are flowing so hard I have to pull over on the side of the road.

As soon as the car is in park, Nicole flings off her seatbelt and hugs me tight. "I'm so sorry, Kens," she says. I let her hold me, soaking up the comfort that she's offering. Leaning on her like I always have these past four years. "I tried to scream and he smacked me so hard I blacked out for a minute. When I came to, we were in the foyer of my house. He had a knife, cutting off my clothes. I fought him and the knife ran deep into my chest. I have a scar on my breast," I tell her. "Maxton he says I'm beautiful, scar and all."

"He loves you, Kensington. You have to know that."

I ignore her statement and keep going. "The pain caused me to stop fighting back. The next thing I know, I hear my mom's voice. She's screaming at him, telling him she called the police. I don't remember what happened exactly. I woke up in the hospital; Dad was sitting vigil by my bed. Mom jumped on his back, Nic. He was holding a knife and she jumped on his back trying to save me. He knocked her off and stabbed her. Over and over again, he stabbed her. She died in the ambulance on the way to the hospital.

"I was released after two days and we had her funeral. Dad and I stayed in a hotel; we never went back to that house. We had a moving company pack our things and we moved here away from it all." I blow my nose and take a deep breath before it's all out. "Two weeks after my mother's funeral, I received a letter from Justin. He told me about his brother being in a gang and how his brother wanted him to be a part of it. About the initiation and how I was the one chosen for him. He went on to tell me that the more time he spent with me, the more he liked me and grew to love me. That when it came time to do the deed and tape it, he backed out. His brother was pissed and beat the shit out of him. That's why he couldn't see me. I would have asked questions. His brother decided to do it himself. He came after me and killed my mother," I say.

"Kensington, I am sorry for your loss. I can't imagine going through that. You know that it wasn't your fault, right? There was nothing you could have done to prevent any of that from happening. He was a bad guy. Bad things happen to good people. You are not to blame," she tells me.

My phone beeps. Picking it up, I swipe the screen.

Maxton: One more hour. Miss you, be safe.

Shit! My confession is going to set us back a good twenty minutes. Wiping my eyes, I quickly text him back.

Me: Slight delay, girl talk. See you in an hour and twenty

Maxton: Are you good, babe?

Me: Yes, we are on the road and I'm on my way to you.

Maxton: Drive safe.

"We better get back on the road and put him out of his misery," Nicole jokes.

I laugh with her at his unnecessary worry and pull back onto the road. I feel a little lighter telling Nicole the entire story. Now Maxton. Someday soon, I tell myself. Soon.

48

Maxton

"MAX, MAN, CHILL. I just talked to Nic and they're almost here," Bright chides me. I can't seem to relax. It's irrational, but something feels… off. Bright and I got here, unloaded the quads, and hung out with the guys for a few hours. They all took their girls into town for dinner. They're bringing back a pizza for the four of us.

Just when I think I can't take it anymore, my phone chimes.

Kensington: Just pulled in

I don't bother to reply. I slide my phone in my pocket and head out to the front door. Bright is hot on my heels. He said I was crazy, but even he was a little worried at their late arrival. I jog down the steps and reach her door as she climbs out. I lift her up and she wraps legs around my waist, holding on. I kiss her, slowly molding my lips with hers. "I missed you, Kens."

"I missed you too, Maxton Cooper."

"I love you." There is no way I could hold it in a minute longer. I hope she forgives me for blurting it out.

"Maxton." Tears fill her already red eyes; she looks tired. "I love you so much," she sobs, burying her face in my neck. Her legs are locked tight around my waist, and I hold her against me. I carry her to the porch and sit down with her in my lap.

"Why the tears?" I ask her.

"It's just been a long day. I told Nicole about my mom on the way here. We had to pull over because I was a blubbering mess." She sniffs.

"You told Nicole?" I ask, surprised.

"Yes, and I promise I'll tell you too as soon as we get home. I don't want secrets between us. If you still feel the same about me after you know, then I'm yours for as long as you want me," she says.

"Kensington, there is nothing you could tell me that would ever make me not love you. Not want to fall asleep with you in my arms and wake up with you in the same spot. Nothing, do you hear me? Nothing will change how I feel about you."

"When we get home," she says. "I just want this weekend with you, and then I will tell you everything."

"Whenever you're ready, Kensi. I'm not going anywhere, babe."

She sits back on my lap, her tired eyes boring into mine. "I love you."

My fucking chest is tight from those three little words. "I love you." I kiss her again, and if it were not for the car I just heard pull up, I would still be kissing her. Instead, I release her lips and help her stand. It's time to introduce the love of my life to some lifelong friends. "There are some people I want you to meet." She nods and releases her legs from around my waist and slides to the ground. Part of me wanted to just introduce her clinging to me like a monkey. She fucking loves me. Best feeling I've ever felt in my entire life. Instead, I pull her close and wrap my arm around her.

She turns to the group that just walked up to us and I start at the left. "Kens, this is Mark and his girl Tabby. This is Rick and his girl Sara, and this is—"

"Justin," she croaks out. I feel her immediately stiffen in my arms.

"Kensington," Justin breathes her name like he can't believe she's here. He fucking knows who she is?

My mind is racing. How do the two of them know each other? I focus on her. "Kens, baby, what's wrong?" I whisper the words close to her ear. She shakes her head no. Her eyes are wide and full of pain and fear? "Kens, you're scaring me. Please tell me what's wrong?" I watch as huge tears fall over her cheeks and my heart aches for the pain she's in. Not getting answers from her, I turn to JT. "How the fuck do you know her?" I yell at him. The scar on her chest runs through my mind. She's been hurt and she's afraid of someone; she's afraid now.

"What the fuck did you do to her?" I take two steps and I'm up in his face. I grab him by the collar and slam him against the side of the house. "You better start fucking talking, JT." That's when it hits me; Justin her ex. "You, you were her ex from high school." I try to remember all I know of what he told me about what happened back then, but rage blinds me. I can see nothing but the huge tears rolling over her cheeks and the pain and fear in her eyes. I slam him against the house and get in his face. "Tell me what you did to her!"

"Maxton!" I hear Bright yelling for me. He probably thinks I'm off my rocker jealous. I'm that too, but right now, I'm fucking livid. I ignore him as I stare JT in the eyes; my fist clenching his shirt is making it hard for him to breathe.

"Maxton!" This time I feel his hand land on my shoulder and he tugs. "Maxton, Kensington. You need to let him go." He's frantic. I release my grip when I hear her name. I look over my shoulder and Bright's face is pained. "She left, Max. She took off running for her car. I didn't get out here in time to stop her." I turn back to JT and throw a right hook into his nose. I release him and he slides to the ground, using the house as his crutch.

I turn back to Bright. "Which way did she go?" I ask.

It's Mark who answers. "She hopped in her car and tore out of the driveway; she headed toward town."

I hear Bright murmur and see he's trying to console Nicole. I walk to her and pull her from him and into my arms. "Nic, I need you to tell me what you know." My voice is pleading.

"Oh, Maxton, she just told me. Today on the way here, she told me. Justin, he's her ex. Oh, God, she was so upset; we have to find her," she cries.

I realize I'm not going to get anything out of her. She's too upset and we don't have time. I need to get on the road. "Come on, man." Bright holds the keys to the truck in the air. I nod and take off in a dead run to the truck. Bright and Nicole are right behind me. We are loaded up and peel out within seconds. Bright heads toward the way Mark said she went while I call her cell repeatedly. She's not picking up.

"She's not fucking answering." I throw my phone on the floorboard and run my fingers through my hair. God, what if she was in an accident. Please keep her safe, watch over her, I silently plea over and over.

"Maxton! Snap out of it," Brighton yells. "Nicole has her on the phone. She's safe, man. She's safe."

I feel hot tears prick the back of my eyes. She's safe. I turn to face Nicole who is in the back seat crying, just listening to the other end of the line. I want to rip the phone from her hands and demand Kensington tell me where she is, but she wouldn't answer for me. So I sit and wait.

"Kens, tell me where you are?" Nicole asks gently. "Are you all right, are you safe?" she asks her. I give her a thumbs up for asking. I'm sure the question was to keep me sane.

"Okay, stay there. I'm on my way." She ends the call and closes her eyes.

"Nicole," I grit out.

"She's safe. She pulled over at the hotel in town. She's got a room and is spending the night before driving back home tomorrow. She's too upset to drive tonight. She's smart, Max," she tells me. "I told her I was on my way. You have to let me talk to her first, and then I'll get her to talk to you. You have to be patient with this; it runs deep," she warns.

"You think I don't know that? That fucking girl is everything. Everything that I am is her; she makes me better. She said she fucking loved me." My voice cracks.

"Maxton," Nicole places her hand on my shoulder, "she loves you. I know she does. You have to let her work through this. I wish I could tell you, I do, but it's not my story to tell."

I clench my jaw and bite my lip. "I just need to be with her. I need her in my arms so I can let her know I'm there. No matter what it is, what his connection is to her, it doesn't fucking matter to me. I just want her."

Bright pulls into a hotel lot and I reach for the handle. "Wait!" Nicole scolds me. "Max, you have to let me talk to her first. Please. I promise I'll convince her to talk to you, but she needs me," she says gently.

"Well, I fucking need her. I can't breathe without her." I rub my chest at the ache that's been there since I saw the pain in her eyes less than an hour ago. "Please, tell her I love her." I lay my head back against the seat and close my eyes.

Bright and I sit in silence. What is there to say? A guy I've known practically my entire life hurt the person who means the world to me. She is my world, and right now, I don't know if she knows that. I don't know if she understands how much I love her, how much I need and want her to be a part of my life. I can't imagine going back to how things were before Kensington.

Brighton's phone finally rings. My eyes pop open and I watch as he answers. "Okay, love you, Nic," he says before hanging up. "She's agreed to see you, but she wants me there as well," Bright says cautiously.

I jump out of the truck and head inside. Bright catches up to me and hits the elevator button. The ride is quiet and fast. Kensi is on the third floor. The doors open and Bright leads the way to her room. We reach the door and he knocks softly. Nicole opens for us and steps back, allowing us to walk in. Kensington is standing by the window looking out. I cover the distance between us in a few longs strides. The emotion that I have been fighting claws its way to the surface as I stand beside her. "Kensington." My voices cracks and a tear falls just from saying her name.

Turning to face me, her hand goes to my cheek and brushes away the tear. I place my hand over hears and lean into her. "Baby, can I hold you?" I'm pleading and desperate and I don't give a fuck.

"Max, I don't—"

I cut her off. "Can I at least hug you? I just need to have you in my arms for a minute. Please, I just, God, Kens, I was so scared," I admit to her.

A barely noticeable nod of her head is what I get and it's enough. I wrap my arms around her and bury my face in her neck. I take a deep breath for the first time since she left. I pull her as close to me as I can get her, and she wraps her arms around my waist. That's when the dam breaks. I lose my shit. I'm crying like a bitch and I don't care who sees it. The tears are a mix of relief, fright, and love all rolled into one huge emotional clusterfuck.

All too soon, she's pulling away from me. "Max, I have things I need to say. I need to tell you everything, and I can't do that with you touching me. It's hard enough telling it. I can't…" She steps away from me and it feels like I'm losing her. "Please, just sit." Her tired eyes plead with me, and I would do anything for her, so I nod and take a seat at the small table opposite of Bright.

Nicole is sitting on the edge of the bed. My girl sits beside her and reaches for her hand. I want to be the one offering that support, but I understand she needs this, so I sit as still as I can and wait for her to tell me whatever it is that made her run from me today.

"Next Friday will be four years." She gets choked up on the words. I start to stand and Nicole glares at me. Bright leans over and places his hand on my shoulder, telling me silently to sit my ass down. Kens is looking at her lap. "My mom was murdered," she finally says. "Justin's brother, Joe, he attacked me and my mom walked in during his attempt. He had a knife; he killed her." She sobs into her hands. Nicole gives me a look, warning me to sit still as she puts her arms around Kensington's shoulders and hugs her.

Kens gets herself under control and starts from the beginning of the story. I sit and listen to her soft voice, laced with anger and pain, and I want to kill JT and Joe. I know that won't bring her mom back, but, fuck,

LEVITATE

I hate to see her hurt. Her eyes are tired and she's pale. I hate what seeing him is doing to her. I hate seeing her like this.

49

Kensington

I MAKE IT through the entire story for the second time today. I'm exhausted emotionally, mentally, and physically. I'm afraid to look at Max, afraid of what he'll say. His lifelong friend's brother killed my mother. I dated a good friend of his.

"Kensi." His voice is thick and I can hear the pain and emotion threatening to break free. "Baby, can you look at me?" he asks.

I suck in a deep breath and lift my head. He's watching me, his eyes glassy with tears. "You with me, babe?" he questions. I nod letting him know that I am indeed with him.

"You're right here." He holds his hand over his heart. "I love you with everything that I am. I'm sorry for what you went through. I'm sorry you've lived with this all these years. Sorry you've been dealing with it on your own. Your story changes nothing for me. I choose you, Kens. Baby, I will always choose you. Every time, no hesitation, no doubts. It's me and you."

Tears, which I don't bother to stop, fall from my eyes. "Kensi," he whispers my name and I need his arms around me. For just a little while, I want to pretend Justin is not a close friend of his, that I didn't just release all the hurt and pain I've been holding in for far too long. I stand from my position on the bed, not able to stay away from him any longer. He mirrors my actions and it's as if our bodies levitate toward each other. *"I want to make you levitate."* His words the first time we made love come back to me and I realize that no matter what the situation is, those words will hold true.

He's now standing in front of me. I reach for his hand and he laces his fingers through mine. "Let me be your rock, Kens."

I lose the fight with his words and lean into him. He doesn't hesitate to pull me tight against him. He murmurs his love for me and holds on tight. I hear him ask Bright and Nicole to give us a few minutes. A few seconds later, the room is quiet. "Kens, you're exhausted; let's lie down." He leads us to the bed. Keeping a hold on me, he pulls back the covers and I slide in. He pulls off my shoes then kicks off his own. He climbs in beside me and engulfs me in his arms. He holds me while I cry and my heart breaks for what we could have had. I will always love him, but how can we go on when he is so close with Justin. I don't think I would ever be okay with that. I know he would choose me, but I can't ask him to do that. I push the thought out of my mind and go back to pretending that none of today's events happened. I just want to feel his love a little longer.

"I got you." His voice penetrates the quiet room. "There is nowhere I want to be more than I want to be right here with you. No matter what the situation may be, that will never change." I feel him kiss the top of my head. "I love you, Kensington James."

I squeeze my eyes closed and fight back yet another round of tears. I don't know how I am going to move on from him. All I know is that I will cherish every moment I've spent with him and pray that it will get me through.

We lay tightly embraced for hours. I'm exhausted but sleep evades me. I know I'm not staying and the ache in my chest from that alone is keeping me awake. Maxton fought it as well. He held me and administered sweet kisses anywhere his lips could reach. I kept my body turned away from his. Getting lost in him is not a risk I can take at this point. I've already tried to talk myself out of leaving a million times. I finally hear his breathing even out and I know he has finally drifted off to sleep. He still has a tight grip on me, so I wait. Wait for him to fall into a deep sleep so I can slip out undetected and sever the connection we share. I just can't be with him, not with Justin in the picture and not with them being friends. I just… can't.

His hold on me loosens just enough that I think I can slip away. I swallow hard to fight off the tears. I need to leave quickly and quietly. As slowly as I can, I lift his arm and slide out from under him. He grumbles and rolls over. I sit still on the edge of the bed, waiting to see if he's going to wake up. He doesn't. Standing quietly, I grab the hotel pad of paper that is sitting on the table and the complimentary pen and write him a note. I don't want him to worry, but he also needs to realize it's over. My stomach twists painfully at the thought. Pushing through the pain and the heartache, I write to him.

Maxton-

You came into my life without warning and changed everything for me.

I never thought I could let myself fall in love with anyone, until you.

I'm sorry I slipped out while you were sleeping, but I couldn't handle the pain in your eyes when you found out I was leaving. When I told you I loved you, I meant it.

You will always be the other half of me. I can't ask you to choose a lifelong friend over me and I can't stay and be involved in any part of his life. I need for you to understand that this is what needs to happen. Please let me go. I need you to know that I will cherish every moment, every touch, every kiss, every single memory from our time spent together. Please take care of you.

Love You, Forever and Always,
Kensington

My eyes are blurry from tears and I'm not even sure what I wrote, but regardless, he will get the point. I left and what we had has to end. Grabbing my keys and phone, I stop by his side of the bed and take in the sight of him sleeping. This is the last time I will ever see him this way. The pain is real, the tightness in my chest, the lead weight in the pit of my stomach, it's real. I'm about to walk away from the best thing that ever happened to me. I place my hand over my mouth to prevent a sob from breaking free. I swallow hard a few times before I'm able to whisper the words, "I love you, always, Maxton Cooper." Then turn and slip quietly out the door.

Keeping my head down, I'm able to make it to the car without anyone asking if I'm all right. I can only imagine how I look with the events of tonight wearing on me. Then again, it is the middle of the night. I'm sure the night staff couldn't care less about my broken heart; they are just here to get paid.

The drive home is long. I drive straight through, just wanting my bed. I pull into the apartment at seven; the sun is just starting to rise. I have to muster up the energy to even get out of the car. I'm emotionally drained; my body is weak and I'm exhausted. I just want to sleep and try to block it all out. Knowing I have my bed waiting for me motivates me to exit the car. I stop in the lobby and get the mail, which will save me a trip down later. I'm expecting paperwork from school regarding my externship. Shit! I forgot all about the extern. I make a mental note to talk to my professor on Monday and start looking for a new site.

Once I'm in the apartment, I toss my keys and my phone on the table and sift through the mail. A letter catches my eye. I take a closer look and see that it's from our attorney. The one Dad hired to prosecute for Mom's murder. My hands start to shake and my palms are sweaty. My heart feels like it's about to beat through my chest. As I attempt to open the envelope, I struggle to pull air into my lungs. I fight through the fear and manage to remove the letter. Sucking in slow deep breaths, I unfold the paper and skim the contents. No, Joe, he wants to talk to me. As if this day hasn't been bad enough. A sob escapes me and I wish more than anything Maxton were here.

I can't breathe. What could he possibly want to talk to me about? My heart is racing. I reach for the back of the couch to steady myself on wobbly legs, and before I know what happens, my world turns black.

50

Maxton

Rolling over, I reach out for Kens and the bed's cold. My eyes immediately pop open and stare at the empty space in the bed where she should be.

She's gone.

I can feel it.

She left me.

Throwing the covers back, I jump out of bed and grab my phone. Swiping the screen, I see it's five thirty in the morning. No messages and no missed calls. I pull up Bright's name and hit send. Grabbing my shoes, I sit at the table. Holding the phone to my ear with my shoulder, I work on putting on my shoes. It's the middle of the damn night and she's alone, upset and not fucking here where she should be. Bright's phone goes straight to voicemail. Of course, he's sleeping snuggled up with his girl, where I wish I were in this exact moment. I slam my fist down on the table and it lands on a pen. Looking down, I see a pad of hotel paper with her handwriting. I read her words and a mixture of emotions swamp me.

I'm worried about her driving at night two hours home by herself. I'm hurt that she left me. I'm pissed off that she's not fighting for what we have. That she's letting them win. I tear the letter from the pad of paper and hastily fold it and slip it into my wallet. I try Bright again and this time he answers.

"Maxton—" I cut him off.

"She's gone, Bright. She fucking left while I was sleeping. She was in my arms, where she belongs. I fell asleep and I just woke up and she's gone. She left a fucking goodbye letter, man. She says it's over. I have to find her; we have to go." I ramble on. I know I'm probably not making any sense and I don't give a fuck. He needs to either get moving or I'm leaving their asses here. I'm going to find her.

"We'll meet you in the lobby in five," he says.

"Make it three. I have no idea what time she left, man. I have to find her." My voice is pleading. That same damn feeling from earlier is back. The same feeling that something isn't right. It hits me that my feeling of needing to stay with her was because of JT. I'm following my gut this time and going to her. I can only assume that she went home. If she's not there when I get there, I'm calling her dad. No holds barred. I need to know she's okay.

"Maxton, you have to calm down. We'll find her," Bright tries to reason with me.

"Calm down. I cannot fucking calm down. She left me. She FUCKING LEFT ME!" I roar into the phone.

"She's upset. I was there, man. I heard her story; I heard about what she went through. I heard her tell us what Joe did to her mother, the letter from JT. She's been holding that shit in for over three years. She needs to process. She'll come around; you just need to be patient."

I hear what he's saying. I felt her pain. Every damn word was like a knife to my heart. Sitting in that chair and not being able to go to her was hell for me. I wanted to hold her, reassure her that no matter what, it's us. I choose her, choose us. I want to prove to her that the trust she has put into me is worth it, that what we have is worth it.

"We're getting dressed. We'll meet you in the lobby."

I end the call without another word. I pull up her name and hit send.

I know she's not going to answer, but I need to call her anyway. The call goes straight to voicemail. "Kensi, it's me. Wherever you are, please be safe. I'm coming home. I need to see you. Fuck, Kensington. I woke up and you were gone, just gone, and I need you here with me. I need to..." I swallow back the tears. "I need you to know that I love you. You hear me, Kens? I love you so fucking much that I don't know who I am without you. Please, baby, just send me a message or Bright or Nic. Just let me know that you're okay. I'm scared as hell. I have this feeling... same as yesterday and... please, just let me know you're safe." Her voicemail cuts me off.

Sliding my phone back in my pocket, I head toward the lobby. Bright and Nicole are there waiting on me and I'm grateful. "I tried to call her; got her voicemail," Nicole says once we are in the truck.

I nod. "Yeah, same here. I'm going to the apartment. If she's not there, I'm going to call her dad."

"Max, she just needs—" Nicole tries to speak, but I interrupt her.

"To be okay. Yesterday I was worried. I couldn't shake this feeling that something was going to happen. I was right. JT..." I clear my throat. "JT is a part of why the girl that owns me is torn apart inside. I could feel something was going to happen, I just didn't know. If I knew, I would have never..."

"We know that," Nicole says gently. "You love her, anyone can see that."

"I have that same feeling now. Only this time it's... stronger. I won't push her to see me or talk to me, yet. I just need to know she's okay."

The rest of the drive is silent. Nicole tries to call Kensington over and over again from all three of our cells and she never picks up. Always straight to voicemail, her inbox is now full.

I make good time. We pull into the apartment a little after seven in the morning. I broke a few traffic laws to make it happen, but finally, I'm here and so is she. I park beside her car and exhale. Once I see her with my own eyes and know she's really safe, I'll leave. A knot forms in the pit of my stomach at the thought, but I won't push her, not yet. I'll give her time to process this, and then I'm fighting for her. She is what I want.

The three of us climb out of the truck and Nicole leads the way up to their apartment. Placing her key in the door, she turns the lock and turns the knob. "Kensington!" she cries and I push through them.

My girl is lying on the floor, out cold. "Call 911!" I scream. I drop to my knees beside her, careful not to move her until I know if and where she is hurt. I gently run my hands over her body, checking for injuries. I don't see anything. She looks like she fell. With blurry eyes, I scan around her to see if I notice anything that might have made her fall.

"Don't move her they said," Bright relays. "They're on the way."

I don't see anything but papers, mail thrown around. I focus my attention back on her. I gently move the hair from her eyes. The only reassuring fact of the entire situation is that her chest rises and falls with each breath she takes. She's breathing; I send up a silent prayer that she's going to be okay. I hold her hand and stroke her hair, just waiting. Taking her in, she's pale; she has dark circles around her eyes. I hate what this has done to her. The tears that I've kept at bay unleash and I let them. My heart is lying on the ground, out cold. I'm wrecked over this girl. Please, God, let her be okay. I repeat this over and over.

I feel a strong hand on my shoulder. "Max, let them take care of her." I jerk my head around to see Bright and Nicole with a swarm of EMT's behind them.

Reluctantly, I stand and step away from her. I don't take my eyes off her. I watch as they check her for injuries and rule out any type of attack. They take her vitals. Her blood pressure is low, but not dangerously so. Nicole asked them. I need to remember to thank her. Words are not something I can form at the moment. I watch as they handle her with care and place her on the gurney. They push her out the door and I'm hot on their heels. "I'm going with her," I tell them as we reach the life squad.

"Sir, are you family?" they ask me.

"Yes, I'm her fiancé." The words roll off my tongue.

"Sir, we—"

"That girl is my entire world. I don't want her to wake up alone and scared. I'm coming with you. I'll keep my mouth shut; I won't interfere." I let them know that this issue is not up for debate.

"Climb in," the female driver says. I don't hesitate. It was going to take an army to keep me from it. I'm glad they are seeing things my way.

I zone out on the ride to the hospital. I think back to all the time I've spent with her. The thought of my life without her in it is unbearable. I continue my silent prayers to please let her be okay. I promise God and anyone else who is listening—my dad, her mom maybe—that I will love her for the rest of my life. I promise to take care of her, to see her through all of this. I just need her to be okay. Her letter said she didn't want me to choose between her and JT. What she doesn't realize is that there was never a choice to be made. She comes first, always. JT and I were friends as kids, our families were friends, but Kensington, she's my entire world.

We arrive at the emergency room and they whisk her away from me. I try to follow them back to a room, but they won't let me. I try for the fiancé bit again, and this time it's not enough. "Sir, you must be family or listed as next of kin. We have a Nicole—"

"That's me," Nicole says behind me. "I called her dad and he's on the way." She steps beside me and lays her hand on my arm. "I give permission for Maxton to be with her," she says with authority. I make a mental note to get her a really good gift for Christmas.

"Ma'am, unfortunately, no one is allowed back until we assess her injuries. Please take a seat and we'll let you know something as soon as we can." The nurse turns on her heel and scurries down the hallway.

"Come on, man. Let's take a seat and let them see what's wrong with her. Her dad will be here soon and we can fill him in," Bright says.

Defeated, I follow him to the waiting room. Its only occupant a guy with a busted lip and what appears to be his girlfriend. Bright and Nicole take a seat on the opposite side of the room. Taking a seat next to Bright, he hands me a piece of paper. "We found that on the floor," Nicole says, leaning around him.

"I'm sure after everything that happened, seeing Justin again, it was a shock to her. I'm guessing it freaked her out and she had a panic attack. Our freshman year, it happened a couple of times. Never out longer than a few seconds. This time… she was out for a while," she says. I watch the tears race down her cheeks before giving the letter in my hands my attention.

Joe, Justin's brother, both were a part of my childhood, Justin more so than Joe. He's the one who killed her mom. The one who attacked her with intentions to hurt her. Joe wants to talk to her. *Not. Going. To. Happen.* I will not let him anywhere near her. I don't care if it's a fucking letter he wants to send her; it's not happening. He's caused her enough pain.

I toss the letter back to Bright and walk to the window. I rest my head against the cold pane. Closing my eyes, I whisper, "Dad, if you can hear me, please save her. I get it now. I never thought I would, but I do. I can't explain to you what she means to me, but I know I don't have to. You already know. Please, if you have any pull whatsoever, bring my girl back to me. We're just getting started. It hasn't even been twenty-four hours since I told her I love her, and I do, Dad. My heart is bursting with love for her. I wish you were here to meet her. She's amazing and smart. She's so breathtakingly beautiful that sometimes when I look at her, I have to remind myself to breathe. I want to build a life with her, give her our last name, and make you a grandpa. I want it all with her, so I need you to help me. Please, bring her back to me."

A strong hand grips my shoulder. "Son," a deep gravelly voice has me opening my eyes. Kensington's dad is standing beside me, his eyes glassy with tears.

"Mr. James." I hold my hand out to him. He shakes his head and pulls me into a hug. I'm reminded that she is all he has.

Stepping back, he says, "I heard you. Just now talking to your dad. I'm so glad she found you, Max. My little girl has been broken for so long. Since she met you, she smiles more; she's actually living again. I cannot thank you enough," he tells me.

"Don't thank me, sir. Loving Kensington is as easy as breathing. I meant every word," I tell him, referring to my one-sided conversation with my father. "Loving her is an honor and a privilege that I would love to have for the rest of my life." I lay it out there for him. He might as well know my intentions.

"That's a long time, son," he replies.

"Yes, and it still won't be long enough. I love her, sir. I want to ask her to marry me, give her my last name, babies, a house, a dog. Anything and everything she wants, I want to be the one to give it to her."

"Are you asking my permission?"

"No, sir. Don't get me wrong, I would be honored for you to give it to me, but I don't need it to love her."

He smiles. "You're a good man, Maxton. I have no doubt you will take care of her. I would be thrilled to have you as a part of our family."

"The family of Kensington James," a nurse calls, walking in to the room. The four of us walk toward her. "This way please." She leads us into a private room just like the one we were just in, only smaller. "The doctor will be right with you." She turns and walks away.

The four of us stand and stare at the door, waiting for the doctor to give us even a tiny shred of information.

"Mr. James?" a tall slender guy says, walking into the room. "I'm Dr. Knolls. I've been treating your daughter. Is it all right to speak freely or would you prefer we step out?" he asks.

I grit my teeth. "No, these three are just as much her family as I am. What's wrong with my daughter? Is she awake?" he asks.

"Yes, she's awake and doing well. It seems she passed out. From the information we got from her, it was a panic attack. Not to mention she was dehydrated and hadn't eaten since yesterday morning. She was able to give me her history. I want to admit her for observation and some IV fluids. She should be able to go home tomorrow. They're getting her set up in a room, and then you will be able to see her.

"Thank you." Her dad reaches out to shake the doctor's hand. I do the same.

I try to relax. The doctor said she's going to be okay. Leaning my head back against the wall, I close my eyes and silently thank my dad and her mom for keeping her safe. Now I just need to see her. To see with my own eyes she's awake and then maybe this tightness in my chest will ease up. I won't be able to breathe with ease until she's back in my arms where she belongs.

51

Kensington

I'VE ONLY BEEN in my own room for five minutes when there is a knock on the door. I expect to see Maxton, but it's the doctor.

"Kensington, we got some of your test results back. I wanted to rule out a few things even though, from the history you gave me, I feel confident what you experienced was a severe panic attack. I did find something in the results," he says, flipping through my chart. "Your blood test came back positive for pregnancy. Congratulations. I'll have the obstetrician who is on call today stop in to make sure everything is okay with the baby from the fall. Where you aware that you were expecting?"

Pregnant. How? "I'm on birth control."

"Are you using any other form of protection? Birth control is not one-hundred percent effective. Changes in things such as medications, antibiotics for example, can alter its ability to prevent pregnancy. And, at times, with no other protection being used there is still that chance."

"No… no other protection, no medications." I'm stunned speechless. Pregnant. Oh, God, Maxton, how are we going to raise a baby together and not be together? How am I going to be a part of his everyday life and not be his, him not be mine?

"Congratulations, Kensington. The obstetrician should be in to check on you and the baby within the hour. There are several people in the waiting room very anxious to see you. Shall I send them in?" he asks me.

"Nicole?" I croak out.

"There is a girl, two guys, and your father. I'll send in Nicole," he says when I don't answer.

Pregnant. My hands cover my stomach. My mother would have been thrilled with this news. Yes, it's earlier than I would have liked, but a baby. Even though I can't have him, I will always have a piece of Maxton. The realization both breaks my heart and makes it soar at the same time. I will have to learn to be around him, or maybe I won't tell him. I've already made my break. I can raise the baby on my own.

"Hey, how you feeling?" Nicole steps into my room.

I don't know if it's her question or just the situation in general, but my eyes well up with tears. She notices and is at my bedside in an instant. "Kens, we saw the letter. Honey, you don't have to talk to him, ever." She leans down and hugs me.

"It was just all too much, you know? I was already a wreck from seeing Justin and learning that he and Maxton are friends, then leaving Max." A sob escapes me.

"Yeah, not a cool move by the way. We were worried sick. Max had another one of those feelings and he broke a few laws getting us back to the apartment. Why did you slip out in the middle of the night?"

"I just... I couldn't stay and see his face when I told him we could no longer be together. I don't want to make him choose, and I can't deal with Justin being in my life," I explain through my tears.

"I get that, Kens. I do, but did you ever stop and think that it's not a choice for him? Maxton loves you. He was a wreck all the way here. There wouldn't be a choice to be made; it's you."

"No. They've been friends for years. He's known me less than one," I justify my reasoning.

She sits on the edge of my bed. "You're pushing him away. You're his world, Kensington. You can trust that he loves you. This is not a game to him, and he would cut off his own arm before he did something to hurt you. I just spent the drive home with him, watching him battle the fear that something was wrong, along with the pain of you leaving. It's tearing him up inside. Just like it is you. Don't fight it. Let yourself be happy; let him love you the way you deserve to be loved."

The room grows silent and I have a million thoughts running through my head. Will he feel the same way when he finds out about the baby? We had a scare after the first time, and he said no matter what happened he would be there, but did he mean it? "I'm pregnant." I whisper the words.

"Did you just...?"

I nod. "The doctor just stopped in to tell me right before you came in. I had no idea."

"Kens, you're gonna be a mommy." She smiles as her eyes well up with tears. "Are you going to tell him?"

She knows me so well it's scary. "I don't know," I tell her honestly.

"Kensington, he deserves to know. You can't keep something like this from him," she scolds me.

"I just need some time to process it all. I just found out," I reply defensively.

"He deserves to know. He's sitting out there waiting to see you. Kens, you should have seen his face when you asked for me and not him. It crushed him."

There's a knock on the door. In walks a woman in a white coat pushing a machine. "Kensington, I'm Dr. Smith." She glances at Nicole. "Is it all right to speak freely?" she questions. I nod in agreement. "Great. I'm here to take a look at your baby. I understand you were unaware that you're expecting and you took a fall earlier."

"Yes."

She continues to explain the process of a vaginal ultrasound since my blood work numbers show that I'm early in pregnancy. She makes sure it's okay that Nicole stays in the room with me and I insist on it. I don't want to do this alone. A pang of guilt hits me because I know he's out there. Max is in the waiting room and he should be here to see our baby for the first time.

The doctor sets up the machine and positions me on the table. The overall process is not as much uncomfortable as it is awkward. I'm staring at the screen even though I have no idea what I'm looking for.

"There," she points at the screen, her fingers lands on a small black circle, "that right there is your baby."

"Baby?" Maxton's deep voice rumbles from the door. It only takes him a few strides with his long legs to get to me. He stalks to the side of my bed. Nicole steps back, allowing him to get close to me. He drops to his knees and grabs my hands. He brings them to his lips. His eyes lock on the screen. My eyes are locked on him. He swallows hard. "We made a baby?" he says.

The doctor clears her throat, causing me to tear my eyes away from Max. I can see the question in her eyes; I nod, letting her know it's okay to speak in front of him. The cat is already out of the bag. "As I was saying, this," she points at the screen, "is your baby. You're very early in your pregnancy; from the measurements, you are four weeks along. Everything looks as it should. I'll prescribe you prenatal vitamins that you will need to take daily. You should schedule an appointment with an obstetrician in the next four to six weeks." She removes the wand, again awkward, gathers her machine and leaves.

"I'm just going to give you two a minute," Nicole says.

Maxton, still holding onto my hands, rests his forehead against my belly. Never able to resist touching him, I run my fingers through his hair. We're silent for a long time, neither one of us saying anything. When he finally looks at me, his cheeks are wet with moisture, eyes wet and red from his tears. "I love you so fucking much, Kensington James." Taking one hand away from mine, he cups my face. "You scared the hell out of me, beautiful. When I saw you lying on the floor," he swallows hard, "I thought I lost you, Kensi." He leans forward and kisses my forehead.

I start to talk, but he places his index finger over my lips. "I got your letter," he says solemnly. "There is no choice, Kensington. You are a part of my soul. You don't walk away from your soul. I need for you to understand what you mean to me." The hand that is now resting on my stomach, rubs gently. "What this baby means to me." He moves to sit on the edge of the bed, his eyes boring into mine. "I don't know if I have the words to explain it to you. You are always in my thoughts. There is not one moment of any day that you are not there. You light up my world. I thought I never wanted this, someone to call mine. Never thought I wanted to be that guy who shouts from the rooftops that he's going to be a dad." He smiles at me and places his hand back on my belly. "You make me that guy. Your love makes me a better man. I don't want to go through life without you by my side. I need you there, Kensi. I need to know, that above all else, I will always have you. You are what I want. You own me heart and soul. I want to wake up with you every fucking day in my arms. I want to fall asleep the same way. I want to raise this baby with you, show him or her what it means to love and be loved. I want you to have my last name. I want every moment of every day filled with us."

Hot tears are racing down my cheeks. How did I ever think I could walk away from him? Mom must have sent him to me. I know she would have loved him. I smile at the thought.

"There's my beautiful girl," he says, tenderly tucking a loose strand of hair behind my ear.

"Maxton..." His lips softly touch mine. My resolve is broken. His words crumbled the last bit of resistance I was hanging onto.

Breaking away from the kiss, his lips trail down my neck and up to my ear. "We made a baby, Kens. A part of me is growing inside of you." He pulls away so he can see my face. "I can't explain how that feels." His hand is back on my belly yet again. His palm is lying flat, his fingers splayed. "I can't wait to take this journey with you."

"I love you," I say through my tears. "I'm sorry I left; I didn't want to come between you. I didn't want you to resent me."

"Never." His words hold conviction. "We're a family, you, me and this little peanut." He holds up the ultrasound picture. "I've never wanted anything in my life as much as I want this with you."

"Knock, knock," my dad says from the doorway. I quickly wipe my eyes. Maxton, however, does not. His cheeks are still wet from the tracks of his tears.

"Hey, Grandpa," Maxton says happily.

My dad stops in his tracks, processing his words. I can tell once it really hits him because his face lights up. It's the same smile he used to give my mother. He's truly happy again in the moment. My baby did that.

"Grandpa, huh?" he asks, walking to the opposite side of the bed from Max.

Maxton hands him the ultrasound picture as confirmation. "That talk we had, it's going to happen. I hope you're with me," Max says to my dad. I have no idea what they're talking about, but Dad seems to understand. He nods and his smile grows even bigger, if that's possible.

"Congratulations." He kisses me on the cheek. "I think I prefer Papaw though, don't you?"

Max and I both laugh at his request. There is another knock on the door and in walks Bright and Nicole. "What did we miss?" Bright asks when he sees the three of us smiling.

"This," Maxton says, handing him the ultrasound picture.

Brighton studies it and then looks up. "What am I looking at exactly?" he asks hesitantly.

"That, young man, is a picture of my first grandchild," my dad says proudly.

"Holy shit! Congratulations, guys." He holds his fist out to Max and they bump knuckles.

"How are you feeling?" Nicole asks and I can read between the lines. She wants to make sure I'm okay with Max and the baby.

I look up at Max, who is already looking at me. "Never better," I say, my eyes never leaving his. He leans down and kisses me on the lips.

"I love you," he says. His voice is firm and loud. He makes sure everyone in the room heard him, causing me to blush. "Don't leave me hanging, beautiful." He chuckles.

"I love you, too."

52

Maxton

THE DOCTOR COMES in and tells us that Kensi will be able to go home tomorrow. I insist that she stays with me. She argues that she's fine. I need for her to understand that I want to take care of them, her and the baby.

Baby.

I'm going to be a dad.

"I can take care of myself," she whines.

I cup her cheek in the palm of my hand. "I know you can take care of yourself. I also know I want you with me. I want to be the one you lean on. I want to take care of you." I place my other hand over her belly. "Both of you."

I watch as her eyes glass over with tears. This is hard for her. She, like me, never thought what we have was a possibility. She didn't see herself finding what we have. It's hard for her to accept that I'm in this.

Forever.

I can tell from the look in her eyes what she's thinking.

"I can do this—"

I place a finger over her mouth to halt her words. "Not going to happen. I know what you're thinking, and you're wrong. I told you I loved you before you... left. I meant it. Baby or no baby, I want you with me."

Her eyes bore into mine. She has trouble trusting and I know that. I'm okay with it. She will see that I'm not going anywhere. She's a part of me and we're having a baby. That's just about as good as it gets. I really wish Dad were here to see this. To meet her and see how amazing she is, to see me become a dad. I will make damn sure I give our baby the love and support he/she needs.

"Don't fight him, Kensi," her dad pipes up. "Let the man spoil you. You deserve nothing less," he tells her.

"See, let me spoil you. You have to listen to your father." I wink at her.

"Since when are you two so chummy?" she pouts.

Leaning down, I place a chaste kiss on her lips. "Since you are the most important person in our world. We both love you; that alone is enough to bring us together," I tell her.

"He reminds me of me at that age. I loved your mother and would stop at nothing to have her." Her dad gives her a sad smile.

"Live life, Kensi. Love hard and enjoy every second." His voice cracks.

"I love you, Dad." Her voice is thick with the tears she's fighting.

I sit on the edge of the bed and wrap my arms around her. She places her hand over mine. "Thank you," she concedes.

Finally! "Never thank me for loving you, for taking care of you. It's what I do." I wink at her, trying to change the mood and dry up her tears.

"Now I just need to convince you to never leave," I whisper in her ear. Her mouth drops open in surprise. I lift her chin to close it and kiss her softly on the lips. "We're a family now, Kensi. The three of us." I settle back against the bed and allow her to lean on me. This is where I'm supposed to be.

53

Kensington

I WAS RELEASED from the hospital and Max brought me straight to his place. I've been here ever since. Nicole had already packed a few of my things and dropped them off. She and Bright have been staying at the apartment. Maxton keeps dropping hints that it's the perfect switch. Not that I would tell him, but I agree. This time with him has been incredible. He's sweet Maxton tenfold.

Rolling over, I look at the alarm clock. It's one in the morning. Today is the anniversary of the day I lost my mother. I've been tossing and turning for hours, two, to be exact. I had to wait for Max to be in a deep sleep before I could wiggle out of his arms. He grumbled but released me. Afraid I'm going to wake him with my restlessness, I climb out of bed and head for the couch.

Curling up in the oversized chair with the throw he bought me, I let the tears fall. I tried to be strong, tried to hold it in. I'm glad he's sleeping, not watching me fall apart. He worries about me, about the baby. He's barely let me move a muscle this week. I'm fine; it was only a panic attack, but he doesn't seem to care. He still babies me.

"Kensi." His thick sleep-laced voice breaks through the sound of my tears. Striding toward me, he scoops me up in his arms and sits in the chair, holding me in his lap. Kissing my forehead, he says, "I got you, baby."

The dam breaks and I let go of the pain. Even though I didn't want him to see it, I'm where I need to be, in his arms. Maxton is able to soothe me with just a touch of his hand. He brings a peace over me that I've never felt. My heart breaks for the loss of my mother, but soars for the love of this man.

"His eyes are what I remember the most. They were dark, full of hatred and glaring at me. He kept telling me he was going to give me what I deserved. I can remember him yelling at me. He said I turned Justin against him. He said I had to pay the price." A sob breaks free and I bury my face in his chest. His arms hold me like a vise, never wavering, letting me know he's there. "He hit me across the face. I tried to fight him; I tried to break free, but the knife. He cut me." Sitting up, I reach over to the end table and grab a handful of tissues from the box. "I can remember all of that, but not her. I remember hearing her voice, her begging him to leave me alone, and then nothing. Fade to black. My next memory is waking up in my hospital bed with my father at my side. I knew it was bad from the look on his face."

Running his warm hands under my shirt, he gently strokes my back, trying to soothe me. "I just keep thinking if I would have fought harder, maybe I could have helped her. If I could have just stayed awake a little longer, I could have screamed for help, and she could still be alive." I barely get the last words out before another round of sobs wrack my body.

"No, baby. It's not your fault. You were trapped; you couldn't save her. Don't think like that," he says, tugging me closer to his chest. I let him hold me while the tears fall. Not saying a word, he lets me work through the pain.

"I just feel guilty. She died protecting me, Maxton."

"I know that," he says softly, "and I understand why she did it." He places his hand over my belly. "Peanut isn't even here yet and I can tell

237

you with everything in me that I would do the same thing for you and for our baby."

I take in his words. I love this baby, too. So much, and for the first time, I think I understand why she did it, how she could put her life in danger for me. I knew she loved me. I just wasn't able to understand a parent's love, a mother's love, until now.

"How do you think she would feel knowing you feel that way?" he questions. He studies me while I let his words bounce around and settle in. "Exactly," he says. My expression must say it all.

"I just miss her so much. I wish she could have met you. I wish she was here to calm my fears about motherhood. I just wish she was here."

"Kensi, baby, I know you miss her. I'm sorry she's not here, but I know what kind of woman she was."

I look up at him with a bewildered expression. "She raised you. You are a part of her, and she's a big part of who you are. You will love our baby just like she loved you. You'll start traditions; the same ones you shared with your mom. I'll do the same. Dad used to take me fishing; I loved it when I was a kid," he says wistfully.

Placing his hand over my heart, he says, "She's here. Every day she's here and we will make sure our baby knows both of them. Your dad is here; he's going to spoil this baby rotten." He smirks.

"Your mom?" I ask him.

He shrugs. "It's been years; I want nothing to do with her. I sure as hell don't want her anywhere near you or our baby. You're my family, Kensi."

"I love you, Maxton Cooper," I say before pressing my lips to his.

54

Maxton

IT'S BEEN FOUR weeks today. An entire month has passed since I found out we were having a baby. As each day passes, the more excited I become. It's amazing how something you thought you never wanted is the one thing that makes you feel complete.

Two weeks after she was released from the hospital, I asked her to marry me. She said yes and our lives have been a whirlwind of changes. Nicole and Bright decided that moving in together was the next step for them. With Kensington moving into the house, it was an easy trade. Bright and Nicole are going to live in their apartment. Kens and I are building our life here, in the place my father worked his ass off for, in the house my mother never took the effort to make into a home.

We started moving her in that very day. I was more than ready to start our life together. I love coming home to her, having every aspect of our lives intertwined. I've even promoted one of the guys at the bar to be a shift leader. I plan to be able to spend my days there and my nights here, with my family.

"Kens, we need to be going, babe!" I yell down the hall. Today is her first OB appointment, and I don't want to be late. She's eight weeks, and from what she's told me, we might be able to hear the heartbeat today. I'm still in awe of the fact that there is a part of me growing inside of her. We can't see the evidence of her pregnancy yet, and I cannot wait for the day we can.

"Hold your horses," she says, laughing as she grabs her coat from the closet. "We have forty minutes and it only takes fifteen to get there."

"Well, you never know what could happen and we are not missing this appointment." I grab her around the waist and pull her against me. I press my lips against hers, kissing her slowly. "We get to hear our peanut's heartbeat today. Get moving, woman!" I smack her ass and step back out of her reach.

She just shakes her head and laughs.

"Let's go, papa bear," she says, leading the way out to the car.

We arrive almost a half an hour early for the appointment. Yes, she was right, but damn it, I'm excited. The waiting room is filled with expectant mothers but no fathers, just me. I wonder what the hell those guys are thinking. I plan to be here every step of the way.

They call us back to a room much faster than I would have anticipated, and Kens is asked to change into a gown. I'm not thrilled with the fact her doctor is a male or that he'll be seeing her in places only I should be. However, I did my research on the guy and he's the best. I will swallow back the jealousy in me to ensure Kensi and our peanut receive the best care possible.

The first part of the appointment consists of the doctor asking all kinds of questions like breast tenderness, morning sickness, and a ton of other things. He reminds Kens to take her prenatal vitamins and to drink lots of water and try to steer away from large amounts of caffeine.

"Now the fun part," he says. He has Kens lie back on the table and pull up her gown. He brings out this contraption that has a speaker attached to it. He places some gel on her belly; I assume it's cold because she flinches at the contact. He places the other end of the contraption on the gel and swirls it around. At first, it just sounds like rushing water, but then I hear it loud and clear. The steady thump, thump, thump of our baby's heartbeat.

"There you go, folks, strong and steady," the doctor says.

I close my eyes and take in the sound. The emotions that are swarming inside me are intense. I'm so in love with this tiny person who I've never met.

"Maxton." Her voice has me opening my eyes and looking at her. Her eyes are filled with tears and she's wearing a blinding smile across her face.

I can't speak. There is a lump in my throat, and even if I could, I wouldn't have the words for this moment. So instead, I do what I do best and kiss her. I kiss her like my life depends on it. I kiss her with all the love in my heart and passion deep inside my soul. Pulling away, I hear the doctor's low chuckle. I speak the three little words that are not strong enough but all that I can think of at the moment. "I love you."

Truth.

55

Kensington

TODAY IS MY wedding day. It's bittersweet for me. My heart aches that my mother is not here, but it's also filled with so much love for the man who I will soon call my husband. I still think Mom somehow sent Max to me. She knew he was the kind of man I could trust and who would love me irrevocably. I know, in reality, it's not possible, but it's my fairy tale and I'm sticking to it.

We decided against a large wedding. I'm packing my last two semesters into one, which, thankfully, is not a huge load. I was ahead of schedule and only needed three classes to finish my degree. One of which involves my externship that allows me to spend time with my fiancé at his business, our business as he likes to remind me.

The wedding is actually being held at our home. I have school, and really, we just didn't want big. Just us, my dad, Bright, and Nicole and that's it. Short, sweet, and simple, exactly how we want it.

"You look beautiful, sweetheart." My dad's voice comes from behind me. I turn to him and smile.

"Thank you." I look down at my simple white silk gown, which is doing nothing to hide my barely there baby bump. I'm fourteen weeks and finally starting to show. Maxton cannot keep his hands off my belly. I would be irritated if it wasn't so sweet. "I wish she was here."

"Me too, Kensi. You look just like her, you know? She would have been so damn proud of the woman you have become." He chokes up on his words. "I'm proud of you too. You fought back against the pain; you allowed yourself to open up and love, to be loved. You couldn't have chosen a better man to spend your life with."

"I never allowed myself to want this." I lay my hands over my baby. "Never thought there would be a man who would take the time to get to know all of me and love me despite it. He does." I look up at him. "He loves me and the baby so much that my heart is bursting with it, Dad."

"I know that, baby girl. I know how he feels. It's the same exact way I feel with you and your mother. I will love her until the day I take my last breath."

I'm wiping away tears when Nicole walks into the room. "I knew it," she says, placing her hands on her hip. "I knew you would be in here messing up my handiwork. Off you go. I'll let you know when we're ready," she scolds my dad.

He chuckles at her, kisses my cheek then hers, and leaves the room. "Now. Let's get you fixed up. Max is liked a caged bear down there. He's going to wear a hole in the carpet if we don't get you beside him soon." She laughs.

When she has me presentable once again, she opens the door and yells for my dad. He appears and holds his arm out for me. We walk into the living room arm in arm. Maxton's eyes lock with mine as Dad leads me to him. As soon as I'm within reaching distance, he reaches out and places a hand on my hip, pulling me to him. My dad throws his head back and laughs a deep belly laugh. "No point in telling you to love her right or to remind you to take care of her, I see," he says.

"Nope, not necessary," Max says, kissing my temple.

We turn to face Brighton. He became ordained so he could marry us? Apparently, it was a long-running joke between him and Max that if the other fell in love and got married, that the other would be the one to marry them. Nicole thought it was hilarious. Little does she know that Bright is not the only one who became ordained. Maxton and Bright did it at the same time. Bright is planning on popping the question soon.

The ceremony, or lack thereof, is short and sweet, again just how we like it. It's more of a formality than anything. We've already pledged our lives to one another and to our baby. Maxton says the best part was finally kissing his wife. Sweet Maxton is here every day. He is the man I fell in love with and the man who just became my husband. Sometimes it feels like a dream, this happiness we have found. If it is, I don't ever want to wake up.

56

Maxton

IT'S A BOY. We found out yesterday that we're having a boy. I don't think I've stopped smiling since the doctor uttered the words. I would have been just as happy with a little girl who looks like her mama, my wife. I think a lot of the happiness comes from getting to see him. We had a three dimensional ultrasound and it was... life altering to be able to see him growing inside of her. Life is good.

Today is Friday and Kens and I are at the bar. We spend Fridays here together more often than not. She now knows the ins and outs of the business; we are partners in all aspects of our life and I would not want it any other way.

She's currently in the office entering invoices into the computer. "Hey, babe, you hungry? I thought I could run down the street and pick up some lunch."

"Yes." She rubs her belly. "Your son and I are starving."

My son.

"How about I go get it? There are a few invoices here that I'm not sure about. You can take a look at them while I'm gone."

"I can—" She holds up her hand, cutting me off.

"Maxton, I am pregnant not dying. The doctor said me and the baby are healthy and doing great. The short walk of what, fifty feet, will be good for me."

"Okay. I'm sorry; I just want to take care of you." I pull her against me and place my hand on her belly. Dropping to my knees, I talk to my boy. "Tell Mommy she needs to get used to me taking care of both of you." I kiss her bump and stand to my feet. I hand her my wallet. "Please take your phone with you." I worry. I will always worry about her.

"I'll be right back." She steps on her tiptoes and quickly presses her lips to mine.

I'm in the middle of taking a look at the invoices when Brian, one of my bartenders, knocks on the door. "Max, there's a guy here to see you," he says.

"Thanks, Brian." I stand to follow him out to the main bar area. When I reach the bar, I stop in my tracks. Standing at the opposite end is JT, Justin. I haven't heard from him since that day at the farm. I'm instantly on alert. Kensington will be back any minute and she doesn't need the stress; it's not good for her or the baby.

"What are you doing here?" I ask, my voice heated.

"I just wanted to explain to you what happened back then," he says.

"You don't need to explain anything to me. My wife filled me in," I retort.

"Wife? Wow, I, uh… I didn't know. Congratulations, man. She's amazing," he says.

My anger rises. "You have no right to talk about her, to think about her. You know nothing about her," I seethe.

"Maxton." Her voice comes from the door behind JT.

Shit! I hop over the bar, needing to be next to her. "Brian!" I yell, he comes over and I hand him the bag of food Kens just brought back." He takes it without a word and walks back to the bar. He stays close, his eyes on us.

I place one arm around her waist and the other rests on the side of her belly by her hip. Protecting them both from him. He will not get near her.

"Kensington." Justin says her name like he's pained to do so.

"Don't fucking—"

She places her hand on my chest to get my attention. "It's okay, Max. I'm good," she tells me. "Just don't let go."

Like I would do such a thing. I raise my eyebrows at her and she chuckles. It's a sound I didn't expect to hear considering the present company. Then my girl surprises me even more; she turns to JT. "Justin, what can we do for you?" she asks as if he is some stranger off the street, not the brother of the guy who murdered her mother.

"I came to explain to Max about then, about what happened."

"My husband is aware of my past and the events surrounding it," she replies.

JT runs his fingers through his hair. "I'm so fucking sorry about your mom, Kens. I was young and stupid and I looked up to Joe. At first, I just thought it was a dumb club. Just a group of guys who would do silly things for no other reason than to say they did. They started out telling me I had to make you fall for me and then break up with you. I wanted to be a part of his group, so I agreed. Then I talked to you that first day and I immediately began to question why the hell I would ever let someone as great as you slip away even to be in some group with my older brother."

He takes a deep breath. I'm barely holding onto my anger, but Kensi wraps her arms around my waist and rests her head against my chest. She's calm, which keeps me in check. "Joe, he was… intense, always was. He knew I was falling for you. I talked about you all the time and spent all the time I had to spare with you. It pissed him off. Then he changed the rules. He said he knew I wouldn't let you go, so the plans changed. I was to videotape the two of us together, having sex. I admitted to him that we hadn't gotten that far yet." I growl at the thought.

JT takes a few steps back. Smart man. "I couldn't do it. I couldn't hurt you like that. I told him so. I told him that I…" He pauses to look at me. Turning away, he focuses his attention on Kensi. "I told him that I loved you and refused. I told him he could take his club and shove it up his ass. The next night after school, he and his buddies jumped me. They were pissed I was backing out. They kicked the shit out of me. That's why I cancelled that night. I didn't want you to see me and ask what happened. I didn't want to lie to you, and I wasn't ready to tell you the truth. If I would have thought for a minute that he would come after you…" He swallows hard and I can see this is difficult for him.

I look down at my girl and her eyes are glassy but she's composed and calm. I hold her a little tighter, rubbing her belly. JT's eyes follow my hand and I can see from the look in his eyes that he is just now realizing we're pregnant. "I didn't know how far gone he was. He was heavy into drugs. I knew he had tried them, but I had no idea it ran as deep as it did. He hid it well from all of us. I swear to you, I didn't know he was coming after you. He beat the shit out of me and I took it. I thought he would leave you alone. I didn't even fight back. I thought he was pissed that I changed my mind." He rubs his hands over his face before he returns his gaze to my wife. "Kensington, I would never let him hurt you, if I knew. When I heard what he had done…" He swallows hard. "When I heard about your mom, I closed up. I wouldn't talk to anyone. I ignored my friends. Max, man, I did it to you," he says. "I wrote you that note, and I know you got it, your dad confirmed as much to Joe's attorney. I just wanted to tell you in person how sorry I am. I know it doesn't make it any better and it will never take away the pain or bring her back, but I am so fucking sorry," he says.

"Why?" she asks. Her voice is soft and calm. "After all these years, why now?" she asks.

"It's always been in the back of my mind. I told myself I needed to leave you alone and let you try and move past it. That you didn't need me tracking you down and bringing the pain to the surface. Then I saw you that day at the farm, and well, I just… I didn't know I would find you here today, that I would have the chance to tell you. I was going to explain it all to Max and tell him I was sorry. I didn't know about the wedding," he glances at our son, "or the baby. I hope you two have a long, happy life and I'm truly sorry for the pain my family has caused both of you." He drops his hands to his sides and walks toward the door.

I don't know what I expected to happen, but I never would have dreamed I would hear the words, "Justin, are you hungry? I bought a ton of Chinese. You're welcome to stay and eat," come out of her mouth.

"Kensi?" I question her.

Looking up at me, she says, "I'm good, Maxton. He didn't make him do it. He did the right thing and he's your friend. I don't think I'll be naming him godfather of this little guy anytime soon, but we can share a meal with an old friend. Besides, you're here, so I know I'm good. He can't break me; you won't let him."

Trust.

Words escape me at her strength, at the kind of person that she is. She's going to be an amazing mother. "I love you hard, Kensington Cooper."

She giggles. "Right back at ya, Maxton Cooper."

57

Kensington

I DECIDED AGAINST walking for graduation. My feet are swollen and, honestly, I just want that piece of paper. Maxton and I talked and I'm not going to work right away. He makes more than enough to support us, and I'm grateful we're able to be provided for so I can stay home with our little man for a while. A professor at the college is looking for a teaching assistant, but the job doesn't start until September when classes start up. She offered me the position and I immediately accepted. It's close to home and decent hours. Max and I will be able to work our schedules with him owning the bar so we will be able to watch the baby with no need for childcare.

Flipping through the mail, I see a package from the college. Ripping it open, I find it's my degree. The piece of paper that says I made it through four years of higher education. Smiling, I set it to the side, making a mental note to pick up a frame. A letter from our attorney catches my eye. After Justin showed up at the bar, I contacted him to let him know I had no desire to speak to Joe. I don't care what he has to say; I will never forgive him regardless of the drugs he was taking. He made the choice to take drugs. There is no forgiveness in me for him. Justin did stay and eat lunch with us; it was awkward, but didn't feel wrong like I originally thought. He did the right thing; he didn't make his brother do what he did. It took me a while to realize that. Do I think he and Max are going to have the same friendship as before? No, I don't. I feel bad about it, but Max assures me that what we have is worth it.

"Hey there, sexy mama", Maxton says as he comes into the kitchen. He steps beside me and kisses my temple. His hands land on my belly as always. "How's my two favorite people?" he asks.

"Good, my back's hurting a little, but I think it's from washing and folding all of those clothes." Nicole threw me a shower last weekend and I spent all day yesterday washing them and organizing the nursery. We are all ready for our little man to arrive.

"Kens, you need to stay off your feet. Come on." He takes my hand and leads me to the living room. He helps me down on the couch and places a pillow behind my back. He places another on the table and props my feet up on it. "You need to relax and stay off your feet," he scolds me.

"She's nesting," Nicole says from behind us. Bright follows behind her. "We brought dinner," she says, pointing to Bright who is holding up two pizza boxes.

"How you feeling, mama?" Nicole asks, leaning over the back of the couch to rub my belly.

"Like I'm as big as this damn couch," I groan.

"You, my darling wife, are beautiful. That's my son that's cooking in there, so watch what you say. You might hurt his feelings," he says, winking at me.

I laugh at his antics. I read somewhere that the baby will recognize our voices when he's born and made the mistake of telling Maxton. He now talks to my belly more than he does me. It's sweet and makes me fall even more in love with him every day.

"So does my nephew have a name yet?" Bright asks. He sets the pizza boxes on the table. Nicole places a bag with paper plates and napkins beside it.

"I'll go grab some drinks. Don't spill the deets without me." She skips off to the kitchen.

"I think so," I tell Bright, "but we're waiting until he's born. Maxton seems to think we need to see him, hold him, before we make our final decision." I roll my eyes playfully. I happen to think it's adorable how involved he's been and how serious he's taking this issue. I can still hear his words the first night we talked about names.

"Babe, this is serious stuff. Our kid is going to be called this the rest of his life; it's got to be good. We don't want him to be made fun of." The look on his face when he said it was priceless!

"So, really, how have you been feeling?" Nicole asks, handing each of us a bottle of water.

"Good. My back has been hurting today, but I think it's because I over-did it yesterday. I got all the clothes washed and the nursery organized. We are ready for this little guy any time now." I smile at the thought.

"You have, what, a week to go?" she asks.

"Five days," Maxton and Bright say at the same time.

Nicole and I both look at them. "It's my baby," Maxton says. "What's your excuse?"

Bright shrugs. "Well, not only do I hear about it at work, I'm excited to meet the little guy. Maybe I can get my fiancée to set a wedding date and we can work on one of our own," he says. His eyes locked on Nicole.

She sits back in her chair and studies him. "Whenever you're ready, I'm in," she replies.

"I get to pick?" he asks her.

"Yep." She pops the p, challenging him.

Brighton looks at Max. "Your little man is due in less than a week. You good in thirty?" he asks. I smile, knowing what they're talking about.

"Absolutely." Max grins.

Bright turns to Nicole. "Max is going to marry us. We figured we both fell hard and that's only fair. You've got thirty days. Tell me what you need and I'll do it. I can even plan the whole thing, just needs to happen in thirty," he says, taking a big bite of pizza.

We all burst out laughing and I have to pee again. "Ugh. Babe, I have to pee yet again, can you help me up?" I ask Max.

A slow trickle runs down my leg. At first, I'm embarrassed thinking that I actually pissed my pants. Then it hits me. Back pain… my water just broke.

58

Maxton

"MAXTON," KENSI SAYS my name and the sound of her voice has me giving her all of my attention, "my water just broke."

Any guy would freak out and, to be honest, I am just a little, but I don't let her see it. Instead, I smile at her and kiss her forehead. "We finally get to meet our boy." I turn to Bright. "Go get the car. Nicole, my phone is on the kitchen counter; can you call her OB, it's under Kensi OB, and let them know we are on our way? When you're done, call her dad and let him know."

"What about the bags?" Bright asks.

"Already loaded," I tell him.

Trying like hell to stay calm, I say, "Let's get you to the car, beautiful." I place my arm around her and help her out the door. Bright is in the driver's seat and Nicole hops in beside him. Kens and I load up in the back and off we go. She's fine until about five minutes from the hospital when she screams out in pain.

I don't say anything; I offer my hand and she squeezes painfully. I rub her back with the other hand, trying to soothe her. There is nothing I can say that will make it better and nothing I can do to take the pain away.

I read in an online forum that I just need to be there to offer whatever she needs.

We finally pull into the ER and there is a nurse waiting for us at the entrance. Kensi's doctor had called ahead, letting them know we were on our way. Taking good care of my girl, it's what I like to see.

She hits the button for the elevator and takes us to the third floor to delivery. We already pre-registered with the hospital, so we didn't have to deal with it today.

"I need you to change into this; do you need me to help you?" the nurse asks.

"No," she grits through her teeth. "Husband."

I grab the gown and wait until the nurse leaves, shutting the door behind her to help Kensi change. Not too long after, the doctor comes in to check her and appears to be surprised. "Kensington, how long have you been having back pain?" he asks her.

"It started yesterday," she pauses to let another contraction pass, "and has been pretty consistent since then. I just thought I had worked too much on the nursery getting things washed and put away."

"You've been in labor. You are already dilated to five centimeters. Any longer to get here and we would have missed our opportunity to give you an epidural," he explains.

"Well, get with it, doc," she retorts as another contraction hits.

The next half hour or so is a flurry of activity. The anesthesiologist comes in to administer the epidural and her pain subsides. However, from the way that the monitor is going crazy, her contractions are coming faster than ever. Nursing staff bring in a bed with lights for the baby as well as blankets and a slew of other items needed to bring my son into the world.

When the doctor finally comes back in, he checks her yet again. He smiles when he says, "It's time, Kensington. Dad, I need you to hold one of her legs. I'll have one of the nurses assist with the other. Kensington, when I tell you to push, I need you to bear down as hard as you can." He watches the monitor and when it spikes, he says, "Push."

This goes on for I don't know how long, and I can tell she's exhausted. "All right, Kensington, one more big push and you can meet your son," he encourages her.

"You got this, baby. One more big push and he's here. We finally get to meet him," I whisper in her ear.

She nods once. "Now," the doctor says and she bears down with every last ounce of energy in her.

Not seconds later, I hear his cries fill the room. Kensi lies back against the pillow and a gorgeous, yet tired, smile crosses her face. Never has my heart felt so full. The doctor offers for me to cut the cord and I decline. My eyes are full of tears and I'd be afraid I would hurt him. I tell him this and he assures me that this will not happen. With a shaking hand, I take the scissors and cut the cord. Nurses whisk him away, cleaning him up, and I focus on Kens. "You did it, Kensi. You did so well. Thank you, I love you so much." I ramble on and on, not knowing how to tell her what I feel in this moment. What this means to me to have them both.

The nurse brings him over and lays him on her chest. We're both crying. I watch as she leans down and kisses the top of his head. "He's perfect," she says.

"Yes, he is. He's perfect," I agree with her.

"I think the name we picked, I think it fits him," she says.

I nod. "I agree." We chose my middle name as his first name. This is also my father's name. We chose her dad's name as the middle name.

"Welcome to the world, Sean Thomas Cooper." I touch his little hand, which breaks free from the blanket, and he latches onto my finger. My heart soars. I love this little guy with everything in me.

59

Kensington

"COME IN," I say at the knock on my door. It's been a flurry activity since our little man was born. Max and I sent the nurse to tell our family that they can come back and meet him. Dad walks in first, followed by Nicole and Bright.

Maxton is sitting on the bed next to me holding Sean. "There is some hand sanitizer right there." He points to the table. My dad doesn't hesitate. He pumps a generous amount into the palm of his hands and rubs them together.

Standing up, Maxton hands Sean to my father, who is sitting in the chair. "Dad, meet your grandson, Sean Thomas Cooper." His eyes glass over at the name and he simply nods, letting us know he gets it.

"He's perfect," Dad says.

"We think so." Maxton puffs his chest out, proud papa that he is. Bright and Nicole take turns holding him, and before we know it, two hours have gone by. They all say their goodbyes with the promise of coming to see us tomorrow when we get home. Nicole and Bright are going to stay a few nights and help us out until we get a routine down, which is something a mother would do, something that neither of us have. We don't dwell on that because we have Nicole and Bright and my dad. We have people who love us and life doesn't get any better than that.

"It's my turn, Gramps," Nicole whines to my dad. The entire room erupts into laughter, well, everyone except Nicole. Even little Sean gave us an Elvis grin as Maxton calls it. The doctor burst his bubble earlier when he told him it was gas. It was hard not to laugh at him. I held it in though, because he was truly upset that Sean was not smiling at him.

Dad finally gets his laughter under control and hands Sean off to Nicole. I watch as a single tear rolls down her cheek. Brighton wipes it away with his thumb and whispers in her ear. Her face lights up with whatever he tells her. It is my prediction that my best friend will be here where I am in no time at all.

"You did good, Kensi," Maxton whispers in my ear.

"We did good," I say, squeezing his hand.

Maxton and I have managed to create a life that most envy, and I thank God every day for bringing him into my life.

Maxton—Three years later

"MY TURN, DADDY," Sean says, climbing up on the couch next to me.

"Hey, little man, is mommy still sleeping?" I ask him.

"Yep," he says, popping his p. "My turn," he says, pointing to his new baby sister who is currently asleep on my chest. She's exactly one-week old today, my daughter, Maggie Mae Cooper.

Kensi and I were worried how Sean would react to sharing our attention, but Maggie's arrival hasn't seemed to faze him. He loves her. Last night, Bright and Nicole stopped by and Sean scolded Bright for touching Maggie's foot without hand sanitizer. "Germs, Uncle Bright," he had said. Already the protector, that's my boy!

"Okay, buddy, remember what I told you. You have to sit really still and hold her head. Your baby sister is precious and we need to always protect her."

He scoots back against the couch, legs straight, arms stretched out, palms up waiting. "I got this," he says with conviction. It takes great effort not to laugh at him. At three, he has his own personality. I'm amazed at some of the things that come out of this kid's mouth. Kensi says he acts just like me, but I can see her in him too. He has her smile.

Easing Maggie from my shoulder, I gently lay her in his arms. I cradle her head while he holds her. Sean's face lights up. Leaning down, he kisses her on the forehead; he's seen me kiss Kensi that way a million times. "I love you, sister," he whispers in his soft voice.

I have to swallow the lump in my throat. Being a dad is… amazing. I love the life that Kensi and I have built, and I love her more each and every day.

"I want to box this moment up and keep it forever," I hear her say. Kensi is standing in the doorway watching the three of us.

Slowly, she moves into the room and sits down beside Sean. "I done, Daddy," he says.

I scoop my baby girl up in my arms. As soon as he's free, Sean is climbing up on Kensi's lap, soaking up some mommy time. Reaching over, I tuck her bangs behind her ear. Her eyes find mine and she smiles. "I love you, Kensington Cooper.

"I love you, too." She smiles.

"What about me?" Sean giggles as Kensi tickles his sides.

"We love you, too," we tell him.

Kensington Cooper.

My girl.

My wife.

My truth.

CONTACT KAYLEE RYAN

Facebook:
https://www.facebook.com/pages/Kaylee-Ryan-Author
Goodreads:
http://www.goodreads.com/book/show/17838885-anywhere-with-you
Twitter: @author_k_ryan
Instagram: author_kaylee_ryan
Website: www.kayleeryan.com
Google +: https://plus.google.com/+KayleeRyan
Pinterest: https://www.pinterest.com/authorkaylee/
tsu: https://www.tsu.co/authorkayleeryan

OTHER WORKS BY KAYLEE RYAN

With You Series
Anywhere With You
More With You
Everything With You

Stand Alone Titles

Tempting Tatum

ACKNOWLEDGMENTS

My family. You make it possible to follow this dream. I continue to receive nothing but love and support from you. There is no way that I could do this without out. I love you!

I have met some amazing friends throughout this process. The indie community is amazing and I am proud to say that I am a part of it. Every time I see a fellow author share my work or that of our peers I can't help but be honored to be a part of this Indie Family.

To my AS101 peeps. I love you all. I have learned so much from all of you. It's a huge relief to be able to bounce ideas and gain suggestions from those of you who are in my shoes or have been there recently.

To my author BFFS – you know who you are. I love the support that we give one another and I am thankful every single one of you.

Sommer Stein you took my vision and exceeded my expectations. Thank you so much for the stunning cover! You never fail to provide a kick ass cover! I can't wait to work with both of you again.

Angela from Fictional Formats you make my words come together in a pretty little package. Thank you so much for making *Levitate* look fabulous on the inside!

Saoching Moose I'm going to keep things simple this time. I love ya girl! I value the friendship that we have created and I cannot wait to meet you in person!

Mary Tatar, I am blessed to call you a friend. You continue to support, me and my work and I cannot thank you enough. Your amazing trailers bring my stories to life. Thank you for being you and always being there.

Love Between The Sheets, thank you for hosting the release day blitz. You ladies are amazing and I don't know what I would do without you!

To all of the bloggers out there... Thank you so much. Your continued never ending support of myself and the entire indie community is greatly appreciated. I know that you don't hear it enough so hear me now. ***I appreciate each and every one of you and the support that you have given me.*** Thank you to all of you! There are way too many of you to list...

To my Kick Ass Crew, you ladies know who you are. I will never be able to tell you how much your support means. I will never forget all that you have done for me. Thank you!

Kaylee, Stacy, Lauren and Jamie you ladies gave up so much of your time to Beta read for me. New scenes, re-worked scenes you ladies were all over it and I cannot tell you how much I appreciate your time and support of my work. Thank you so much for all that you do.

Kaylee (2) I never thought it possible to meet someone online with common interests, name, personalities and become such fast friends. I am blessed to have found the friendship that we have formed. I value our daily talks and messages. You have talked me through scenes and provided support in all aspects of my work as well as everyday life... I love ya girl!! Thank you for being you.

Last but not least, to the readers. Without you none of this would even be worth the effort. I truly love writing and I am honored that I am able to share that with you. Thank you to each and every one of you who continue support me, and my dream of writing.

With Love,

Kaylee Ryan

Bruce County Public Library
1243 MacKenzie Rd.
Port Elgin, Ontario N0H 2C6

CPSIA information can be obtained at www.ICGtesting.com
Printed in the USA
LVOW10s1532170915

454594LV00019B/1409/P

9 780986 180019